A wave of awareness swept over Lennon, making her knees weak

She tried not to sigh, tried to maintain some semblance of control as Josh's lips worked their way down her temple with tiny kisses. And she just might have managed it if Josh hadn't chosen to lean back against the wall.

Lennon went with him, off balance, forced to press her hands against his chest and hang on. He braced her against him with his thigh wedged between hers, his hard muscles zeroing right in on the spot that made her ache.

A moan slipped unbidden from her lips and Josh caught the sound with his kiss. Delicious, dangerous excitement whipped through her. She was completely under his control...vulnerable, and she found the sensation both familiar and utterly irresistible.

Their breaths clashed, his ragged breathing as unchecked as hers, his mouth insistent, his kiss urgent. She scarcely had the strength to remain upright. Josh's mouth trailed away.

"Ah, *chère*." His voice was throaty and rough with passion. "You tempt me beyond my control. Either we stop now or I drag you into the nearest bedroom."

Blaze™

Dear Reader,

My life usually involves family and friends jet-setting around the globe while I stay at home, waiting for postcards. But for once I actually got to make the trip—to New Orleans, a city I adore. My cousins Nick and Marguerite were wonderful hosts, touring me from the French Quarter to the bayou in a spanking new Corvette, which left me positively inspired to write a romance set in this awesome city.

Meet Lennon and Josh. Lennon's a woman who knows what she wants—a husband, and not one of those romance-hero, make-her-crazy-with-lust kinds, either. She wants the stable, share-life's-ups-and-downs variety. Josh is Mr. Wrong incarnate—a real-life romance hero who's determined to convince Lennon he's Mr. Right.

Blaze is the place to explore red-hot romance, a place where you'll find spicy adventurous journeys to happily-ever-after. I hope Lennon and Josh's story brings you to happily-ever-after, too. Let me know. Drop me a line in care of Harlequin Books, 225 Duncan Mill Road, Don Mills, Ontario, Canada M3B 3K9. Or visit my Web site at www.jeanielondon.com. And don't forget to check out tryblaze.com!

Very truly yours,

Jeanie London

Books by Jeanie London

HARLEQUIN BLAZE
28—SECRET GAMES

ONE-NIGHT MAN

Jeanie London

Hope you enjoy my red-hot romp!

Jeanie London

HARLEQUIN®

TORONTO • NEW YORK • LONDON
AMSTERDAM • PARIS • SYDNEY • HAMBURG
STOCKHOLM • ATHENS • TOKYO • MILAN • MADRID
PRAGUE • WARSAW • BUDAPEST • AUCKLAND

To Susan Kearney, for everything.
And special thanks to Wanda Ottewell,
editor extraordinaire—wow!
I lucked out, big-time ;-)

ISBN 0-373-79046-5

ONE-NIGHT MAN

Copyright © 2002 by Jeanie LeGendre.

All rights reserved. Except for use in any review, the reproduction or
utilization of this work in whole or in part in any form by any electronic,
mechanical or other means, now known or hereafter invented, including
xerography, photocopying and recording, or in any information storage
or retrieval system, is forbidden without the written permission of the
publisher, Harlequin Enterprises Limited, 225 Duncan Mill Road,
Don Mills, Ontario, Canada M3B 3K9.

All characters in this book have no existence outside the imagination of
the author and have no relation whatsoever to anyone bearing the same
name or names. They are not even distantly inspired by any individual
known or unknown to the author, and all incidents are pure invention.

This edition published by arrangement with Harlequin Books S.A.

® and TM are trademarks of the publisher. Trademarks indicated with
® are registered in the United States Patent and Trademark Office, the
Canadian Trade Marks Office and in other countries.

Visit us at www.eHarlequin.com

Printed in U.S.A.

1

"IF I HAVE TO LOOK at one more penis tonight," Lennon McDarby whispered while lifting the glass panel from the display case, "I'm going to scream."

This penis stood a good sixteen inches tall. The mammoth proportions would have made the sculpture crude had it not been crafted from marble with exquisite attention to detail.

And the piece was just one of many, because all the artwork in the Joshua Eastman Gallery had a connection to sex. This artist's theme for *The Promise,* as the work was titled, was of the oral variety. The marble penis was half of a pair. Its partner—an equally detailed sculpture of a woman's mouth—depicted lips opened wide enough to swallow sixteen inches.

Lennon sighed. The sound echoed in the empty gallery. She didn't even have to glance at her watch to know midnight had come and gone. She'd become intimately acquainted with late nights these past few weeks while helping her great-aunt ready the collection for the opening. Lennon wouldn't even think about how she'd blown off her own work, despite a looming deadline, to spend every waking hour in the National Trust Artists' Museum.

But the collection finally neared completion, and Lennon cast a satisfied glance around the entrance hall. Along with *The Promise* and Great-uncle Joshua's portrait—which presided over the room, welcoming guests to his memorial art gallery—a compelling array of artwork and artifacts represented each category of the collection. Select paintings, prints, drawings, photographs, sculptures and decorative artwork were displayed in and on various cases and shelves, introducing visitors to the scope and quality of the Eastman Gallery's unique objets d'art.

Sex, sex and more sex.

With a tired smile, Lennon surveyed *Solitaire,* a 1792 watercolor of a nude young man stroking himself in a beautiful wash of transparent colors. Auntie Q had displayed the painting, declaring, "We want men to feel welcome, and this piece will prove they've been playing with themselves since long before *Playboy* hit the stands...."

On another wall hung a 1750 oil on canvas depicting a pastoral scene of a couple making love on a riverbank, a work that had been commissioned by Madame de Pompadour herself.

One of the more unusual items in the hall was a basin and ewer set, a gorgeous example of "Saint-Porchaire" ware, one of the rarest types of Renaissance ceramics. Ingeniously mounted on a low stand, the pieces had been fashioned into a makeshift bidet long before the bidet had come into vogue as a tool for personal hygiene. Lennon thought the set made an attractive addition to the entrance hall. Tasteful. Subtly erotic.

Since Auntie Q and Great-uncle Joshua—*honorary* great-uncle, as he and Auntie Q hadn't been married—had devoted their lives to collecting these erotic pieces, the least Lennon could do was figure out how best to display them. Back to *The Promise.*

Repositioning the giant penis on the black velvet display base, she leaned back on her haunches to consider the effect. Still not right. She yawned widely, wondering if she would ever be content with the result.

"Playing with a penis shouldn't put you to sleep, dear." Auntie Q's lilting voice broke the late-night quiet.

Rocking back on her heels, Lennon swung a weary gaze toward her great-aunt. Auntie Q—Quinevere McDarby to the rest of New Orleans's society—stood silhouetted beneath the arched entrance, surveying the exhibition hall as grandly as a fairy queen.

And that's exactly how Lennon thought of her. With her white hair and brilliant blue eyes, Auntie Q was petite, quintessentially feminine, and had been as exquisite in her youth as she was darling in her dotage.

"It's so late nothing can keep me awake, Auntie."

"The right man could."

Too tired to argue, Lennon said, "You should be resting."

"Why? I'll have plenty of time to catch up on my sleep when I'm dead. Until then..." At Lennon's stricken look, Auntie Q tutted reassuringly. "Shh, dear. I went online to check the weather report. If I didn't, you would have, and I want you to finish your to-do list so the bachelors and I will have your undivided attention during the gallery opening."

"I'm all yours this weekend."

The cheeky old girl winked. "You should say that to a man sometime."

Lennon only smiled, not up to another debate about her love life or lack thereof, and attempted to steer the subject toward the million and one things still left to do before the reception tonight. "What's the forecast?"

"Cool Gulf breezes for the next two days, if I care to trust the weatherman. I don't. I've arranged a contingency plan in case the weather doesn't cooperate and we have to move the reception out of the sculpture garden."

"Good idea, but I've got my fingers crossed the weather will be fine."

She'd said a few prayers, too. Lennon wanted this weekend to come off without a hitch. The opening of the Joshua Eastman Gallery—the newest addition to New Orleans's largest art museum—represented two years of Auntie Q's hard work, a memorial to the man she'd loved for most of her life.

"Great-uncle Joshua would be touched that you're opening the gallery to showcase his antiquities collection." Sinking back onto the floor, Lennon glanced up at the portrait that hung above the display case.

Great-uncle Joshua peered down at her boldly from the canvas, a handsome man with deep green eyes and striking black hair. He'd sat for the portrait during the prime of his life, long before Lennon had been born, and she thought he looked like a real-life romance hero. As a romance writer, she was qualified to make that assessment.

Auntie Q followed her glance, her wizened expression softening as she gazed upon the man she'd loved in life. "He bequeathed me his collection specifically to keep me busy after he passed, otherwise he'd have opened this gallery himself. I'm sure he's up there right now, throwing roadblocks in my way every time he doesn't like one of my decisions."

"Roadblocks?"

Auntie Q waved a thin hand impatiently, sapphires and rubies flashing when her rings caught a gleam of light from the after-hours lighting. "There's simply no other explanation for why the painters painted the decorative arts exhibition hall the wrong colors. I mean, really, dear. Each and every paint can mislabeled? The project supervisor getting the flu just as the painters were about to start the project? And I'd have never been out of town if not for the opportunity to acquire that exquisite Italian Renaissance majolica dish that Joshua had been trying to purchase for a decade. All Joshua's doing. He hated the bold colors I chose to offset the collectables.''

Frankly, Lennon thought the natural tones now gracing the walls of the exhibit better suited the collection of rock crystal vessels, ivory carvings and gilt and silver miscellany. But if Auntie Q believed Great-uncle Joshua sat up on a cloud critiquing her decorating choices, who was Lennon to argue?

''You made the right choice conceding to his wishes then,'' she said. ''The hall looks great.''

''It does indeed. All in all, I think he's pleased.''

''And so are a lot of people in New Orleans. You're giving the art world an invaluable contribution.''

''Not everyone is happy.'' She held up an envelope, which Lennon, in her exhaustion, hadn't noticed before.

''Oh, no. Not another one.''

''I'm afraid so, dear.''

Lennon didn't need to open the envelope to discern the thoughts of the harsh critics who'd opposed the gallery's opening. She and her great-aunt had already had a few unpleasant run-ins with protestors. ''Well, I still don't understand the trouble.''

''Every collection has detractors.'' Auntie Q gave a shrug, though Lennon knew each negative comment struck her hard. ''The point is to showcase Joshua's collection. He wanted people to embrace our collective erotic art history. 'Don't need a royal family to enjoy the royal family jewels,' he always said.''

That he had. As a young man, Great-uncle Joshua had earned his fortune importing and exporting antiquities; throughout his later years, he'd become a collector and philanthropist. As far back as Lennon could remember, memories of her great-aunt and -uncle had always involved exciting treasure hunts to track down artwork and collectibles from all over the world.

That their idea of treasure included all forms of *erotic* artwork throughout history was a detail Lennon had become acquainted with only in adulthood.

"Are you sure you've chosen the right work of art to display beneath Great-uncle Joshua's portrait, Auntie?" Leaving the glass display case on the floor, she pushed herself to her feet and eyed *The Promise* skeptically.

Auntie Q glided into the room. Meeting her halfway, Lennon plucked the letter from her grasp, tucked her finely boned hand in her own and led her back toward the portrait.

"Georgia Devine is an up-and-coming young artist," she said. "Joshua loved boosting new artists' careers. That's why I'm exhibiting this piece." She walked the few steps to a wall display that featured an exquisite seashell-and-pearl necklace. "This is a Reina Price original. I just acquired it last year when she opened her own gallery."

Lennon didn't think there was any comparison between the huge sculpture beneath the portrait and the necklace designed to resemble a woman's genitals in soft pastel shades.

"This is a gorgeous piece," she said, moving closer for a better look at the fine detail. "I mean really gorgeous. I wouldn't mind seeing this artist's other work."

"We'll go together, dear. After the opening."

Lennon nodded. "This piece would be perfect beneath the portrait. It's beautiful, tasteful, not...well, *crude.*"

"Crude?" Auntie Q glanced back at the sculpture as though the thought hadn't occurred to her. "That gorgeous white marble? Think of yin and yang. *The Promise* symbolizes the wholeness of the universe, the sun and the moon, the unity of man and woman. What's crude about it?''

The sheer proportions, for one thing. The blatant suggestion of oral foreplay, for another. Not that Lennon would try explaining that to Auntie Q. A waste of breath. She didn't have anything against oral sex per se, but seeing it so deliberately displayed, almost flaunting... ''I prefer the subtler pieces, I suppose.''

''The sculpture makes you uncomfortable because you haven't seen a penis in a while.'' Before Lennon could comment, Auntie Q tugged her hand. ''Come on, let's find you a man.''

They walked the few steps to the foyer adjoining the entrance hall. A dozen easels flanked the arched entrance, displaying promotional photos of the bachelors to be auctioned off during the gallery opening.

Auntie Q studied the photos, a respectable assortment of candid gazes, carved jaws and arresting smiles. ''Any thoughts on whom you'll bid for?''

Oh, she'd had thoughts all right. Lennon took a deep breath and waited until her great-aunt had turned her assessing gaze back before admitting, ''Actually, I've been giving the bidding a lot of thought. Not only will the auction raise funds for the collection, but it's an opportunity to find Mr. Right.''

Auntie Q's face suddenly became wreathed in smiles and excitement. ''Mr. Right, Lennon? Really? Are you *finally* going to allow yourself to fall in love?''

Lennon nodded. ''I'll be thirty in May. I've finished college, traveled the Continent with Mother and established my writing career. It's time to settle down.''

''Are you talking about marriage?''

''Yes.''

''Marriage would be delightful, but don't you think

you're getting ahead of yourself? Shouldn't you be in love with a man before deciding to marry him?''

"That's where the auction comes in." Taking a deep breath, Lennon chose her words carefully. "These are the most eligible bachelors around. They're all reputable, self-made men, from the best families. Where better to find a husband?''

That laser-blue gaze narrowed. "And where does love fit in?''

Lennon faced her great-aunt squarely. "My definition of love differs from yours a bit, Auntie. To me, love doesn't necessarily include what you always call 'grand passion.'''

It definitely didn't include grand passion.

"You're a McDarby," Auntie Q said. "Passion is our special gift. It's what we live for. You're just a late bloomer.''

"I'm not a late bloomer. I do passion. I'm a romance writer, for goodness sake.''

Auntie Q shook her head, as though shaking loose whatever might be obstructing her hearing, since she clearly didn't think she'd heard Lennon right. "You do passion on a computer, not in real life. When was the last time you went on a date?''

Lennon dragged her memory for a recent date to prove her point. Wow, had it really been that long? Apparently so, judging by her great-aunt's smug expression.

"Okay, so it's been a while," she admitted. "But I signed a three-book contract and haven't had time to do anything but write. It was a career opportunity I couldn't pass up.''

"A while, indeed. You haven't dated since before your book contract, since that handsome young man who handled promotion for the Saints. What was his name, Craig...Cliff—''

"Clint."

"Clint, that's right. He had a promising future, dear."

A very promising future that involved delicious sex and equally delicious memories. Clint had been whirlwind romance material, not marriage material. There was a big difference. By the time she and Clint had parted ways, Lennon had needed a vacation to convalesce.

"Romance heroes are for affairs and books," she explained. "Nice stable men are for marriage."

Auntie Q blinked. "Are you saying you don't marry heroes?"

"I want to marry a man I like, a man I respect and will still respect through all the ups and downs of marriage and rearing children."

"And you don't think you can respect a man you can love?"

"No, no," Lennon said with a huff of exasperation. "It's not that I can't respect a man I love, it's just that I want a solid, stable…*comfortable* marriage. I want to love my husband. And not that 'grand passion' kind of love, but the caring, companionable kind. The minute passion gets involved, love becomes an emotional roller coaster."

"Emotional roller coaster?" Now it was Auntie Q's turn to huff. "Of course it's an emotional roller coaster. That's the beauty—the excitement, the anticipation, the joie de vivre. It makes life worth living."

"Passion makes *affairs* worth living. And affairs are wonderful, but I need a rest afterward." Lennon spread her hands in entreaty. "You know as well as I do that the minute a man knows a woman is in love with him, he's got the upper hand. He makes her crazy just because he can."

"But it's the best kind of crazy, dear. It's a feeling of being alive, of being cherished—"

"I don't want to marry a man who'll drive me nuts. I want a husband who'll be my partner and stick by my side no matter what life offers. I don't want one who'll consume my thoughts every single minute and distract me from everything else...."

Lennon lost her steam when she saw Auntie Q goggling like a pixie who'd been zapped by a lightning bolt. Apparently the thought of separating love and passion hadn't occurred to her.

But Auntie Q had a mind as sharp as a Cajun spice. Understanding quickly dawned upon her, revealed in her impish features, and she cut a gaze back to the portrait inside the entrance hall. "Give me strength, Joshua, please."

After fifty-five years of discussing all aspects of her life with Great-uncle Joshua, Auntie Q hadn't been able to break the habit after his death. She still talked to him whenever she felt the need, no matter where she was or whom she was with. Lennon wondered if he ever answered her.

She couldn't hear a thing but the drone of the museum's climate control system as it cycled on, which was truly a shame. She could have used an advocate about now.

Taking her great-aunt's thin hands in her own, she gazed down into that dear old face, needing Auntie Q to understand. Her great-aunt had been the mainstay of Lennon's life, the doting darling who'd pinch-hitted for Lennon's mother, who'd devoted her own life to chasing her Mr. Rights.

As usual, Mother was nowhere to be found to act as an advocate when Lennon needed one. She was currently residing in Monte Carlo chasing Mr. Right number forty-two.

But Lennon had long ago learned to make her own decisions, because sometimes her mother's affairs *d'amour* had easily accommodated a child in tow, at other times not.

During those times Auntie Q had always stepped in, bringing Lennon back to the huge family house in the New Orleans Garden District.

By the time Lennon had been ten, jet-setting around the globe for her mother's wild affairs had lost its appeal. She'd longed for the stability of a home, a school and friends of her own, and the enduring love of her kind and fun Auntie Q.

Mother hadn't argued when Lennon had asked to stay in New Orleans. She hadn't asked Auntie Q if it was okay, either. She'd just kissed their cheeks on the veranda and departed with a breezy, "Call me when you're ready to come home."

Twenty years had passed and Lennon still hadn't called. Neither had Auntie Q. And never once had her great-aunt ever seemed to mind the lifestyle adjustments that assuming the responsibilities of a child had entailed. She'd been the most loving of surrogate parents, and Lennon wanted her approval.

"It all boils down to Mr. Wrong and Mr. Right," she explained. "A man who's right for an affair isn't what I want for my marriage."

Auntie Q sighed. "If this is about your mother and the choices she has made, Lennon, don't let her knack for choosing rogues frighten you off."

"Mother chooses rogues because she lives for that rush of lust. She's a junkie. As soon as the thrill wears off and her fantasy man starts to look real, she's gone."

Gazing into her great-aunt's face, Lennon frowned when she saw worry there. "I enjoy the rush of lust, too, Auntie. You know that. I may not have had a romance in a while, but I've had some wonderful ones. I'm not frightened of passion, just rational about it. I want a real marriage, not some up-and-down roller-coaster ride. I know what my needs are, and I choose to fulfill them.''

"Love shouldn't make you rational. It should make you crazy, even a bit foolish. It should make you feel alive.''

"That's fine for an affair. I want stability in marriage.''

"Why can't you have both? Look at your great-uncle and me. We endured fifty-five years of the most wonderful relationship.''

"You and Great-uncle Joshua lived a fifty-five-year love affair.'' Lennon couldn't bring herself to point out the obvious: Auntie Q had been Great-uncle Joshua's mistress. "You once told me that you felt lucky because you shared your life with the man you loved. Living the legend, you said, because your namesake, the real Guinevere, hadn't been so lucky. I always thought that was so romantic, but—''

"But we didn't have a real marriage,'' Auntie Q said. "No, dear, we didn't, but we shared our lives and never once regretted the difficult choices we were forced to make.''

"I know.''

What her great-aunt and -uncle had shared had been special, even more so because their love had endured though they hadn't met until years after he'd committed to an arranged marriage. At the time, a man didn't divorce simply because he'd found a more suitable partner—even if his wife had decided she wanted a marriage in name only after providing an heir.

Though Auntie Q and Great-uncle Joshua had made the best of the hand life had dealt them, and had fun in the process, Lennon didn't envision a future for herself even remotely similar.

She wanted home and hearth and babies. Lots of babies. Little girls to share tea parties with and little boys to help catch bugs in glass jars. She would work her writing schedule around her family's needs and revel in the joys of being a wife and mom.

Auntie Q must have recognized her resolve, because she said, "Your mind's made up." It was a statement.

"It is. I've given my future a great deal of thought. Mr. Right for a marriage is what's right for me. I don't want a husband I'm head-over-heels in lust with. I want a husband I like, love and respect. I want a life companion."

"A life companion?" Auntie Q rolled her gaze heavenward. "Old people have companions. I'm not even old enough for one and I'm eighty-two."

Lennon didn't point out that her assistant, Olaf, who cared for her in myriad capacities, could be considered a companion. She gently squeezed her great-aunt's hands instead. "Trust me, Auntie. I know what I want. And with the bachelor auction, you've provided me the perfect place to find him."

"You need grand passion."

Lennon peered back into the entrance hall at her great-uncle's portrait. Maybe it was the night lighting or staying up long past her bedtime, but Lennon recognized the underlying excitement in his green eyes, the zest for living that had been so much a part of the man she'd known. And admired.

Great-uncle Joshua had been the only steady male presence in her life while Lennon was growing up. A kind, fun and very noble man, he'd had the ability to make her great-aunt feel like the most important person in his world. And Lennon, too.

He'd been a part of every important step in her life, from dance recitals and graduations to helping her cope with her flighty mother. She'd always considered her great-uncle family-by-love. He may not have been officially related, but he'd always encouraged and supported her, and she still thought of him as her ideal, a man she modeled her romance heroes after.

"You had grand passion, Auntie," she said, guessing that if Great-uncle Joshua had been free to marry, Auntie Q would probably have considered life perfect. "Maybe if there was another man as wonderful I might consider a different sort of marriage. But Great-uncle Joshua was one of a kind."

Auntie Q regarded her from beneath a wrinkled brow. "I really wish you'd reconsider."

"I know what I want, and it's not a life full of emotional upheaval. I want to marry a man who'll help me create a stable, *normal* family. I wouldn't change a moment of my life with you, but we're not exactly normal, are we?" She smiled lightly, hoping to ease her great-aunt's concern. "Besides, I've had my share of affairs and romances. I'll settle down with a man I can love, and keep passion for my romance novels."

She kissed her great-aunt's cheek. "Now will you go to your office and try to catch a few hours of sleep? The museum directors will be here at the crack of dawn and we won't have a chance to slow down before the reception. I still don't know when we'll find time to check into the hotel."

"We'll manage, dear." Auntie Q squeezed her hand. "Why don't you come, too? A few hours wouldn't hurt you, either. You'll want to look fresh for the bachelors."

Lennon couldn't tell if this remark meant Auntie Q had accepted the game plan or not. Her bright eyes and easy smile didn't reveal a thing. Too late and too tired for more debate when she still had so much to do, Lennon let the matter drop and focused on settling Auntie Q in her office, before she herself returned to the entrance hall to tackle *The Promise.*

Smoothing the black velvet drape over the display, she maneuvered the pieces around like men on a chessboard. The penis at a forty-five degree angle from the mouth. No. Too far apart, the pieces didn't appear like part of any yin-yang whole. She moved them closer and thought the penis looked as if it stood sentinel over the mouth.

The Promise was the first piece of artwork the guests would see after Great-uncle Joshua's portrait. Possibly the first, if their gazes didn't follow the lines of the room to the portrait. The arrangement had to be right.

One hundred eighty degrees southeast? Ninety degrees northwest? The penis lying on its side, its huge marble head touching the open mouth?

No, no, no. With a disgusted groan, Lennon snatched the penis off the base and dropped it into her lap. There, no penis at all. Worked for her. And displayed alone, the mouth looked sort of like a huge white rose. Rather attractive, really.

Laying an arm on the display base, she wearily rested her head on the crook of her elbow and decided Auntie Q was probably right. She just didn't like the sculpture because she hadn't seen the real thing in a while.

2

If Josh Eastman hadn't known better, he'd have thought he'd walked into a storybook illustration of *Sleeping Beauty*. Security lights washed the new gallery's entrance hall with a pale gleam, illuminating the beauty asleep at the foot of his grandfather's portrait. This woman was a late-night fantasy, all long, long legs and sleek blond hair.

Her filmy skirt and clingy sweater drew his gaze to willowy curves curled around a low display case, and to smooth golden skin where her bare arm draped over the black velvet.

But Josh knew better. She might be a sleeping beauty, all right, but not from any child's version of the tale. Not with a huge marble erection propped upright on her lap.

Sleeping Beauty could only be Lennon McDarby, all grown up.

Moving silently into the new gallery, he drank the espresso he'd picked up in the museum's security office and surveyed the woman before him. She'd been, what?—ten, maybe eleven the last time Josh had seen her, right before he'd headed off to college. A skinny girl, all arms and legs and conversation about things he couldn't have cared less about.

He hadn't thought much about her since, though he'd heard of her from his grandfather and Miss Q. But who'd have guessed that gangly kid would have grown into this golden vision? Not him.

Even if Josh had guessed, he'd never have pictured the erection—which wasn't, incidentally, the only erection around. A watercolor nearby showed a man servicing his own needs.

"Don't blame you a bit, pal." He rested his gaze on a sleeping Lennon. "She's definitely something to look at."

Definitely.

She was the best sight he'd seen in a long time. More sexy than all the art in the room combined. With her long slender curves, silky blond hair and gold-dusted lashes fanned out in half circles on her cheeks, Lennon couldn't look more delicious if she'd been spread out on a bed.

Unless she'd been naked.

Now there was an image to inspire more than a few late-night fantasies. Lennon, all gleaming gold skin and sleek curves, with her eyes closed and her lips parted as if awaiting his kisses.

An image that made Josh long to kneel down beside her, peel away her clothes and wake this sleeping beauty with a kiss right now, because the very idea of tasting those pouty lips and touching all that smooth golden skin clouded his thoughts and inspired an upsurge in his pulse rate.

Josh shook his head to erase the image. How in hell was he supposed to help Miss Q by protecting Lennon this weekend, when he'd spend his time protecting her from himself, instead of the bad guys?

A damned good question. This woman was passion personified. The closest he'd ever come to his perfect fantasy. And except for the unusual piece of art resting strategically on her lap, the only thing to mar the view was the portrait of his grandfather, which loomed above her head to remind Josh why he'd come. Guilt. Loads of guilt. Otherwise he'd never be in this new gallery wing at the crack of dawn. In the French Quarter during Mardi Gras, no less.

Josh didn't celebrate Mardi Gras, hadn't for years, anyway. When he'd been a kid, his grandfather had routinely commandeered him from his parents and grandmother, all of whom had believed the party in New Orleans proper was nothing more than a peasant festival. The real action, as far as they were concerned, took place uptown, in the mansions of the Garden District.

He hadn't partied with his grandfather at Mardi Gras since he'd been seventeen years old. A lifetime ago. Nowadays, Josh scheduled himself out of town during the first half of February, and he'd managed that task for the past five years running.

This year he hadn't been so lucky. A self-employed private investigator, he was just wrapping up a missing person case that had ended with a corpse, and he'd spent the past two weeks giving depositions to multijurisdictional authorities.

Just his luck. If he hadn't been in town tonight, his answering service would have fielded the call that had turned out to be the last person on the planet he'd expected to hear from—Quinevere McDarby, his late grandfather's mistress and the woman he'd known as Miss Q throughout his youth.

She'd worked him over in a big way, and here he was with the unenviable task of breaking the news to her great-niece.

"Lennon," he whispered quietly, not wanting to startle her. "Lennon, wake up."

She inhaled deeply, a soft sound that rippled in the quiet, and made the slight parting of her pouty peach lips seem as enticing as if she'd brushed that sexy mouth across his skin.

Josh swallowed hard. Without even opening her eyes, grown-up Lennon was having an absurd physical effect on him. An effect that had to be the combined result of his too-long-ignored libido and the giant phallus sitting in her lap. With that giant open mouth propped on the display case, firing his imagination with all sorts of tempting images, no wonder the seam of his jeans suddenly dug into his crotch.

She tipped her heart-shaped face up and blinked open whiskey-colored eyes. Eyes he hadn't thought about in years, but suddenly remembered with startling clarity.

Startling being the operative word, because Lennon shot bolt upright at the sight of him, inadvertently rolling the sculpture off her lap. It hit the carpeted floor with a thump.

"Penis envy, *chère?*"

She dragged her wide-eyed gaze down to the marble sculpture. Her mouth popped open. With jerky, panicked motions, she grabbed the huge phallus and lifted it off the floor.

Even with the low lighting, Josh could see the flush of color stain her cheeks as she repositioned the sculpture on the display base. But her flush was nothing compared to the heat rushing through him at the sight of her fingers wrapped around that smooth marble.

Taking another gulp of espresso, he barely noticed it scald his throat on the way down. "Long time no see, charity case."

He called her by the nickname he'd coined during a long-ago conversation where he'd lamented his grandmother's never-ending disapproval. Lennon had countered with her own tale of being quasi-orphaned and totally dependent on her great-aunt's charity. He remembered thinking that she'd had the better deal.

Shooting a startled glance at his grandfather's portrait, Lennon shook her head as if trying to shake off sleep, before turning back to stare at him.

"Black sheep!" She continued the name game, using a soubriquet he hadn't heard since the last time he'd seen her, and that she remembered it pleased him. "What are you doing here?"

He didn't answer. Instead, he extended a hand and helped her stand—a fluid movement that drew his attention to every curve between her head and her toes. Then he noticed her whiskey gaze glued to the cardboard travel cup he still held in one hand.

"Espresso, black," he said.

"Do you mind?"

He handed her the cup and watched as she sucked down an appreciative swallow. Her eyes shuttered briefly and she sighed as if she'd never tasted anything as good. "It's uncanny."

"What?"

"How much you look like your grandfather."

He gazed up at the portrait again. No denying it. The resemblance was nothing short of remarkable—a fact that came as a mild surprise. His grandfather had been close to sixty by the time Josh had been born, so the only memories he'd had of the man in his prime had been from photos. No getting around the fact that besides their dark coloring and green eyes, the facial structures matched almost identically.

Though Josh had spent most of his adult life establishing himself independently of the Eastman family, he found it ironic that the shirt his grandfather had worn while sitting for this portrait some forty-odd years ago was the same green-gray shade Josh had on right now.

"Except for the hair," Lennon observed, gaze darting back at him. "You've got a ponytail."

He shrugged, unsure whether this was good or bad. The length of his hair had been a grooming concession for his latest investigation. When he went undercover with drug dealers, he looked the part. With all the red tape and police reports he'd been wading in lately, he hadn't found time for a haircut.

"Life been treating you all right?" he asked, deciding that if her luscious appearance was any indication, she'd been treated very well.

"Sure has, thank you. How about you?"

"Better than I deserve."

Except at the moment. Somehow when he'd agreed to help out Miss Q, he'd still thought of Lennon as a girl.

A big mistake, he now realized, but one that didn't surprise him. Bottom line was he hadn't thought much about Lennon, Miss Q or any of his own family since he'd gone to college and devoted his life to breaking away from his controlling grandmother.

She'd been hell-bent on grooming him to pick up the reins of the family art import-export business. The business hadn't interested Josh, but the art had, so his grandfather had encouraged him to explore where that path might lead. There'd been tension between his grandparents over which direction Josh's life should take. His parents had routinely swung back and forth between the opposing factions, wanting their son to be happy, yet wanting the demanding matriarch to stop making all their lives miserable with her efforts to get her way.

Thanks to youthful stupidity, Josh had simply walked away from the fight. He'd had a big chip on his shoulder at the time and felt as if he was disappointing everyone. Swapping the family mansion in the Garden District for a refurbished warehouse in the art district, he'd cut himself off so completely from his family's social circles he may as well have been living on another planet.

His grandmother had written him off as a lost cause, but

his grandfather and his parents had kept in touch through the years. They told him what happened in their lives, tried to find out what was happening in his. But Josh rarely picked up the phone himself. More often than not, he'd used work as an excuse to avoid meeting his mom for lunch, or dropping by his dad's club for a drink, or making an appearance at his grandfather and Miss Q's annual Mardi Gras masque.

With age and experience came the knowledge that he might have handled his rebellion with more maturity and less rebellion. He suspected that if he'd just stood up to his grandmother, he might have found his grandfather and parents supportive of whatever path he chose. Which was why he'd rushed to Miss Q's assistance tonight. He owed his grandfather at least this much.

"Listen, charity case, we've got a problem," he said. More than one, actually, but his starved libido was technically his problem and not hers.

"I assumed. Why else would you be here? Is your family all right?"

Josh nodded, surprised that she would inquire about people who'd never had the time of day for her. Then again, he shouldn't be surprised. Quinevere McDarby had reared her, and she was a woman who opened her heart to everyone. Including him.

Which was another reason he'd come tonight.

Miss Q had always been full of the hugs and approval Josh had professed not to need, but had secretly placed himself in the line of fire for. He remembered thinking that fate had played a nasty trick by not allowing his grandfather to meet Miss Q long before he'd met Josh's own grandmother.

Then again, if his grandfather had met Miss Q first, Josh would never have been born. That just proved how satirical love could be. One of the reasons he made no time for it in his life. He did short-term relationships. Period.

"The family's fine." At least he hadn't heard otherwise. And what was the cliché? No news is good news....

"Then what's up?" Lennon took another long swallow of espresso, appeared to brace herself.

"A few hours ago, Miss Q left the museum to get some papers from your car. Someone assaulted her with a flash-and-bang grenade. She wasn't hurt, but we think it was a protest of my grandfather's collection."

"What are you...Auntie Q...someone threw..." Lennon's features blanked in the sort of stunned expression he knew all too well, from being a frequent bearer of bad news. She finally zeroed in. "A *grenade?* As in...*hand grenade?*"

"A flash-and-bang," he explained. "It's a nonlethal stun device used to disorient an enemy."

A clever device, and one he'd been grateful for on more than one occasion. But the way Lennon gaped drove home the differences in their interpretations of nonlethal.

A flash-and-bang grenade was useful in his line of work, but he doubted Lennon had ever heard of one, which reminded him why he didn't invite pretty, pouty-mouthed blondes into his life for more than a quick visit.

"It's a nonfragmenting type of grenade," he offered, hoping to reassure her. "The kind that doesn't explode."

Lennon didn't look reassured. "Josh, you must be mistaken. Auntie Q is in her office, asleep."

"It's almost six in the morning and I just put her in the car with Olaf. She's on her way home."

"I'm confused." Lennon ran a shaky hand through her hair, sending waves of honey-gold tumbling around her face, and inspiring thoughts about what that silky blond hair would feel like beneath his fingers. "Auntie Q couldn't just go out to my car. We're in a secure museum. The security guard has to let her out of the building after hours."

"The guard was asleep. She didn't want to disturb him when she can disable the system for the Eastman wing herself."

Apparently Lennon didn't have any trouble believing her great-aunt capable of that sort of recklessness. A frown creased her smooth brow and she shivered.

Plucking the cup from her hand, Josh marched her toward a nearby bench and forced her to sit. He didn't dwell on the awareness that ripped through him the minute he touched her bare arm. And he refused to acknowledge the naked lovers twined around each other on the canvas directly above her head.

"She's okay?"

"She's fine. The noise startled her."

"Thank goodness." Breathing deeply, Lennon cradled her face in her hands. She shivered again.

"Are you okay?"

Looking back up at him, she nodded. "But I don't understand why you're here. Where are the police?"

Josh shrugged. "Miss Q decided she doesn't want an investigation. She's afraid the museum will postpone the gallery opening. Instead of reporting the incident so the authorities can conduct an inquiry, she hid the discharged grenade in her handbag, lied to security and called me and Olaf."

"Where have I been while all this has been going on?"

He glanced over his shoulder at the phallic sculpture resting beneath his grandfather's portrait. "Given the way you were hanging on to that penis, *chère,* I'd say you were dreaming."

"Josh." Scowling, she grabbed the coffee cup and slugged back the remains defiantly.

He couldn't contain a laugh at her look of outrage.

"Well, I can't say I'm surprised," she finally said. "Auntie Q isn't about to let anything come in the way of this opening. Great-uncle Joshua loved Mardi Gras. 'A celebration of being alive,' he used to call it. She has had her heart set on this weekend ever since he died. I won't even bother trying to convince her otherwise."

Great-uncle Joshua. Damn, but that reference to his grandfather brought him back a lot of years. Lennon wasn't related, yet his grandfather had been as much a part of her family as his. Her posthumous concern for this memorial showed a graceful acceptance of the sordid triangle of man-family-mistress that Josh couldn't help but admire.

Though he'd grown up knowing his grandfather divided his time between two families, he couldn't help perceiving the entire situation as strange. True, people had done things differently back then. Otherwise his grandmother might have divorced his grandfather after realizing she wanted no part of marriage save the social and economic position it provided her.

She hadn't. Instead, she'd suggested her husband tend his needs outside their marriage. Her solution had offended his noble grandfather, who'd resisted for well over a decade—until Quinevere McDarby had come to work for Eastman Antiquities. Thus the Eastman-McDarby connection had been born, and this gorgeous woman before him had become a part of Josh's life.

"I tried reasoning with your great-aunt," he admitted. "Didn't work."

"So she wants you to investigate. Isn't this a little out of your normal line of work? I heard you freelance for a bunch of government agencies. Looking for missing people and heavy stuff like that."

Evidently Lennon knew a lot about him, and for some reason the realization pleased him. He nodded.

"How'd Auntie Q rope you into this, then?"

"She called me Josh Three and I caved. I haven't been called that since she gave me the nickname to distinguish me from my father and grandfather. It was a time warp."

"Joshua Eastman *the third* sounds so…highbrow."

"Confusing." At least while he'd been home.

"That's it?" Lennon eyed him doubtfully. "All a girl has to do is call you Josh Three to get her way with you?"

"And heap on the guilt. Works every time."

She tipped the cup at him and said, "Aha! I knew it."

"She laid a whole trip on me. Told me that she and my grandfather had been watching every move I've made during my career. She knew all about my college education, the civil and criminal programs, the certifications and the police training seminars. She even knew the exact date when I graduated with my master's degree." He shook his head, still staggered by Miss Q's revelation. "She said they'd thrown a party for every damned milestone, that they still had the right to celebrate my accomplishments, even if I chose not to be there."

"Whoa. She worked you over big time."

"Like a pro." He had to force a smile. "She resorted to threats, too. Told me my grandfather would haunt me for the rest of my life if I let her—or you—get blown into bits all over the parish. Then there'd be no one left to fund-raise for the Eastman Gallery until the museum can afford to support it. It would be sold off piecemeal…all my grandfather's acquisitions, his life's work—"

"Gotcha." Lennon laughed, then sobered. "Is she in danger?"

"After fifteen years in my business, I've learned it's

never wise to ignore this type of incident. I can't rule out the possibility of a threat, and that's enough for me.''

Lennon nodded and jumped on his reasoning like a speeding bullet. ''We've already had some trouble.''

''What sort of trouble?''

She rose in a lovely display of slim curves and sleek lines, then strode toward his grandfather's portrait to retrieve an envelope from beside the display case below. ''Negative letters and some picketing. Given the, er, *sensitive* subject matter…'' she said, studiously avoiding the marble sculpture propped erect beside her. ''There are always supporters and detractors.''

''Let me see.''

She sat back down and passed him the envelope, which he opened to reveal a bold message in computer-generated type: ''Erotic art is just an upscale name for smut. Smut doesn't belong in our museums.''

''Have they all been like this—computer printouts with no signatures?

Lennon shook her head, sending pale hair slipping over her shoulder in a sleek wave. ''Most, but not all. Some have been handwritten.''

''I'll investigate and find out what's going on.''

''Thanks. But I'm still worried about Auntie Q's safety.''

''For the time being Olaf will be a more than adequate bodyguard. Not too many people would want to mess with him, based on his size alone, and he promised me he won't let her out of his sight. But I've got to tell you that Miss Q has the exact same concerns about you.'' Josh paused for effect before adding the kicker. ''She wants me to be your bodyguard.''

A golden brow arched skeptically. ''Oh?''

''She hired me for round-the-clock protection. She's

afraid if there's a personal threat it might place you at risk, since you've been active in opening the gallery, too."

"What do you think?"

He brushed stray hairs from her cheek, knowing he had no right to touch her, yet unable to help himself all the same. "I'd hate to see anything happen to you, *chère.*"

She leaned away from him and forced a smile—an act of sheer determination if ever he saw one. "Well, it's very nice of you to be concerned, but you don't want to get stuck baby-sitting me through all the erotic activities we've got scheduled."

Josh could think of any number of erotic activities he'd willingly get stuck in with Lennon, but before he could see past images of her long legs naked and twined with his, she said, "I'll be fine. I understand why Auntie Q is worried, but no one has thrown a grenade at me."

He shrugged. "I promised."

Leaping off the bench, she handed him the empty coffee cup, cocked her fists on her hips and glared at him. Josh settled back against the wall while she came up with an astonishing number of reasons why she didn't need protection.

He didn't buy a single one. Her heart-shaped face revealed barely suppressed panic. He considered the possibility that he wasn't the only one who'd noticed the chemistry between them. The lady clearly found something disturbing about sharing close quarters for the long weekend.

"What's the trouble, *chère?*"

"I just told you—"

"The *real* trouble. You've got loads of reasons, but no explanation why having me undercover as your bodyguard won't work."

To say Lennon looked offended would have been an understatement. Josh bit back a smile.

Going undercover as Lennon's *anything* worked on a personal and professional level. His connection to the McDarbys and the Eastman Gallery would be an asset to solving this mystery. And this mystery needed to be solved. The whole flash-and-bang attack struck him wrong on a gut level. He'd learned long ago to trust his gut.

This attack meant someone had been waiting outside for Miss Q—or more likely both of them—to leave the gallery and head to Lennon's car. And though that someone had obviously meant to frighten rather than physically harm, that someone already knew too much about the McDarby women. He'd known their schedule, what vehicle they were driving and that he'd catch them together without Olaf, who'd been sent home before midnight to tend to details there.

For anyone to know this much about their activities meant they were being stalked. And stalkers made Josh nervous.

"Olaf can keep an eye on me, too," Lennon suggested.

Josh didn't think so. "Olaf will have trouble keeping up with Miss Q. From what I hear about the schedule, you two will be so busy entertaining and fund-raising, it'll be impossible for one of us to keep track of you both. You need me."

"I refuse to let people see me being…*guarded.*"

That Lennon's argument had deteriorated into semantics about appearances meant he almost had her.

"Miss Q hired me, *chère,* so I'm on your tail until you convince her to fire me."

Lennon scowled. "You said Olaf took her home?" Before he had a chance to answer, she spun on her heel, gifting him with a lovely shot of her departing backside. "Let's go. I'll talk some sense into her."

Josh followed. Inclining his head at his grandfather's portrait as he passed, he decided he wasn't sorry he'd picked up the phone tonight, after all. The ensuing fireworks should prove entertaining, and he quite enjoyed being on Lennon's tail.

3

"I'LL WAIT IN THE CAR while you unload the suitcases,"
Quinevere told her assistant from her comfortable seat in
the limo. No sense standing on the sidewalk when she
needed a moment to collect her thoughts and evaluate her
game plan. "I want you with me when I meet with the
sales director."

Olaf caught her gaze in the rearview mirror. "Problems?"

"I want to check on a few details and make sure the
hotel doesn't make any last-minute changes to our room
assignments."

He held her gaze before nodding, curiosity written all
over his smooth features. With his dark skin and bald
brown head, Olaf looked like he'd be at home in a South
American jungle. He was also strapping enough to make
any prizefighter think twice about raising a fist his way.
Exactly how his Goliath proportions and Scandinavian
name factored into his French Guianese–Creole background
was a question Quinevere had frequently asked through the
years, but had yet to receive a straight answer to. She'd
known the boy since he was nine years old and didn't think
he'd ever get tired of spinning outrageous tales about his
unusual name, not when she suspected he knew how much
she enjoyed his fabrications.

And that wasn't all he knew. The smart, streetwise kid
Joshua had brought home from a trip into the jungle had

matured into a keenly intelligent and insightful man. He eyed her in the mirror with a look that told her he wasn't for a second buying her explanation about room assignments.

"Why are you worried, Miss Q?" he asked. "I thought the LeBlancs confirmed their reservation yesterday."

She smiled. She would let him in on her little secret when she was ready and not a moment before. "They did."

"Then what's the trouble? The extra room?"

Evidently Olaf didn't want to wait until she was ready. He knew something was up and intended to pick her brain. "I'll have management release the extra room from our block. With Mardi Gras, I'm sure they'll have it booked before we unpack."

"I wouldn't do that. I'd hang on to it for a day in case Mrs. DesJardin changes her mind again."

Quinevere grimaced. "Oh, phoo on Lisette. I'd forgotten about her. She's just yanking my chain to see who shows up before she consents to grace us with her presence."

"You're right, but think about *Tête-à-tête*. You don't want to miss the chance to acquire the drawing for the collection."

"Or a monetary contribution to alleviate her guilt if she decides she can't part with the piece." Quinevere wanted Lisette to feel good and guilty if she hung on to the superb black chalk on paper, a François Boucher original. "You're right. I'll keep the spare room, but I've got to confirm that the room assignments will stay exactly as I've arranged them. No last-minute changes."

Olaf narrowed his gaze, but he knew when to ask questions and, more importantly, when not to. She silently thanked Joshua for leaving behind someone so intuitive to help care for her. Most of the time a blessing…

"I'll see to the luggage," he said, maneuvering his six-foot-plus frame from the front seat.

Closing the door behind him, he sealed her in the cool interior of the car. "Olaf dotes on me almost as much as you did, Joshua," she whispered above the hum of the running engine. "And he's going to help me fix this mess, whether he knows it or not."

She sighed, leaning back into the plush leather seat and fixing her gaze through the tinted window on the valet entrance, where Olaf supervised the bellhops.

"I intended the auction to provide Lennon with a place to fall in love, not choose a companion. If I didn't know my great-niece so well, I'd think this was another trick of yours."

The drone of the engine was the only reply. But Joshua could hear her, she knew, and he would approve the steps she'd taken to disabuse her great-niece of the ridiculous notion that she should marry for anything but passion.

Life was far too precious to waste even a second. If Lennon wanted safe, companionable love, she should adopt a pet. A cute little Maltese, maybe, or a needy mutt from the pound.

Companionable was not a defining quality in a husband.

"Boring," Quinevere said with a shudder.

Some women might be content with that sort of life, but not Lennon. Even though she'd been buried in her writing lately, she'd had relationships before with some very suitable men. Nice, healthy romances that had put color in her cheeks and a sparkle in her eyes. She thrived on love, so why she'd convinced herself she would be content with a companionable man while keeping grand passion reserved for her books...

Then again, why wouldn't Lennon think passion belonged outside marriage, given the examples she'd seen?

Her mother had made a career of one-night stands or affairs that never lasted much longer, while Quinevere's relationship with Joshua... She twisted the antique sapphire ring on the third finger of her left hand, finding comfort in the motion, feeling a connection with the man who'd given her the beautiful piece to symbolize their marriage of the heart—a marriage not recognized by the laws of Louisiana.

"There were times, my love, when I wished we could have lived more conventionally, maybe even had our own family," she whispered, a sad, lonely sound that contrasted sharply with the activity outside the car. "But I knew what I was getting into when I decided to spend my life with you. I've never once regretted my choice.

"Oh, Joshua, all Lennon has ever seen is that she can't have marriage and passion together. We showed her that, and her mother did, too. Why else would she think she has to choose?"

A heavy sort of sadness—the kind that weighted a person all the more because there was no way to rewind the clock and say things that should have been said long ago—seeped through Quinevere like the muggy air of a New Orleans summer afternoon right before a rainstorm.

Oh, Joshua. Tears prickled her eyes—she cried so easily now. Whether her tears were a function of old age or simply loneliness for the man she'd chosen to share her life with, Quinevere couldn't say. She only knew that she wanted so much more than companionship for Lennon, a great-niece who was her daughter in every way but by birth.

Blinking furiously, Quinevere caressed her wedding band and took a deep breath. "I've got this under control, my love. I've got a plan to get Lennon back on the right track again, and maybe even that grandson of yours, too. I can't join you in the ever after until I've taken care of the details down here."

And that meant ensuring those she and Joshua left behind had a chance to find happiness, too.

By the time Olaf appeared at the passenger side of the car, Quinevere managed a smile. Perhaps with luck, and Joshua's divine assistance, she'd soon smell grand passion blooming beneath her nose. Given the way Lennon had fought tooth and nail this morning to convince them she didn't need Josh Three around, Quinevere suspected she'd smell grand passion blooming sooner rather than later.

Especially given Josh's reaction to Lennon.

He'd sat in her parlor, just as comfortable as you please, all respect and attention and stoic deliberation of Lennon's rants, but his beautiful green eyes had twinkled devilishly.

Quinevere recognized that look. She'd seen it in his grandfather's eyes too often not to know exactly what it meant.

Josh Three was interested in Lennon.

So Quinevere had simply told her great-niece to cope with her bodyguard or stay home. That was that. Lennon had chosen to cope.

Ah, *l'amour.*

"WHAT DO YOU MEAN you can't upgrade my suite to one with two bedrooms?" Lennon asked the desk clerk incredulously. "I know there's a spare suite with the art gallery reservations."

This was the Château Royal, a hundred-seventy-year-old establishment in the French Quarter known for its five-star hospitality. That was why Auntie Q had chosen this hotel. That and the fact it was within walking distance of the art museum. Fighting Mardi Gras traffic from their home in the Garden District didn't make sense when they had activities scheduled between the hotel and the museum practically all weekend.

"We've been told we're not allowed to reassign any rooms."

"But I'm with the art gallery."

"I'm sorry," the desk clerk said apologetically. "You'll have to take it up with the coordinator."

Auntie Q.

She should have known. No doubt her great-aunt had foreseen the trouble with Lennon and Josh's room arrangement and wasn't about to allow for plan B.

Lennon wouldn't give in so easily. "I'm booked in the Carriage House. Can't you just move me into the main hotel?"

"It's Mardi Gras." The desk clerk shrugged in entreaty, silently begging Lennon to cut her some slack. "I don't have a suite in the main hotel to give you."

Staring at the uniformed clerk, she tapped her credit card on the desktop. Didn't this woman realize she was asking her to share a king-size bed with her new bodyguard?

Of course not. How could she know? Most of the *normal* population—which included anyone not related to Auntie Q—couldn't appreciate the ramifications of living with a great-aunt who played life by her own rules.

But Lennon knew what that king-size bed would mean— an awkward conversation about sleeping arrangements. It was bad enough being forced into such close proximity with a man who looked like a romance hero in 3-D, a hero who didn't seem to mind the logistics of guarding her body 24–7.

Sure, this assignment probably seemed like a dream to a man who routinely hunted down criminals, bail jumpers and the ilk that hid from government authorities, but it was a nightmare as far as she was concerned. She'd known it the instant she'd awakened to find Josh staring down at her with those green bedroom eyes.

At first she'd thought she'd been dreaming, that the handsome man in the gallery portrait had come to life. Which was certainly an understandable reaction on her part, given how exhausted she was and how much Josh looked like his grandfather.

But once Lennon had realized who her visitor was, she'd recognized trouble in Josh's potent gaze, in the quick smiles that made her heart beat too fast. He'd been watching her sleep and she knew with that fluttery sense of intuition deep inside that he'd liked what he'd seen.

"Is there a problem?" Mr. Hero himself asked, suddenly appearing behind her.

Yes, a big one, but Lennon wasn't going to tell him that. She could sense him towering over her, and his voice resonated through her like a caress.

Jeez! Who'd have guessed the black sheep would have grown up to be the stuff sinfully delicious heroes were made of? Not her, for sure. She hadn't thought much about Josh Eastman since she'd been ten years old. She may have heard about him from his grandfather, but for some reason Great-uncle Joshua hadn't mentioned how seriously attractive his grandson had grown to be.

Taking a deep, calming breath, Lennon turned around and lifted her gaze.

His eyes, greener than the lawns along Rue St. Charles, gave her a jolt. *Another deep breath.* "They can't upgrade my suite to a two bedroom."

"I don't mind sharing a bedroom with you, *chère.*"

He smiled, only his wasn't a smile as Lennon had ever thought of one. His smile lit his face with arresting candor, drew her attention to how his white teeth dazzled in contrast to the dark shadow of stubble along his chiseled jaw.

For her last three books, she'd begged her editor to find a cover model with such strong, cut features, only to have

Ellen laughingly tell her that those heroes didn't exist anywhere but in the stories she wrote.

Wrong. She'd be sure to tell Ellen when they next spoke.

Turning back to the desk clerk, Lennon handed her the credit card, but Mr. Hero plucked it from the clerk's grasp.

"Use mine," he whispered in her ear, a burst of warm breath that tickled her hair and sent goose bumps down her arms. "You're my client, which means I pick up the tab from now until the case is over. Standard procedure."

Lennon didn't argue. The man was a reputed professional, after all, and she had no desire to wind up scattered in pieces all over the parish. She had to do whatever she could to help Josh contain any threat to her great-aunt's safety.

But she didn't have to abandon her own plans.

Auntie Q may have thrown her a curve by providing her with a roommate, but Lennon was here to scope out Mr. Right. Josh Eastman was *not* Mr. Right. Near as she could tell, he lived in the wrong part of town, worked in the wrong career, and he didn't even look the part of a decent husband with his too-long black hair, rugged hero face and green bedroom eyes.

And, jeez, he must be nearly as tall as Olaf, a strikingly obvious fact as he towered above the bellhop after they arrived in the Carriage House. An intimidated bellhop, if the way the young man jumped at his directions was any indication.

Lennon wanted to rear *normal* children, and any child of Josh's might grow to be a giant. Not such a bad thing for sons, when she thought about it, but she didn't want her girls to tower above their classmates. Of course, tall girls could always become fashion models or basketball players....

That settled it. Josh was Mr. Wrong incarnate. And how

difficult would it be to find Mr. Right with Mr. Wrong dogging her heels all weekend? Lennon didn't want to think about it.

Placing her laptop on the table, she checked out the suite. As a turn-of-the-century addition that occupied the rear of a lovely inner courtyard, the Carriage House afforded her privacy.

If not for her new roommate, the suite would have been perfect. Though not large, it comprised a bedroom and living area spacious enough for a neat arrangement of antique chairs and a sofa. With fourteen-foot-high ceilings and French doors that opened onto a small balcony, the airy layout should offset the addition of her unexpected guest. Hopefully.

"That looks like the last of it, sir," the bellhop said, and Lennon couldn't miss the hopeful note in his voice. "Was there anything else you needed?"

"That's it." Josh tipped the boy.

Lennon hoped he'd been generous, given the ridiculous amount of electronic equipment he'd brought, and decided he must have been when the bellhop disappeared with a smile and an enthusiastic, "Let me know if you need anything else."

An adjoining suite with another bed would have been nice.

But Josh seemed more interested in taking stock of their surroundings than with the sleeping arrangements.

Lennon opened her laptop case and checked the battery. She'd brought it to try and catch up on her deadline. This manuscript was due on her editor's desk by the end of the month, and she had to leave time to edit, make corrections, then add Ellen's revisions…. Lennon shook her head. She just couldn't think about all she had to do without getting overwhelmed.

Heading into the bedroom, she exhaled in resignation. What she'd considered quaint and charming on her tour of the hotel a year ago seemed completely inadequate now. The petite Queen Anne sofa occupying the living room would be nowhere near large enough to accommodate a man of Josh's size, leaving this king-size sleigh bed as the only alternative.

Hefting her garment bag over her shoulder, Lennon headed back out to the living room.

Josh stood from where he'd been crouched beneath the table, presumably connecting a surge board to the power supply. "Problem with the closet?"

"I want my things out here, where I'll be sleeping."

His green gaze caught hers, potent with amusement, making Lennon suddenly feel self-conscious. "Problem with the bed?"

"No. But there are only two places to sleep—this sofa and that bed." She glanced through the doorway at the item in question. "A rollaway won't fit because the suite's so small, and the sofa won't work for you. You can have the bedroom."

Josh followed her gaze and a smile curved his lips. "All right, charity case, let's cover some ground rules." Half sitting on the edge of the table, he folded his arms, drawing her attention to the way his strong biceps stretched the cotton of his white Henley shirt. "I'm here to protect you, and I can't do that if I'm asleep in the bedroom while you're out here." He inclined his head toward the balcony. "Especially with those French doors. Anyone could break a pane and come in for a visit. Not safe."

The man had dressed in jeans, a casual outfit markedly similar to the one he'd shown up in at the gallery. While it wasn't inappropriate for check-in at the Château Royal, he might have worn newer jeans, or at least a pair that didn't ride so low on his hips they were distracting.

"All right." She willed the observation from her mind and hoped she sounded nonchalant. "If my suggestion won't work, what do you recommend?"

"We've only got two choices, *chère.* I sleep out here with you or you sleep in there with me."

"Are you offering to sleep on the floor so the bad guys have to crawl over you to get to me?"

"That wouldn't be my first choice, no. I'm not real fond of tile floors when there's a bed big enough for two." His smile widened, carving deep lines in his cheeks and narrowing his eyes to lushly fringed slits. "Afraid you won't be able to resist me?"

Lennon sighed. The only things missing were a cape and a sword to make him a perfect rogue. "I'll control myself."

Eyeing him with what she hoped was unruffled coolness, Lennon swept back into the bedroom with her garment bag. She wouldn't dignify his teasing. He might find the situation amusing, but she had concerns. How could she concentrate on finding Mr. Right with Josh under her nose—and in her bed?

She had no easy answer, but luckily Josh gave her time to mull over the problem while he remained in the next room unpacking his equipment. She did manage to put their sleeping arrangements from her mind—until he turned up in the bedroom with his own garment bag.

Hanging it over the bathroom door, he helped himself to a seat on the bed. "I need to assess potential threats. I've studied the information available online and what the press has written, but you need to fill in the blanks."

Lennon smoothed a dress into place on the rack, giving herself a chance to school her expression and calm her jangled nerves. Josh wanted to discuss business. She could do that—she could discuss *anything* but sleeping arrangements. Especially with him sprawled out on the bed he expected both of them to sleep in.

"What can I tell you?" Good, her voice sounded normal.

"Define a 'risqué buffet of events designed to advance understanding of erotic antiquities'."

She recognized the quote from the invitation. "Tonight starts with a cocktail party in the sculpture garden. Let's see…" she ticked off the events on her fingers to keep track "…then there's a scavenger hunt, masque, musicale, poetry reading, several fine art showings featuring different artists, a modeling session and of course, the bachelor auction."

"A modeling session?"

Judging by the frown etching his chiseled jaw, Lennon could see he didn't know what to make of that one. "Try your hand at becoming a model or an artist."

"Exactly how are these events risqué?"

"Aside from featuring erotic art?"

"Obviously."

"Well," she drawled, wanting to rattle his air of bored calm, as if lying on a bed discussing risqué events was all part of his normal workday. "The modeling studios are set up like boudoirs, with props to create a sexy mood, and locked doors for privacy. The photography equipment is digital, of course, so our guests can get creative without worrying about anyone else seeing their artwork." She inhaled a deep breath for dramatic effect. "Just pop the disk out of the camera and take it home to view or print."

Even from this distance, she could see the lightning flash of surprise smoldering in the depths of his eyes. Lennon paused in her unpacking, holding a slinky beaded sheath in front of her, and met his gaze with a carefully blank expression of her own.

He must have seen right through her, though, because he

recovered with impressive speed and rose to her challenge. "What's risqué about the masque?"

"The guests have to impersonate characters who've contributed to enhancing erotic culture."

"I hope you're going as Lady Godiva. Riding naked through the village...I'd say she did her bit to support the arts."

At his quicksilver grin, Lennon's heart thudded dully in her chest. "I can't tell you or I'll spoil my debut."

She couldn't tell him or he'd know her bravado was all an act. She might sound unaffected by discussing risqué events with this man, but she wasn't. The sight of him sprawled across that shiny bedspread—long muscled lines of his body making it impossible not to think of how it would feel to snuggle against him—disconcerted her completely.

Mr. Wrong, Mr. Wrong, Mr. Wrong.

His grin widened, and Lennon suspected her efforts went for nothing, because he probably already knew she was bluffing.

"Seeing you dressed in nothing but hair will be worth the wait, *chère.*"

He was definitely on to her.

Lennon jammed the sheath dress onto the rack and tried to segue back to business, without appearing to admit defeat. "Auntie Q likes to mix business with pleasure, so fund-raising isn't so dry and stuffy. Talking business with Lady Godiva should liven things up, don't you think?"

"The Eastman Gallery could expect some hefty donations."

"Humph." Lennon didn't need to turn around to see his grin. She heard amusement loud and clear in his voice.

"Okay, I got the risqué part. Now I need to know how

the finances work, but let me grab something to take notes on.''

From the corner of her eye she saw him sit up and swing his legs over the side of the bed. Lennon waved him off and said, ''I'll get something. Where?''

''My briefcase on the table.''

She sailed out of the room without a backward glance, relishing the activity and the breather from being bombarded with testosterone at close range. ''Do you think money could be the motive, Josh?''

''I always cover all the angles. You never know what'll motivate people.''

Lennon didn't reply, just dug through his briefcase and told herself to get a grip. She couldn't think of Josh as a romance hero. Sure, he looked the part of some Navy SEAL or Cold War spy, but he needed a quick demotion to a more human plane.

Palming a day planner from his briefcase, she weighed its worn leather cover in her hand. Businessmen used day planners. Businessmen from the twenty-first century. Day planners hadn't been around when swashbuckling romance heroes had inhabited the earth. Except the hero she currently wrote about. A spy for England during the Napoleonic Wars, he was also a titled lord, which meant he had an estate to manage and would own a leather-bound journal to record his activities, one very similar to this....

Arrgh! Heading back into the bedroom, she tossed the day planner at Josh, ignored his politely murmured thanks, and sought refuge in the closet. ''The finances are really very simple. In a nutshell, your grandfather bequeathed his collection to Auntie Q along with the pieces they owned jointly. She took those and included some she owned herself and donated them to the museum. Together, they included a financial endowment large enough to construct the gallery and the sculpture garden.''

After hanging up her dress for the cocktail party, she stowed her empty garment bag on the closet floor, out of the way. ''Technically, the museum owns the collection now, but there's overhead it can't swing until the exhibition starts bringing in income. That's where the fund-raising comes in. We need to collect enough to carry the Joshua Eastman Gallery until it establishes a name for itself.''

Lapsing into silence, she stacked her shoe boxes to the sound of Josh's pen strokes.

''Sounds like a lot of work,'' he finally said.

''It has been. Pulling this together has consumed Auntie Q for the past two years.''

''I'm sorry my grandfather wasn't around to help her.''

Lennon didn't have to turn to know he watched her. She sensed his gaze, felt her heartbeat thud in response. ''Auntie Q's convinced he meant to keep her busy after he died.''

''What do you think?''

''She's probably right.'' Steeling her nerves, Lennon swung around, leaned back against the wall and tucked her legs beneath her. ''Great-uncle Joshua used to talk about his plans for this gallery. It was his passion. But whenever I'd ask when he was going to break ground, he'd just smile and say he wasn't done collecting yet. He told me not to worry, though, that he'd been given Auntie Q as a gift to help him focus on what was important, and that she'd make sure things got done. I remember thinking he knew he might not be around to get the gallery started because he was older than she was.''

''You knew an entirely different side of my grandfather.''

She heard regret in Josh's voice, a realization that he'd

missed out on something special. She wanted to reach out and smooth the tight edges from his mouth, say something to erase his hurt, but squelched the crazy urge. She had no right to comfort this man. She hadn't seen him in years and hadn't really known him even back then.

Sure, he'd sometimes showed up on their doorstep, and Auntie Q had whipped out her stash of cookies. But Lennon had been eight years his junior and not particularly interested in hanging around to listen to whatever her great-aunt coaxed out of him.

"Damned bizarre situation." His gaze pierced the distance, and Lennon felt the connection as if it were physical. Two people bound by the actions of others, each clinging to their parts of the whole and wondering what they were missing.

Then, in an instant, Josh shuttered his expression behind a grin. "Are you scarred forever?"

"Naw. Just focused. Despite the unusual gestalt of the situation, what's not to like about love?"

"Ah." He gave a brisk shake of his head that sent his black ponytail brushing his collar. "The romance writer."

"I can write it however I like it."

"And how do you like it, *chère?*"

The intensity of his expression made her pulse quicken. "If you want to know, you'll have to read my books to find out."

She hadn't meant her reply as a challenge, but it was definitely taken as one. She could see fire leap into Josh's eyes, his smile broaden appreciatively.

"I'll keep that in mind." Swinging those long legs over the side of the bed, he planted his booted feet on the floor. "Right now I've got to get hotel security on the phone about the letter that was waiting for Miss Q when she arrived. I want them to question the desk clerks to see who dropped it off. Be ready to leave for the cocktail party at four.'' He crossed the length of the bedroom in a few quick strides. ''I'll need a copy of your guest list. Miss Q said you had one.''

Lennon nodded, feeling a bit off balance, disappointed that she'd been so easily dismissed from their bantering.

She squelched that feeling fast. ''I'll get it for you. Josh?'' she added, causing him to stop in the doorway. ''Auntie Q got a threatening letter last night at the museum, one this morning at home and another today when she arrived here at the hotel. Do you think whoever's harassing her may decide that frightening her isn't getting the point across? Do you think he might try to really hurt her?''

His expression sobered, but he met her gaze with a promise in his. ''Don't worry. Olaf and I won't let anything happen.''

For the first time since Josh had shown up, Lennon felt that perhaps Auntie Q had been right to call him.

4

A MAN WHO HADN'T HAD SEX since creating his own fireworks with a flight attendant over July Fourth weekend had no business holing up with a woman who looked like Lennon, Josh decided. Not if he expected himself to act with any self-control.

Dressed for the cocktail party, she was a vision in a clingy dress that molded her curves as though she'd been dipped in gold. Delicate chains flashed around her neck and wrists, drawing his attention to all the creamy skin exposed in between.

And her legs... Those strappy sandals should have been illegal the way they showed off graceful ankles, defined sleek calves until her legs seemed a mile long.

Josh's pulse kicked hard, a reminder that July Fourth weekend had been *seven months ago.*

"Wow, black sheep. You clean up nicely." She paused in the bedroom doorway and eyed him in a way that he didn't think his several-years-old tux warranted. "If I didn't know better I'd think you actually still belonged in our world."

"Must have me confused with someone else." The thought of making small talk at this party tonight was killing him.

"Nope, don't think so." When she smiled, shiny peach lipstick made her lips look ripe for kissing. "You may not choose to live the part, but you can't rub off good breeding. It sticks like sugar on Monkey Bread.''

''Makes years of chasing bad guys a total waste.''

''Not necessarily.'' Slinging the gold-chain strap of a handbag over her shoulder, she sauntered into the living room, each fluid stride making her dress shimmer over sleek curves.

Josh swallowed hard.

Popping open her handbag, she rooted through its contents, the smooth fall of blond hair sexily hiding her profile. ''I thought I stuck my key in here. Lipstick. Blush. Mints.''

''I've got mine.''

''Ah, key.'' She glanced at him, apparently ignoring the fact that she wouldn't be out of his eyesight long enough to need her own key. ''All set.''

''Let's go. We need to do a walk-through of the gallery.'' Preceding her to the door, he held it wide as she passed through, catching a whiff of her subtle spicy scent.

''I'm ready.''

And Josh was, too—damn his long-ignored libido.

But the protesters they encountered when their cab pulled up to the museum's main entrance soon demanded his attention.

''I can't believe they're here so early,'' Lennon said, peering out at the small crowd crossing streets and turning corners. It was a group of seemingly normal people Josh might expect to see commuting home on a Friday night for a weekend of watering lawns and family picnics.

Except for the signboards.

Don't Confuse Art With Pornography!

Keep Smut away from our Local Treasures!

Lennon inhaled deeply, as though steeling herself for the unpleasant encounter ahead, and reached for the door handle.

"Not yet, *chère*." Josh stayed her hand, before telling the driver, "Circle the block. We'll let museum security deal with them, so Miss Q and Olaf won't have to when they arrive."

He retrieved his cell phone, dialed and waited for the call to connect. "Josh Eastman with private security for the Eastman Gallery. I've got protesters outside the main entrance...."

While they drove around waiting for security to disperse the crowd, Josh scanned the nearby rooftops for any signs of a threat and pondered the connection between the messages on the protesters' signs and the letters Miss Q had received today.

Their messages mirrored almost exactly, but the format of the letters surprised him. To date, Miss Q had received only handwritten and computer-generated letters, yet both messages today had been pieced together from cutout magazine letters, like cheesy warnings from a B flick.

The connection between the messages and the protesters' signs seemed obvious—too obvious. He mentally filed the concern, and by the time the entrance had been cleared and he'd paid the driver, Josh decided to have security arrange for the police to patrol the museum to keep any other such groups from forming.

Protesters provided the perfect cover to involve the police without raising the museum's suspicions about the flash-and-bang attack. But unfortunately, the process took another thirty minutes and put them way behind on the walk-through of the sculpture garden and the new gallery.

As it was, they arrived at the reception along with the guests, but Miss Q didn't seem to mind.

"Did you case the joint?" she asked breathlessly, apparently relishing being part of an active investigation.

Josh let Lennon explain about the protesters, and then mentioned the security measures he'd implemented.

"Oh, Josh Three," Miss Q said. "I just knew you'd take care of everything. Now I don't have to worry about this letter that was waiting for me when I arrived." She plucked a folded white envelope from her handbag and handed him what proved to be another cut-and-paste warning: "Museums shouldn't have XXX ratings!"

"How'd you get it?" he asked.

"From the clerk at the information desk. He said someone left it on the counter."

Any of the protesters could have slipped inside the building unseen, so Josh didn't hold much hope of discovering who'd delivered it. "I'll talk with security."

Miss Q beamed as though he'd made her day, and Josh couldn't help feeling pleased that he'd reassured her. Her approval had always had a way of pumping him up.

"Olaf," he said, extending his hand.

"Mr. Joshua would expect us to keep his ladies safe."

Olaf obviously meant business. Josh recognized the outline of a shoulder holster under the man's formal wear. The way his pants pulled suggested another weapon tucked in the waistband. And if his personal arsenal wasn't enough, he hovered over Miss Q like a Saints' defensive lineman.

"Agreed."

Miss Q darted an approving gaze from one to the other. "I'm not surprised about the protesters, though. Given the amount of coverage the media gave us today."

"I haven't had a chance to look at the paper yet." Lennon frowned. "They haven't said anything awful, have they?"

Olaf met Josh's gaze and laughed, a sound like the rumble of an avalanche. "Miss Q and Lennon resent the collection being termed a pornography exhibit."

"Pornography, bah!" Miss Q waved an impatient hand. "It boggles my mind to see how many narrow-minded and misinformed people there are in this world. Sensuality is part of every culture. Even the earliest tribes had sexual rituals. Why shouldn't those rituals be appreciated as part of history?"

"No reason I can think of," Josh said. "I'm sure you and the Eastman Gallery will heighten society's awareness."

Miss Q beamed once more. "The media is doing its part, too, which is why we have detractors lining up at the doors. Nothing negative today, though, except Agnes, the old bat, made sure the cultural society wasn't officially connected."

"Agnes is the current president of the society," Lennon whispered as an aside.

Josh nodded.

Miss Q fixed a laser-blue gaze over the rim of her champagne glass. "Agnes is miffed because I didn't ask that smarmy grandson of hers to participate in the bachelor auction."

Lennon shrugged. "Some might consider him a good catch."

"Wilfred the weird, dear? Perish the thought. He may have money, but he didn't earn a penny of it. It's all his grandfather's. Not to mention that Olaf caught him slinking around Bourbon Street with a *person* as tall as he is, who was dressed prettier than a debutante at her coming out party, if you take my meaning."

Lennon must have, because she barely swallowed back a laugh at her great-aunt's delicate description of a crossdresser.

"If that's where his tastes lie," Josh said, "then you're right not to include him in the auction. His grandmother would only be more annoyed if no one bid on him."

Olaf laughed. Lennon arched a fine golden brow.

Miss Q passed her glass to Olaf and clapped delightedly. "You're absolutely right, Josh Three. We couldn't have that. The whole point of this weekend is to educate the public about erotic antiquities and convince the tight fists around here to contribute to the gallery, either with art from their own collections—if I deem the pieces worthy, of course—or by donating monetarily."

"With the lineup of risqué fund-raising events you've got scheduled, I'm sure you'll meet your goals," he said.

Miss Q's eyes glowed with amusement. "There's something to appeal to everyone—the art exhibition, the masque, the scavenger hunt. I hope you'll find something that appeals to you."

Glancing at Lennon, Josh remembered pressing against her in the cab. He'd find something to amuse him, no doubt.

"When you're done in the garden, dears, I want you to go talk to Louis Garceau and his cronies. See what they think about our first edition of Shakespeare's *Venus and Adonis*. What a coup. Your grandfather and I tracked down that book right before he died. There was thought to be only one surviving copy and Louis has been trying to corner me to ask about it."

She scowled. "You tell him it has been authenticated and any true literati would know the difference between a 1593 first edition and a facsimile reprint. That literary set always annoys me." She lifted her gaze to Josh, blue eyes twinkling. "They get so academic about an orgasm. I always thought the whole point was *not* to think while I was having one."

"It's more fun that way," Josh agreed.

Lennon said, "Auntie Q!" in a singsong exhalation that clearly conveyed her exasperation, but Josh found the old woman's humor refreshing. He'd spent too many years at

functions that were exercises in patience because his grandmother didn't know the meaning of the word *fun*.

Plucking two flutes of champagne off the tray of a passing waiter, he handed one to Lennon. "If you'll excuse us,
Miss Q, Olaf. We've got to interrogate your guests."

"You shouldn't encourage her," Lennon cautioned, once
out of earshot.

"Why?"

"She doesn't care who's around, and she's worse than
a sailor when she gets going. When Great-uncle Joshua was
alive, they could get me blushing so hard I thought my
cheeks would melt."

"Sounds like you went to the fun parties."

"You think?" She eyed him as if that thought hadn't
occurred to her before.

Josh didn't want her thinking he'd resented sharing his
grandfather. Lennon had been dealt her cards just as he had.
Neither of them had been given much choice.

"Come on. Let's go talk to your guests." Taking her
hand, he led her onto a cobbled path that led around the
garden.

A live band played on the piazza in front of the fountain,
filling the garden with mellow strains of jazz. Twilight
glazed everything in a starry haze, making it damned hard
to differentiate between the walkway and shadowed reces-
ses in the foliage. Josh could only follow the jagged slices
of artificial light cast by strategically placed lamps.

"This place is so spread out," Lennon observed, mirroring his thoughts as he tried to map the layout mentally.
"Another grenade could come from just about anywhere,
couldn't it?"

"Not unless the assailant wants to be hauled off to jail."
At her look of confusion, Josh explained, "A twelve-foot
security wall surrounds the perimeter. The only entrance to

the garden is from inside the gallery, and museum security has it covered.''

''Oh.'' Looking relieved, she cast her gaze around. ''And Olaf promised Great-uncle Joshua he'd care for Auntie Q, so I know he will.''

''He will. I'm not surprised he transferred his attention to Miss Q rather than stay on at Eastman Antiquities. He picked the better of the jobs.''

Given his choice of staying on as part of the Eastman empire or tending a flighty, but sweetheart of an old lady and her gorgeous niece, Josh would have found himself part of the McDarby household, too.

''That's very nice of you to say.'' Drawing to a halt in a bower, Lennon lifted her gaze, the amber glow in her eyes deeper than ever in the lamplight. ''I know you won't let anything happen to me, either. You've come to the rescue like a knight in shining armor.''

Her voice was light, teasing, but there was no question in it, only a solid assurance that she trusted him to do what he'd promised. That she felt so safe with him came as something of a surprise. He wasn't expecting that, hadn't had anyone who meant anything rely on him in a very long time. Apparently Lennon meant something. Why? Because of her connection to Miss Q and his grandfather? Or because he was attracted to her?

And he was attracted to her in a big way. Just being with her heightened all his senses. A breeze kicked up, preventing him from sweating in his tux, but not enough to raise the hairs along Lennon's bare arms. The guests' chatter crackled above the music like the buzz of an electrical wire.

Lennon made him aware in a way he couldn't remember ever having been aware of a woman before, on some emotional level he'd always managed to ignore. Ignoring Lennon was impossible, so he resorted to evasive maneuvers.

"Who's this?" He motioned to a nearby sculpture.

Lennon followed his gaze to the marble sculpture that occupied the bower. "Calliope."

"The muse of epic poetry?"

"Careful, black sheep, your classical education is showing." Lennon's whiskey-smooth eyes glinted with amusement and she cocked her head sexily to survey the sculpture.

Josh surveyed her, not nearly as enthralled with the sculpture as he was by the way the delicate gold-link chain she wore around her neck dipped into the shadows of her cleavage.

When an accented male voice rang out, "Lennon, love" he dragged his gaze from the lovely lady to see a man with a pencil-thin mustache and a goatee hurrying toward them.

A suspect.

"Get ready." Lennon passed Josh her champagne glass and extended her hands to the newcomer in a gesture of fond welcome. "Louis, I was looking for you. Auntie Q said you wanted to hear about *Venus and Adonis.*" She dutifully lifted her face as the man brushed kisses on both cheeks.

"She wouldn't tell me a thing, the devil, except to say I could find you in the bushes with a man." Swinging a narrowed gaze to Josh, he extended a hand. "Louis Garceau."

"Josh Eastman."

One look at Louis's open mouth confirmed the type of reaction Josh could expect from Miss Q's guests this weekend. In polite New Orleans society, his grandfather's relationship with Quinevere McDarby had been accepted, even respected for its endurance. But his grandfather's life with

Miss Q had not crossed over into his life with the Eastman family.

Never the twain shall meet. Josh's classical education must be failing him because he couldn't remember who'd said that, but with regard to his family, truer words had never been spoken.

Louis finally found his voice. "You're Joshua's…?"

"Grandson," Josh supplied.

"Isn't it wonderful he's here to open the gallery?" Lennon jumped in, and he could tell by her strained smile that she hadn't anticipated this reaction.

"Wonderful," Louis agreed. "But I can't believe you're keeping him to yourself. You simply must bring him over to meet Grant and everyone, or you'll be banished from the literati."

Lennon laughed lightly. "Banished, Louis? I didn't realize I was part of your set."

"We're all holding out hope for you yet." Louis smiled. Motioning them toward the path, he said, "Come, Josh, let me introduce you around. Perhaps you'll have better luck at convincing Lennon to write something real."

"Real, as opposed to what?" Josh returned Lennon's glass, gauging her reaction to the objectionable comment.

She smiled benignly. "As opposed to genre fiction."

Louis didn't seem nearly so compassionate as he hurried them down the path toward the piazza. "So when will you give in?"

"When a publisher offers me a six-figure advance and enough promotion for a shot at a sixty-percent sell-through."

"Writing isn't about money, Lennon. It's about producing something of lasting literary value with a worthy message."

"What was the message of your last book—how far into

depression you could possibly drive your reader?'' A smile accompanied her question, but Josh heard the bite below. So did Louis Garceau, if his frown was any indication. ''After I finished that story, I walked around for three days feeling like someone had murdered my best friend.''

''I evoked your emotions, didn't I?''

''Mission accomplished.'' When Louis turned a corner, she caught Josh's gaze and rolled her eyes. ''But I prefer to leave my reader with a smile and a satisfied sigh.''

''It's not real satisfaction.'' Louis glanced back at them.

''That's the whole point. I get my fill of real every time I pick up the *New Orleans Daily Herald* or turn on the news. I'll take fantasy in my leisure reading, thank you, and leave you literary heavyweights to mourn the state of the world.''

''You should always have a moral to your stories.''

'''There is no such thing as a moral or immoral book. Books are well written, or badly written,''' Josh quoted, deciding he'd never make it through the night if all the guests proved as annoying as this pompous ass.

''Oscar Wilde.'' Garceau looked surprised.

''He was in good company. My grandfather thought art embraced all forms of expression. You have another opinion.''

Garceau gave a nervous laugh. ''No. No, not really.''

''No? I must have misunderstood you then.'' Josh stared the man down, indicating that this topic of conversation had just ended.

Then he segued into interrogation. ''What brings you to the opening? The Eastman Gallery of erotic antiquities doesn't exactly fall into the conventional classical category. Erotica seems related to Lennon's romances, don't you think?''

Though he looked as though it pained him to admit it,

Garceau agreed. The man even went so far as to rationalize his participation in the gallery opening, and to qualify the existence of erotic artwork among the classics.

Josh listened without comment, mostly because Garceau didn't pause long enough to draw breath. He ranted, once flinging his arm around in a display of such exaggerated eloquence that only the agile movements of a waiter saved them all from being covered in champagne.

Lennon caught Josh's gaze above her glass, a slight lifting of her golden brows that accused him of instigating this diatribe.

Josh only smiled. A short-lived amusement, because the rest of the literati set showed up, and they multiplied Garceau's rant by five. Not good.

With Lennon's help, Josh wrestled the conversation back to the gallery opening and everyone's motive for attending. Eventually, the group answered all his questions, before degenerating into a debate on the pros and cons of literary fantasy versus literary reality.

Josh cast his vote for fantasy—the reality of this party was killing him. Interrogating this crew wasted time he could have spent questioning other suspects. As far as he could tell, Louis Garceau and his chums circulated among the philanthropists only to drum up readers for their writing.

Lennon's frown suggested she was just as unhappy with the conversation. Pausing as they returned to the piazza, she handed her empty flute to a passing waiter and refused another.

"Listen, Josh, I appreciate what you tried to do back there, but defending me from literary elitism isn't part of your job description. Just keep me safe from the bad guys, okay?"

"Ah, *chère,* you're asking me to stand by and do nothing

when a man is impugning a lovely lady's art. My grandfather would expect better from me.''

Folding her arms across her chest, Lennon gifted him with a glimpse of the gleaming skin above her cleavage. His heart began a tempo similar to the impatient tapping of her strappy sandals on the cobbled path.

''Unfortunately, there are too many people who don't consider what I write to be of any literary value,'' she said. ''They're entitled to their opinions. I choose to ignore them.''

Josh chose not to. The idea of anyone ragging on Lennon's work didn't sit right. ''Garceau's entitled to his opinion. But not at your expense.''

''I was only teasing about the knight in shining armor business.'' She frowned again, a slight dipping of her brows that warned him she was gearing up for an argument.

After being forced to listen to Louis Garceau and his chums, Josh wasn't in the mood. The only logical thing to do was grab two glasses from a passing waiter and ply Lennon with champagne to distract her.

But Josh didn't feel logical.

He grabbed her hand and brought it to his lips, instead. ''Do you need a knight in shining armor, *chère?*''

5

JOSH PRESSED HIS MOUTH to Lennon's skin. Not quite a kiss, but a preface to a kiss. A slow, sweet sort of beginning that introduced passion to the moment. The way he imagined a knight might try to charm a lady.

She gasped, a soft, surprised sound that couldn't compete with the buzz of voices and strains of jazz music, yet hummed right through him. Her slim fingers molded around his hand like it had been modeled for a perfect fit.

His breath burst gently against her skin, then gusted back against his lips with her taste upon it, warm and just spicy enough to make his pulse rush hard. To block out the noise of the party around them. To make it seem as if they were the only two people in the world.

Josh had never been this aware of a woman. Then again, he'd never been any woman's knight in shining armor before.

It was an absurd idea for a man who spent his life hunting down criminals, and he had to force back a laugh. Only Lennon could make him feel this way. And that shouldn't surprise him, since Miss Q had reared her.

Miss Q had always had a way of bringing out a lighter side of life. He remembered the fun-loving woman who'd always been game to try her hand at deep-sea fishing, or to hop an airboat for an impromptu tour into the bayou. She was as opposite his stern grandmother as Mardi Gras was to a funeral.

In his youth Josh had responded to her ebullience, had often felt daring and gallant in her presence. Which didn't really explain why he was caught up in the feeling now. His life currently involved computer searches, long stake-outs and even longer stints undercover. He didn't have time to pursue women from a world he'd left behind.

But at this moment, with his mouth touching Lennon's sweet skin, work was the last thing on his mind.

"Do you need to be rescued, *chère?*"

Catching her gaze above their hands, he smiled when her kissable lips parted. Her gold eyes were wide with surprise, and Josh knew—man, he knew in his gut—that he wasn't the only one feeling the chemistry between them.

"No." He heard the alarm in her voice as she tugged her hand from his. "I don't need to be rescued."

She took a step back, a clear retreat from the moment, from the intensity of *them,* but Josh pulled her back toward him when she almost collided with a passing waiter.

"Josh!" She caught sight of the impeccably dressed waiter and turned around hastily. "Oh, excuse me. I'm so sorry."

The waiter inclined his head in dignified ac-knowledgment, and Josh let her fingers slip away, then felt curiously bereft of her warm touch.

Finally deciding to do the logical thing, he grabbed two champagne flutes and dragged her back into the crowd, not giving Lennon a chance to recoup. He didn't want to deal with her reaction when he needed to analyze his own and figure out why she affected him this way.

They drank. They ate. They mingled. After a few tense exchanges, Lennon finally recovered enough to chat with guests, commenting on and debating the various pieces in the gallery.

Josh recovered enough to discuss his own appearance

there, a fact that attracted more interest than either his grandfather's collection or Miss Q's risqué events. Putting that interest to good use, he grilled guests about their reasons for attending and gauged their reactions to Lennon.

Slowly—too damned slowly for his taste—he mentally drafted a sketch of the guests and potential suspects. The bachelors participating in the auction were high up on his list, but not because they had means, opportunity or motive for threatening Miss Q. No. Something else was going on. Josh could tell by the way they honed in on Lennon like gorgeous-blond-seeking missiles.

And this latest one was a winner.

Lincoln Palmer, a cosmetic surgeon who apparently ran a highly successful practice in Kenner, took Lennon's hand and brought it to his mouth in a move reminiscent of Josh's own a short time earlier. Only this guy didn't inspire a reaction from her that even remotely resembled panic.

"Finally, a woman I can't improve with my medical tricks."

If Lennon knew he was feeding her a line, she didn't let on. "Now, Linc, if that woman existed, you'd risk going out of business."

"But think how beautiful the world would be."

With an attention to detail honed by years as a P.I., Josh summed the man up with a glance. Doc Linc must be making a dent in prettying up the world himself, judging by his knife-creased profile and chiseled jaw, which suggested he was familiar with both the executing and receiving end of a scalpel.

"Josh Eastman." He stepped in front of Lennon and thrust out a hand.

Doc Linc didn't look pleased by the interruption, and Josh got the impression he'd been trying to ignore that Lennon had an escort, but he recovered quickly enough. "The man of the hour. Everyone is talking about your surprise appearance.''

Apparently Doc Linc wasn't the only one displeased. Lennon stepped in front of him, leaning back on a high heel to tread painfully on Josh's toes in the process.

''Wouldn't have missed it,'' he rasped. ''How'd they rope you into the auction?''

Doc Linc raked another leering gaze from the top of Lennon's shiny blond hair to her strappy sandals. ''You can actually stand next to this exquisite woman and ask me that? I'm hoping Lennon will bid for me.''

Lennon's smile suggested she might consider it, which meant Josh had better figure out whether Doc Linc was on the suspect list. None of the other bachelors had withstood his interrogations long. Time to see how the doc held up… ''So tell me, what's your connection to erotic art and the McDarbys? Are you an enthusiast or a collector?''

In an apparent attempt to impress Lennon with his art world connections, Doc Linc generously spilled his guts. To hear the man tell it, art appreciation ran in his blood like plasma, compliments of some Palmer ancestor who'd picked up a brush to paint a mural on a church wall several centuries ago. While money didn't seem to factor into this appreciation, Doc Linc's knowledge of the McDarby women seemed extreme for their casual social acquaintance.

He had an impressive recall of exactly which art pieces in the gallery Miss Q had donated herself and which she'd owned with Josh's grandfather. He knew how much Lennon had been helping Miss Q with the gallery, the date of her next book release and that she'd first been published in the fourth grade, when her teacher had submitted an essay Lennon had written to a local historic organization.

Doc Linc had done his homework, and his diligence

made Josh suspect he was doing more than just his bit to fund-raise. Exactly what, Josh couldn't say, and before he could find out, Lennon ended his interrogation, cornering him in a grotto sheltered from the piazza by a hedge and a low stone wall.

"What's your problem, Eastman?" she hissed, tapping a strappy sandal impatiently on the cobbled path. Temper made her cheeks flush and her eyes flash—a potent combination.

"You mean aside from becoming the self-appointed Eastman family representative?"

"With me. You've commandeered my last five conversations."

"I'm here to investigate. That means asking questions."

"We were asking questions fine—and a lot less obviously, I might add—until I started talking to the bachelors."

Okay, so she'd nailed him. Driving a finger into his collar, Josh eased aside fabric that suddenly had a viselike grip on his throat. As long as she was calling a spade a spade… "I got tired of watching you hone your flirting skills on every male below the age of sixty."

"Flirting?" Her eyes widened, and she sputtered indignantly. "*Flirting?* Are you talking to me?"

He had the urge to kiss the angry words from her lips. Damn. If he made more time for sex in his life, he wouldn't be caught with a hard-on when gorgeous blond romance writers got in his face.

Regrettably, he hadn't. Time to deal with the consequences, which meant a pulse zipping through his bloodstream like class five rapids. "Yeah, I'm talking to you, *chère.* We're here to question suspects, not play *The Dating Game.*"

Her lashes flew wider, and she stared up at him as if he were a stranger. *"The Dating Game?"*

The squeak in her voice told him she didn't expect a reply. To Josh's amazement, she thrust a fingertip into his chest.

"You're here to interrogate the guests, black sheep. I've got my own agenda. And even if I was flirting—which I wasn't—it's none of your business." With a huff, she spun on her heel and stormed off, leaving him to dodge the handbag that swung wildly in her wake.

Technically, she was right. Josh couldn't say why her flirting grated on his nerves. This wasn't a date. This wasn't even a real job. Not the kind he normally took, anyway. Lennon attracted him, sure, and he attracted her—even if she refused to admit it—but that in no way implied exclusivity.

Ego, maybe? No one had asked, but Josh would lay odds that more than one person tonight was wondering why he and Lennon were working the crowd, stuck together like peanut butter and jelly.

Pushing away from the wall, Josh followed her, smiling as her rounded backside swayed with each quick step she took. This might not be a real job, but it sure was a sweet one.

She slowed when he caught up to her. "Okay, Josh, truce. I'm sorry you've had to field questions about being here."

Her tone had lost its edge of annoyance, and this lightning-quick mood swing revealed another dimension to his protectee. Her anger blazed hot and fast, but appeared to burn out just as quickly.

"I didn't realize you being here would raise so many questions. Auntie Q must not have, either."

Josh wasn't so sure about that. But the word was out and

he couldn't do a thing except hope his family didn't hear about his participation in the gallery opening.

"No problem."

He hoped. This wasn't his family's way. What balanced the Eastman-McDarby connection in high society was that each faction respected the boundaries—and never crossed them.

His grandfather and Miss Q had swung with one circle of friends—the cultural, fun set—while his grandfather and grandmother had swung with another.

Josh hoped those circles never intersected. He also hoped the newspapers would gloss right over his involvement here, or else his grandmother would get wind that her family had just endorsed an erotic memorial to her late husband, and Josh would have some serious explaining to do.

Never the twain shall meet.

A credo to live by, Josh knew. That fact, combined with struggling to keep his hands off Lennon, was giving him the makings of a killer headache by the time the party moved back to the hotel.

"I've had enough, Lennon. Let's go out to the suite." He had a long night ahead of him running database checks on the guests.

She resisted his efforts to haul her from the hotel bar, where the guests had congregated to continue their discussions of watercolor paintings and marble sculptures. "But I really should stay and—"

"Let's go." Wrapping an arm around her waist, Josh steered her toward the door. He wasn't in the mood to watch her shine that high-beam smile on any more bachelors tonight.

She waved a rushed goodbye, but jerked away from him as soon as they stepped into the cool night air of the courtyard. "Josh, I need to socialize with those people. This weekend is the only opportunity I'll have to really get to know them.''

''I'm running background checks.'' He slipped his fingers around her elbow, halting her retreat. ''You'll know more about them than you want to. Trust me.''

She stopped resisting. ''Really?''

''Really.''

His revelation seemed to override her objections, because she fell into step beside him.

''What kind of information do you check?''

''The usual—DMV violations, credit reports, tax status, employment history, medical records, arrests.''

He could practically see her brain working, and wondered whom she wanted inside information on. She didn't say, but that glint in her eyes hinted that he'd find out soon enough.

''What time do things get going in the morning?'' he asked, letting her unlock the door with her key, before brushing past her to check out the suite.

''The gallery tour starts at eight. There's a breakfast beforehand. We should be out of here by six-thirty.''

He motioned her inside. She walked in, sliding the shoulder strap of her handbag back up her bare arm in a sexy move that made her dress ride high on her thighs. Josh's headache faded beneath a surge of blood heading in the opposite direction.

''Wow,'' she said as she passed the table he'd set up as his workstation. ''It looks like central command in here.''

Josh didn't have to ask what kinds of television programs and movies Lennon watched. And in all honesty he supposed that, to a layperson, his communications equipment might resemble something out of a spy movie. One desktop PC acted as server to three portable systems, all configured to perform separate searches and functions. Add those to the peripherals—printer, Global Positioning receiver, video-conferencing equipment, fax machine—and Josh had a mobile office that enabled him to work effectively from just about anywhere.

"I'll be able to run your guests through the national databases."

"You're allowed to access those?"

"The Freedom of Information Act—it's a beautiful thing. Especially if you know how to make it work for you."

"What other kinds of things can you find out? Could you find out if someone had a nasty breakup with an ex-girlfriend?"

So she wanted to know about a man. "If the ex filed a restraining order."

"If not?" Propping a hand on the back of the chair, Lennon tried hard to affect a pose of nonchalance.

Josh didn't buy it. Shrugging off his jacket, he dragged a chair around and sat down, settling in for what looked like a long haul. "Why don't you tell me what you want to know?"

She considered him, the pursing of her full lips and her narrowed eyes suggesting some inner battle. Finally, she drew a deep breath, which, from his vantage point, did amazing things to her chest, and said, "I want information on the bachelors. Stuff I'm not likely to read about in *Who's Who.*"

"No," he repeated. "I told you I'm conducting an investigation, not running some sort of dating service."

"I'm not looking for a dating service, Josh." She inclined her head, sending tawny-gold hair spilling over a bare shoulder, obviously unsure whether she'd heard him right. "I'm looking for a husband."

He could only stare until her words finally clicked.

You're here to interrogate the guests, black sheep. I've got my own agenda.

Recalling the comment she'd made earlier, he said, "You're scoping out potential bridegrooms. That's your agenda."

Her chin raised a notch, but she held his gaze steadily. "The bachelor auction is the perfect opportunity to meet Mr. Right. I'm thinking about my future. And I want someone…" she hesitated, plainly floundering for the right word "…*suitable.* I'd really like your help."

He wondered if she had any idea how mercenary she sounded. "Did it ever occur to you to just go out and fall in love like normal people do, *chère?*"

A hint of color crept into her cheeks and her gaze darted away to settle on his computer equipment. "I intend to fall in love, but I want to make sure it's with the right kind of man."

"It's as easy to love a rich man as a poor man, hmm?"

The second the words were out of his mouth, Josh knew he'd hit a nerve. Everything about her was tentative, from the uncertain tilt of her chin to the way she clasped her hands as though trying to keep them still.

"No. No, it's not like that."

He thought about asking her to clarify the differences, because he'd obviously missed them, but decided he really didn't want to know. "I won't help."

"Why not? You're investigating the bachelors anyway—"

"No."

Shoving the chair back, he stood, but before he'd cleared the table, she'd approached and placed a hand on his arm.

"If it's money, I'm willing—"

"It's not money." He covered her hand with his, liking the cool, satiny feel of her skin even though the thought of

Lennon scoping out potential bridegrooms with left-brain deliberation left him feeling annoyed and somehow…let down.

Josh shouldn't be surprised. He'd been around enough debutantes to know marriages were "arranged" with considerations other than just love. His own grandmother had tried to push him into a marriage with one. He wasn't sure why Lennon's search for Mr. Right bothered him…unless on some level he'd expected more from Miss Q's great-niece.

He stared at her, at the imploring expression on her heart-shaped face; felt the connection of skin against skin. Lennon glanced down at their joined hands and he wondered if she felt the same warmth he did, the same physical jolt that made him want to run his fingers up the length of her smooth arm and explore her texture, her taste.

His fingers tightened over hers. Awareness flared in her gaze, but she didn't pull away.

He did.

"I can't help you, Lennon." His collar seemed to constrict around his throat, making it difficult to breathe.

Turning his back to her, Josh booted up his system, glancing at the fax machine to see if anything had come through. Nothing. The tray was as empty as he suddenly felt inside.

Hearing the tinkle of metal and the click of heels over tile, he turned to find Lennon adjusting her handbag on her shoulder and heading toward the door.

"Where are you going?"

"Back to the bar." She must have recognized his surprise, because she said, "Olaf is there with Auntie Q. If you need to work here, then fine. Work. I promise I'll stay within screaming distance."

"No."

She spread her hands in entreaty. "Look, I'm not trying to be difficult here, but I don't have a choice. I've only got this weekend. If you won't help me find out about these men with your Freedom of Information Act, then I have to find out the old-fashioned way, which means I need to be downstairs in the bar. I'm going."

Without waiting for his reply, she continued toward the door, clearly intending to leave. After a moment of disbelief that she would openly defy him when he was only ensuring her safety, Josh went after her. In a move he'd used a hundred times before—usually to tie up bad guys—he caught her wrists and spun her to face him.

Her expression transformed from shocked surprise to angry bravado, but he knew if he let her go, she'd march right out the door. For lack of a better alternative, he dragged the strap of her handbag down her arm, looped it around her wrists and fastened it to the sturdy wooden finial on top of the armoire.

"No, *chère,* you aren't."

He expected her to demand to be released. Hell, he wouldn't have blamed her if she kicked him with one of those strappy sandals. What Josh didn't expect was that surprised, vulnerable, *melting* look on her gorgeous face.

That expression changed the moment completely.

The sight of her shouldn't have aroused him, shouldn't have sucker-punched him in the gut and made him want to double over with the strength of the blow.

But it did.

With her arms high in the air, bound securely at the wrists, Lennon—all flowy blond hair and sultry eyes— couldn't go off searching for Mr. Right, couldn't retreat from *him.*

Her slender curves spread out before him, she was subject to his control, his whim. He ached to hear her sigh his name—an ache that conflicted with every rational objection.

She gasped, a stunned whimper, though he saw no fear in her eyes, or her face. His gaze trailed downward, over the pulse jumping wildly in her throat, the chest rising and falling sharply, and then he saw. Then he *knew*.

Her nipples strained through the wispy dress, peaked to silken pearls that proved she was as excited as he.

Josh's groan carried over the sounds of their ragged breathing, and he caught her mouth with a desperate demand. *Satisfy me. Fulfill me.*

Her lips yielded beneath his, slanted open to receive him with a warm velvet demand of her own, driving him with an urgency to possess that he'd never before known.

6

OH, NO, THIS WASN'T happening. This couldn't be happening. Lennon should be fuming. She should shove Josh away and draw the line between them. He'd gone too far. But she had no hands. They were tied, *tied,* above her head by a slender gold chain. She should be mortified.

She should *not* be kissing him.

But she was. And she didn't want to stop. Even if her hands were free, Lennon wouldn't push him away. Not with this delicious, dangerous excitement whipping through her. Not when she was bound, completely under his control, *vulnerable...* She found the sensation both unfamiliar and utterly irresistible.

Their breaths clashed, his ragged gasps as unchecked as hers, his mouth insistent, his kiss urgent. She didn't mean to encourage him, but her lips parted and his tongue was suddenly there, tangling with hers, filling every recess of her mouth, exploring, tasting.

A soft sigh slipped from her lips, one more unexpected reaction to this man.

What was happening here? Lennon had no comparison to make. She'd never felt anything like this before. His mouth possessed hers with a demand that made her hot and dizzy and needy. Her breasts had grown heavy and tight. Her nipples tingled. The dull thump between her thighs amplified.

She didn't think Josh had intended to kiss her. He'd

seemed as surprised as she, as powerless to resist the thrill of the moment, this crazy rush of excitement. They'd stumbled upon the tantalizing here, the forbidden and unknown.

The unknown was electrifying.

Lennon wasn't sure what would come next, and the desperate edge to Josh's kisses suggested he barely maintained his control. But she knew, as surely as she knew her own heart raced out of control, that he wanted *next* to happen.

And some barely functioning part of her brain realized he wouldn't touch her until he was sure she wanted *next,* too.

These were uncharted waters for Lennon. She'd never traveled on the edgier side of sex before, except in her novels, where her hero and heroine could explore to their hearts'—to her heart's—content. She'd taken her characters to erotic places before. Erotic for the characters on the page. Vicarious thrills for her.

Should she give way to the wisp of sanity telling her that edgy sex meant passion, and risk? But this was Josh. He'd never hurt her. She knew that with absolute certainty. If she told him to stop, Lennon knew he would.

But she didn't want him to. She wanted him to touch her, because she couldn't touch him....

Arching her back, she pressed full length against him.

It took only one startled breath to register the heat of his hard body. All scorching passion and muscled male. All sinewy ridges and subtle hollows and lean power. A physique honed to breathtaking strength.

It took Josh only one low growl to accept her silent invitation. Thrusting his rough-velvet tongue deeper, he whipped an arm around her, anchored her against him.

Lennon melted. She had no strength to remain upright, would have sunk to her knees had he not held her so tightly, or had her wrists been free. They weren't. Arms raised, breasts jutting, she was stretched out before this man, vulnerable and wanting and subject to his hunger.

He was hungry. With strong fingers he nudged up her hem, bunching gold silk around her hips, revealing her bottom to his exploration. His fingers dug into one silk-covered cheek, not painfully, but purposefully. Lifting her up onto her tiptoes, he pulled her impossibly closer, until the ridge of his erection nestled securely in the juncture of her thighs, a steely presence through the sheer hose.

A thrill shot through her, dark, tense. She shouldn't be so aroused but couldn't help herself. She had no ability to reason, could only react. Satisfaction filled her at the realization that he was as aroused as she.

And then he ground that thick ridge between her thighs, zeroing right in on the knot of nerve endings there. The exquisite pressure dragged another moan from her, increased the throbbing between her legs as if he'd turned up the volume. Indeed, he had, tracing her lips with his tongue, strokes that made her warm breath gust against her skin.

Lennon shivered, a sensation that pumped strength into her legs so she could balance on her tiptoes, rock her hips and ride his erection. Through the fabric of his trousers his hard shaft swelled against her, working the exact spot that made her knees collapse and her breath shudder from her chest in sharp bursts.

Josh growled and his mouth trailed away, sweeping a hot path along her jaw and down her throat, his tongue flicking, his teeth nipping. Lennon arched against him in reply, using his erection to feed the ache inside her, to coax tortured groans from him.

The hand he held around her wrists was only a formality. The chain of her handbag, too, because Lennon wasn't going anywhere while this man trailed his fingertips down her bare arm. Not while he braced his legs apart and held firm against her. Not while this wild pulsing between her thighs made her press against him.

His breath grew harsh and fast. He dragged a finger along each inch of her skin, a sweeping caress that traveled over her shoulder, around her neck. He explored, discovered, exposed just how defenseless she was to his erotic attention.

The tension inside her coiled even tighter, and Lennon trembled again, stunned by the intensity of these sensations, by her response to this man. She wanted to feel his mouth on hers again, but his lips were otherwise engaged....

His hot breath soaked right through the thin silk of her dress, through the wispy lace of her bra to burst in a hot gust over her nipple.

Lennon jolted against him, unprepared for the lightning heat that shot through her, but oh so ready. Josh lifted her breast to his mouth and, with his sooty black head bent low, used his teeth to coax her nipple to a point through the fabric.

She whimpered—there was simply no other word for it. Even to her ears, the whimper was the most needy, deprived sound she'd ever heard, a sound that echoed how much she wanted Josh to free her breast, to possess her in a way she'd never allowed any man to possess her before, had never even thought to.

He took such liberties, this man. And though she'd known him most of her life, he was a stranger....

"Ah, *chère*." His voice was throaty and rough with passion. "You tempt me beyond my control. Either we stop now or I take you into the bedroom."

With his mouth still hovering above her breast and his warm breath tickling her skin, Josh tipped his head back and met her gaze, his own smoldering with the power of his confession.

"Lady's choice." His thick whisper punctuated their shallow breathing and the silence that emphasized that they were two people alone in a suite with one king-size bed.

Scarce centimeters below his mouth, Lennon's chest rose and fell, each broken breath lifting her breast until it almost brushed his lips. The wet mouth print on the rumpled gold silk was a blatant reminder of the intimacies she'd just allowed him, of the abandon she'd felt under his control.

And surely his thoughts mirrored her own, because his lips curved upward in a smile, his white teeth flashing devilishly against his dark skin and hair. He was plainly waiting for her to decide whether they would take the next step to explore this surprising chemistry between them.

Josh Eastman was *not* Mr. Right. He was Mr. Wrong personified, a romance hero straight off the pages of one of her novels. The term "grand passion" took on a whole new meaning with this man, and she'd crumbled beneath his attentions, had gloriously gone to pieces in his arms.

This was exactly what she'd told Auntie Q she didn't want in her marriage—this unsettled, uncertain, out-of-control feeling, as if her next breath might pitch her over the edge of a cliff.

While the wild abandon she'd just experienced in Josh's arms didn't frighten her, Lennon didn't want to find out Auntie Q was right, that she was a late bloomer who needed this sort of passion to find fulfillment. Was she willing to give up her dreams of husband and babies to surrender herself to grand passion?

Josh watched her as if he could see right though her. And he waited, his potent gaze reminding her of how she'd abandoned herself to him. Of how much he wanted her to abandon herself again.

The moment became charged, their closeness filled with questions for which she had no answers. Her wrists ached where the chain bound them. Her dress was still bunched around her hips, exposing her parted thighs.

Her world narrowed to the way this man held her close, how his breath caressed her breast through her dress. Lennon didn't know whether to embrace this side of herself or be ashamed.

When Josh broke the contact, reaching above her head, Lennon's breath hitched audibly. For the space of a heartbeat, she thought he would untie her. But suddenly a fresh red rose he'd plucked from a vase appeared in his hand. With a slight smile, he brushed the fragrant bloom across her lips.

"Got more than we bargained for with that kiss, eh, *chère?*" Dipping his head low, he brushed his mouth across hers as gently as he'd touched her with the soft petals.

The scent filling her nostrils was all Josh, a strictly male scent touched by a hint of the fragrant bloom that would remind her of him until the day she died. Her pulse beat through her veins, slow, languid. Her eyes fluttered shut when his cool silky hair grazed her cheek.

"Ever since I saw you asleep with that sculptured erection in your lap, I've wanted you, Lennon."

His softly voiced admission had the effect of a New Orleans summer rainstorm. It cleansed away her uncertainty and doubts and made everything that had passed between them so very right.

She wanted him, too.

He trailed the rose down her throat as light as a whisper, his mouth following in its wake, gentle brushes of firm lips and soft breath triggering the most amazing flutters inside her, emphasizing how powerfully her body responded to him.

Tracing the bodice of her dress, he circled the rose around the wet fabric until her nipple crested again.

"You want a husband and I can't be one of those. But how about giving me a chance to prove you've still got time to enjoy yourself before the wedding?"

He only wanted a chance.

"You're definitely not husband material." She laughed weakly, a bit hysterically to her ears. "I'm looking for Mr. Right and you're Mr. Wrong in the flesh."

"Should I be offended?"

He sounded as though he'd already decided she'd impugned his masculinity, and she forced open her eyes, felt another flutter at the sight of him poised so erotically over her breast. "If you wanted to be my husband, I suppose you might be offended. If you want to be a romance hero, it's a compliment."

"Define romance hero."

"Romance heroes are fantasy men," she said—an outward show of bravado, when inside she was still rattled and completely relieved that he'd dragged them through what might have been an incredibly awkward moment. For her at least. "Romance heroes are the stuff of grand passion. In books there's always a happily ever after. In real life they're meant for sweeping affairs that leave you smiling every time you remember them."

That green gaze held hers. "So you marry Mr. Right, and have sweeping affairs with Mr. Wrong?"

She nodded.

"And I'm Mr. Wrong?"

"Personified."

His gaze dropped to her breast, watched her nipple strain toward his touch as he traced lazy circles with the rose petals. "Are you in the market for a sweeping affair?"

"I might be."

"If I help you scope out Mr. Right?"

She hadn't thought of that, wasn't thinking of much except holding still, when she wanted to rub her body against his like a cat needing to be stroked.

"Are *you* in the market?" The repercussions of lust with this man were beyond her comprehension right now.

The answer blazed in his eyes, a green fire that scorched her. "If you let me tie you up again."

The arm he'd locked around her waist tightened, anchored her against him, his rock-solid erection emphasizing his point.

Those crazy flutters inside her rioted to get out. "I'll think about it." She didn't know what else to say, couldn't ever remember being more overwhelmed in her life.

Josh straightened, and that devilish half grin flashed. "Me, too, *chère*. Me, too. I'll be thinking about it for a long time."

The rose suddenly disappeared and the moment was broken. Taking a step back, Josh worked one-handed the knot that bound her wrists. "Will you stay now?"

"I'll stay." No question. What would be the point of leaving? How could she think about any man now but the one who'd just kissed her?

Josh let her handbag fall to the floor. The chain strap clinked as it coiled into a pile at their feet, a tinkling reminder of her pleasurable imprisonment. Her wrists sprang free and she wobbled slightly on legs that felt as though her muscles had been tied into knots.

Josh steadied her with a strong arm. Taking one of her hands, he lifted it, surveying the indentations where the chain had bitten into her wrist. As if he could erase the marks, he pressed a soft kiss to her skin, making Lennon shiver.

"It's after midnight, *chère*. Are you heading to bed?"

No, not bed. Not unless she could go there with him, and Lennon simply wasn't ready to take that step just yet.

She didn't think she could bear crawling into bed beside him, to act as if nothing had just happened. Not if she expected to sleep.

She glanced at the antique ormolu clock. "It's not too late. Maybe I can still get some work done. What about you?"

Was it too much to hope that he'd go to bed, leaving her to crawl in bed later when he was safely asleep?

The somber glance he cast at his computer equipment answered that question.

"I've got a long night ahead of me. I'm calling room service for some coffee. Do you want anything?"

"No, thanks." Nothing on that menu would help Lennon figure out what had just taken place between them, what could take place if she abandoned her search for Mr. Right.

JOSH CALLED ROOM SERVICE. While he placed his order, he watched Lennon boot up her laptop. Gold silk shimmered with her motions, a champagnelike effect over slender curves that meant this ache in his crotch wasn't going away anytime soon.

He had no business lusting after Lennon—nothing about the situation worked. He did flings; she wanted a husband.

A husband. He wasn't even sure what to make of that revelation yet. Or of Lennon's spin on Mr. Right and Mr. Wrong. What was it about romance heroes that had her convinced she could only handle them in small doses?

Sounded like a job for an aggressive P.I. And Josh was aggressive if nothing else. At the moment he questioned whether he possessed more aggression than intelligence, because an intelligent P.I. wouldn't be interested in probing the life secrets of his beautiful blond protectee.

Lennon was from a world Josh didn't belong to anymore. He had no use for cocktail parties or cultural philanthropy.

He tracked down missing people, and he'd rather spend his time off fishing in the bayou. Or at a Saints game. Not dealing with endless obligations to family and friends, which was exactly what she—and he by association—was doing at this art gallery opening.

If that wasn't enough, he'd already stirred up enough speculation by appearing at tonight's event. The last thing he needed was to stir up even more by openly consorting with the great-niece of his late grandfather's mistress. His family would go through the roof, and he'd have to deal with the fallout.

Even though at some time in his disreputable past the thought of annoying his family would have satisfied him, nowadays Josh plain didn't want to deal with their reactions. He could almost hear his grandmother: *"I never thought I'd live to see the day when history would repeat itself."*

His father would scowl and pour a brandy. Not because he'd disapprove of his son's affair, but because he wouldn't want to deal with his mother's diatribes any more than Josh did. Josh's mom would be the one rushing around trying to appease everyone and bring back peace to the family. A bad scene all the way around.

So why wasn't Josh worried? Damned good question.

Placing the telephone receiver back in the cradle, he watched Lennon settle herself in a chair, one smooth motion of supple muscle that made his crotch throb hard. And when she swept that honey-blond hair off her shoulders, he could see the fading marks from the chain that had bound her wrists.

Did Auntie Q hire you to be my knight in shining armor, too? Lennon had asked him just hours ago.

Miss Q hadn't and he wasn't, but that didn't change the fact that he felt more than protective toward Lennon. She did things to his libido he'd studiously avoided for two decades.

Josh hoped like hell the coffee would get here soon. If he had any sense at all he'd drink enough to stay awake all night. The thought of sleeping while Lennon stretched out on the bed beside him…well, *that* was a joke worthy of a good chuckle.

"What are you working on?" he asked, swinging around the table to sit in front of his own system.

"I'm revising. This manuscript needs to be on my editor's desk soon and the gallery opening has put me behind."

He tapped the keyboard to wake the system from sleep mode. "A romance novel?"

"I write historical love stories set in Georgian England and the Regency period." She never lifted her gaze from the screen. "I'm calling this one *Milord Spy,* but that's just a working title. My editor will change it to whatever she thinks will sell best."

"Georgian England and the Regency?" He had to dig deep to remember exactly when those time periods were. He remembered crazy old King George, but that was about the closest he got. "Are there any knights?"

"No."

"*Milord Spy,* hmm? Who's he spying on?"

Lennon still didn't glance up, but her fingers tapped speedily on the keyboard before she replied. "On the heroine. He has evidence that she's a traitor to the Crown during the Napoleonic Wars."

"Is she?"

"No. But he doesn't know that. He's trying to seduce her into revealing her involvement."

Josh typed in his password. "Not very gallant, is he?"

"Not yet, but he will be. Think story conflict. The dark

moment. He's going to have to choose between his love for the heroine and his honor.''

Lifting his gaze, Josh glanced at Lennon. She still stared at her screen, fingers tapping mad bursts on the keys.

''What does he choose?''

''Love, of course.''

Of course. Did Lennon demand that kind of sacrifice before she got involved? And where was the damned coffee, anyway? ''She doesn't want much, does she?''

The clicking stopped abruptly and Lennon lifted her whiskey gaze from her laptop, leaning on an elbow to peer at him around his monitor. A slow smile touched her mouth. ''He made the right choice. It's a romance, black sheep. There's *always* a happy ending. He keeps his job and gets the girl.''

Josh rocked back in his chair and snapped his fingers. ''Oh, that's right. You write fantasy, not the real stuff.''

Lennon's smooth golden brow dipped downward in a frown. ''It's a fairly common misconception. But hey, each of us to our own.''

Josh thought her opinion was rather generous, but didn't comment when she went back to typing.

With a sheer effort of will, he set one system to running the names from Miss Q's guest list through the Department of Motorized Vehicles, while another one performed credit checks. More difficult to access than some local and state databases, financial records could effectively eliminate money as a motive for threatening the gallery and its coordinator, which would clear at least one helping off his plate.

But it was damned difficult to focus on taking the databases through their paces with Lennon sitting so close. Her bursts of typing didn't bother him, rather it was her presence that was doing him in. Now that he knew how it felt to kiss those pouty lips, Josh couldn't pretend he'd rather do anything else.

He got up when room service arrived, only to find that caffeine didn't alleviate persistent erections, rather it kept him awake enough to appreciate the full effects of being horny. And it didn't help that Lennon had slouched down so low in her chair that every time he moved, he brushed her knee.

Josh tried to lose himself in the search. Work usually provided the cure-all for anything that ailed him. Not tonight, though. Tonight, dodging the Fair Credit Reporting Act only brought an accumulation of payment histories, liens and recent bankruptcies that pieced together profiles of the guests.

When he learned Louis Garceau had recently declared bankruptcy to the tune of some hefty numbers, Josh had to wonder about a man who valued literary elitism over the more practical aspects of survival. Did Garceau hang around with moneyed philanthropists just to find endorsements for his literary works, or did he have another, more ambitious reason for being here?

Josh jotted down the question on a notepad and dodged another brush with Lennon's knee. Then it occurred to him that her keyboard was silent and had been for a while. Leaning back, he stretched his arms to ease the tension building in tight neck muscles, and glanced around his monitor. And found out why Lennon hadn't complained that their knees kept bumping like too many crayfish in a bucket. She was asleep.

Her lashes painted golden half circles above her cheeks and brought to mind the way her eyes had fluttered closed when he'd kissed her. She looked as gorgeous asleep as she had with those soft sighs tumbling from her lips.

She also looked uncomfortable with her chin propped on

her palm. The only heroic thing for Josh to do was get her to bed, because if she moved, she'd wake up with her face in her keyboard.

She'd dubbed him Mr. Wrong, after all, and Mr. Wrongs were romance heroes. Time to be heroic. All part of maintaining an image and living up to expectations.

Getting to his feet, Josh whispered, "Come on, Lennon. Time for bed."

She jolted, and sure enough, her elbow slipped out from beneath her. Fortunately, being the hero he was, Josh steadied her with a hand on her shoulder.

"I'll shut down your system."

Lennon didn't argue, but sleepily allowed him to steer her toward the bedroom. For a hopeful moment, Josh thought he might have the pleasure of tucking her in, but one glance at the king-size bed pulled Lennon from half-asleep to fully conscious faster than he could have unloaded his nine-millimeter.

"It's okay. I'm awake." She still sounded groggy, but had recovered enough to shrug him off. "Thanks."

Her hackles were up, and Josh knew a lost cause when he saw one. "Sleep by the wall, *chère*," he said, before leaving her to perform her nightly ablutions alone.

The door slammed behind him.

Pouring the dregs from the carafe of coffee, Josh took a fortifying swig before sitting in front of Lennon's laptop. He was looking for the Save function when a phrase caught his eye.

The pearl of her womanhood.

That warranted a second glance, and Josh scanned the document, wondering if reading a writer's unpublished work constituted any sort of crime. None that came to mind, and Lennon had been the one to suggest he read her books.

The hard planes of his face softened as he explored the dewy folds of her body with knowing fingers, his thumb centering on the pearl of her womanhood. Pleasure spread through her like the heat of the summer sun. Her muscles grew languid, melting, her head much too heavy a weight for her neck. Sinking back against the pillows, she curled her fingers into the coverlet, lifted her hips as the first sweeping stroke of his tongue blazed along the folds of her sensitive flesh.

"Well, well, *chère*. What have we here?" Josh stared at the monitor. "A glimpse of the way Lennon likes it."

He'd never been one to ignore opportunity when it fell into his lap, and didn't intend to start now. Information specialists put information to good use. He was one of the best. Even better with proper motivation. And the thought of lovely Lennon climbing into bed was the best motivation he could think of.

The lovely young lady in the story was losing her virginity in this scene. While reading all the problems associated with a virgin sacrificing her maidenhead didn't do much for him—personally, he preferred reading Clancy and Uris—the thought of Lennon sitting nearby working on this steamy scene did crazy things to his already-strained libido.

Had their earlier brush with bondage inspired her?

Josh could only wonder. Had he made Lennon feel this way when he'd tied her up tonight? She'd sure as hell made him feel like pounding his chest in a rare testosterone burst.

Scanning the screen, Josh searched for a hint of the woman who had such an unexpected effect on him. And he found her in her characters' actions. The hero in her story was gentle with his innocent lover, but he possessed her in an undeniable exchange of power that hinted of the various sexual places he would explore with her—once he'd familiarized her with the basics.

Before backing out of the file, Josh made note of the name, *Milord Spy,* then familiarized himself with her desktop.

A Love All Her Own. A Love to Believe In. Daughter of Midnight. He opened *Lord of Shadows* and scrolled randomly through the document, landing on page 267.

His lovely lady recognized his need, and his reluctance, but she intended to take what she wanted. Suddenly her slim fingers were between his legs, unfastening his trousers, and he could have done nothing more than brace his back against the sturdy oak chest if the Regent himself had appeared and bade him stay her hand.

She unleashed his beast, her fingertips brushing his hot length, provoking a need that had him grinding out a curse and reaching blindly for her.

Looked as if Lennon liked to be in control, too. The well-crafted scene simmered with sensuality, and Josh shifted uncomfortably on the chair, closed the file and opened another.

"I intend to make you breathe my name on a sigh." His throaty promise filled the shadows between them, whispered across her ear until she shivered with anticipation of his touch. Then with one insistent thrust, he gave her what she wanted, sank his finger deep into her heat. "I plan to explore every inch of your sweet flesh until you want me more than you ever wanted before."

Josh would have felt like a damned voyeur if his head hadn't been filled with images of enacting these scenes with Lennon. He'd never make it through the night if he kept this up. Fortunately, he found a folder containing more practical files, and headed into those, hoping to alleviate the trouser seam digging into his crotch in what was becoming a regular annoyance of late.

Electronic Press Kit. Magazine Interview. Web Site Updates. Not only could he handle these, but reading her biography revealed something he found very interesting.

Lennon McDarby published her first work in the fourth grade, when an elementary teacher submitted her essay in a contest sponsored by a historical organization.

Josh would bet money Doc Linc had read this biography or some variation of it, which meant he'd researched Lennon online. And that got Josh thinking in an entirely different direction.

Who was to say that their stalker wasn't some psycho trying to get a response from Lennon? Terrorizing her great-aunt would get one. She was a writer, and as such, a personality up for public scrutiny. Maybe she didn't have the exposure of a celebrity, but she'd surely have…

A Web site.

Heading back to his system, Josh ran a search on Lennon's name and pulled up a disturbing number of hits— both Web sites and bulletin board discussions devoted to her novels.

Within minutes, Josh had titles, reviews and even industry statistics that indicated the romance market was bigger business than he'd ever realized. And apparently Lennon had earned a name for herself there.

Her official fan site and her publisher's pages provided a wealth of promotional information that told him everything about Lennon the writer, but nothing about the woman.

The bulletin board discussions were much more interesting.

Several boards provided a forum for her fans to log on and voice opinions of her latest works. Lennon herself made the occasional appearance to promote an upcoming book or discuss a topic of interest. There were discussions devoted strictly to Lennon's fictional sex scenes. From what he saw, reviewers and readers alike touted her as one of today's spiciest genre novelists.

From what he'd read, he decided that Lennon liked fairy tales. Cinderella stories where the hero rescued his heroine. Beauty and the Beast stories where the heroine rescued her hero. Lennon might be approaching marriage pragmatically, but the woman he met through her writing wanted a romance hero.

And he just happened to be in the mood to be one.

Keying in the commands to save the URLs of several interesting discussions, he printed a hard copy of Louis Garceau's credit report, plus those of several other guests whose financial history raised a red flag in his mind.

He would start a file on each of these guests and spend tomorrow grilling them. Even Doc Linc. Though the plastic surgeon's financial status appeared routine, his interest in Lennon had been anything but. And Josh wanted to see if Lennon pursued the husband hunt with as much enthusiasm in light of what had transpired between them tonight.

Heading into the bedroom, he steeled himself for the possibility that she was indeed the mercenary debutante that he'd first supposed. But his instincts told him differently. After spending the past few hours getting to know about her, he was convinced more than ever that there was more to Lennon than her bridegroom search might indicate.

And as he glanced upon her sleeping form in the big bed, Josh was more determined than ever to find out.

She'd erected a wall of pillows to separate her sleeping space from his, and lay curled close to the wall, apparently fast asleep. Josh smiled. Like those pillows were going to protect her from him.

He stripped, then climbed into bed, dismantling her barrier with a grin. A hard-working guy deserved a pillow or two to sleep with, right?

Though Lennon lay as close to the wall as she could get without actually wedging herself into the crack there, she obviously hadn't factored in that her bedmate was six-three and probably close to double her weight. It took only three good bounces to cause her to roll against him.

She emitted a soft sigh, but didn't wake. Josh tucked her into the folds of his body, his knees curled behind hers, her bottom warmly cradling his soon-to-be-raging erection.

She wore a cotton pajama set that she must have thought was more pragmatic than sexy, but the material was so lightweight it might not have been there at all. Josh buried his face in her hair, inhaled deeply and willed himself to enjoy the moment.

He may not want to be a husband, but he fully intended to take a stab at being Lennon's hero.

7

LENNON KNEW without opening her eyes that she hadn't slept nearly enough. Her entire body felt weighted and heavy, and a few groggy minutes passed before she realized she felt weighted and heavy primarily because of the muscular arm and thigh pinning her to the mattress.

Josh.

Sometime during the night her blockade had miraculously disappeared, leaving her pressed against a sinewy male physique, the stuff romance heroes were made of. Had their nightly movements pushed the pillows away, or had Josh deliberately removed them?

Lennon didn't really want to know.

Not when she could enjoy the result relatively free from any logical arguments. Her brain was still muddled with sleep and she was far too drowsy and warm to be analytical.

Josh's even breathing suggested he was still asleep, so she didn't have to deal with him. Nope, she could just lounge in this delicious man's arms. What a way to start the day.

And to think she'd believed her editor that the romance heroes in her imagination didn't exist in real life. Josh proved those hard-muscled, bedroom-eyed, very irresistible heroes did indeed exist, primed and perfect for a grand and glorious love affair.

If she'd been in the market for an affair, of course.

The whole point of this weekend had been to scope out

a suitable man. But how could Lennon pay attention to any man but the one who presently held her?

She couldn't and she knew it. She just didn't know what to do about it yet.

Enjoy the moment, she reminded herself. Enjoy the thrill of knowing this handsome man wanted her. Enjoy the feel of his arms around her. Josh's chin rested on top of her head, an anchor of sorts, one that drew her attention to just how perfectly their bodies fit together.

His broad, square shoulders and firmly muscled chest shielded her from any threat. One hard thigh braced against hers. The other he'd thrown over her legs, and along with the arm he'd wrapped around her, it effectively locked her into immobility. No doubt Josh would argue that he was protecting her, but whether that was true or not, the end result was the same—she couldn't move. Not without him knowing.

Lennon didn't want to move. There was something so delicious about lying here, his penis—not erect, yet not lifeless, either—nestled neatly against her bottom. He radiated enough heat to warm St. Louis Cathedral in a cold winter. Heat that penetrated through her pores and set her blood on fire.

Lennon had no idea how much time had passed before the expansion of the male parts wedged between her cheeks suggested she wasn't the only one dreaming about all the wild sex they might have if she'd indulge in one last fling.

"Good morning, beautiful." Josh's gravelly voice whispered against her ear. "Sleep well?"

"Well protected."

He chuckled, a low burst of throaty sound that rippled through her senses and evoked a very real shiver.

He tightened his grip around her, whether to punctuate his resolve to protect her or to take full advantage of the moment, Lennon couldn't say. Every inch of her skin was so sensitive to his touch, she had to bite back a moan.

She really shouldn't have gone so long without a lover. While writing romances was a creative outlet, it wasn't a physical one, and Lennon was a healthy woman with healthy needs.

Chalk up another positive for marriage: regular servicing of her sexual needs.

Sex without passion? Who'd want it?

The voice echoed in her head—a voice that sounded remarkably similar to Auntie Q's—and Lennon squelched it. "Would you mind letting me up?"

"You've got me lying in bed, hot and hard and ready...." He brushed his erection against her bottom again just to make sure she hadn't missed it. "And you want to get up?"

"Yes, I do."

"Ah, *chère,* you're breaking my heart."

"More like deflating your ego."

Josh laughed good-naturedly. "That, too." And he rolled away, leaving her gasping at the sudden absence of his body heat.

Propping himself up on an elbow, he stared down at her, his eyes heavy-lidded from sleep, the stubble along his jaw emphasizing the intimacy of the night they'd just passed together. "You want the bathroom first?"

Lennon shot a glance at the door. It was one thing to change clothes and get ready for the cocktail party together, another entirely to share the intimacy of morning showers and daytime preparations. Ugh. But any squeamishness about sharing one bathroom immediately vanished when Josh climbed out of bed.

He was naked.

Lennon had seen naked men before. She'd seen some

really handsome naked men, too. And if that wasn't enough, she worked day in and day out creating *absolutely flawless* naked men for her readers. So she really shouldn't be rendered breathless by the sight of this one.

But she was.

Straight-legged, broad-shouldered and *beautiful* were the only words she could find to describe him, wordsmith though she was. He had the kind of chest that graced the covers of romance novels, all cut planes and angles and silky dark hair that arrowed to knifepoint sharpness below his navel.

Josh was clearly a physically active man, which Lennon supposed shouldn't come as a surprise, given his line of work. But seeing him displayed in all his tanned glory drove home the fact—especially with that very impressive morning erection jutting from between those sculpted thighs.

Lennon was also no stranger to impressive erections. Those she hadn't become personally acquainted with, she'd seen en masse in the Eastman Gallery or while researching new sexual themes for her books. This man's erection, while really, *really* impressive, shouldn't be making her heart leap into her throat on every beat.

His amusement revealed that he knew exactly how he affected her. Or maybe he remembered last night, when she'd melted in his arms and submitted to his kisses because he'd tied her up....

Tied up. Submitted.

Lennon almost smacked her forehead in disbelief at her own stupidity. How could she have possibly missed this?

Submission was the sexual fantasy of *Milord Spy*.

To recreate the theme accurately in her book, she'd spent days online, researching women and men who practiced submissive lifestyles with their partners. She'd even joined a chat to ask questions, and had found the chatters to be friendly people who'd been generous in sharing their stories.

No wonder she'd responded to Josh last night. Sure, he was romance hero gorgeous. Sure, he was scrumptious with his roguish grins and bedroom eyes. And, sure, he kissed like a devil and had hands that knew exactly what to touch and when. But Lennon had submission on the brain, submission embedded in her creative subconscious as she wrote her latest story.

Last night she'd been living her fantasy—her *current* fantasy, because with each new book and each new hero, her sexual fantasy changed. On her editor's advice she'd become secretive about upcoming themes. Ellen said it helped create anticipation for her new titles, or so the marketing department insisted.

"Would you like to visit the bathroom first?" she offered magnanimously. "Because I want to jump in the shower."

Looking rather deflated, Josh spun on his heel and walked away, giving her a prime view of his attractive bottom.

Mmm. Hopping off the bed, Lennon raced to the phone and dialed room service to order coffee, feeling suddenly as though her already promising day had just taken a turn for the better.

All indications seemed to point in that direction, anyway, because Josh quickly reappeared, still defiantly naked, giving Lennon another chance to admire male perfection in the flesh.

Then she swept past him to take possession of the bathroom. "I ordered coffee. I won't be long."

She locked the door behind her.

A steaming hot shower buoyed her mood even more. She shampooed her hair and then conditioned, mulling over the finer points of knowing she wasn't a closet submissive who was going to have to soul search and face up to her sexual preferences.

She was a perfectly normal, healthy woman who created fantasies for other perfectly normal, healthy women. And the thought of living one of her fantasies was very tempting indeed. Josh would be a no-risk type of guy. He'd already told her he wasn't interested in marriage.

On the other hand, though, could she really pass up this opportunity to get to know the bachelors? When else would she ever have the chance to scope them out all at once? This would definitely be a missed opportunity. Doubly so, because she had her own private investigator running background checks on those bachelors. *If* she could convince him to share his information.

Then again, she'd kissed the private investigator and wasn't really interested in talking with him about the bachelors—wasn't interested in *talking* at all.

She had the opportunity to live out a fantasy here—the fantasy of her current book, which could provide such incredible inspiration to her muse. If she were writing about sex while actually having sex with Josh, her readers would be in for one hot read.

Just the thought made Lennon smile.

The sound of the opening bathroom door didn't.

She peered around the thankfully *not* see-through shower curtain to find Josh—still naked—walking in.

"Josh, I locked that door!"

"I'm a private investigator, *chère*," he said, as though that explained why he should know how to pick bathroom door locks.

Coming to a halt in front of the vanity, he narrowed a stare at the heavy jacquard shower curtain, the downward tilt to his mouth suggesting he wouldn't have minded X-ray vision right then.

Lennon's heart throbbed in slow, measured beats. A brushfire sparked her skin and she was grateful for the shower curtain so he couldn't see her nipples harden.

Taking an instinctive step into the hot spray, she wondered what she'd do if he brushed aside the curtain and joined her.

"I need to get a move on if you want to be out of here by six-thirty."

"Oh." She didn't sound disappointed, did she?

He cocked his head toward the vanity. "Mind if I shave?"

"No."

Though she would have preferred to be alone, she refused to give him the satisfaction of thinking he'd rattled her. Not when he looked so smug and unaffected.

Perching one muscular buttock on the vanity top, he leaned over the basin to fill it.

Lennon forced her attentions back to her shower by a sheer act of determination, though her imagination ran wild with images of him scraping the stubble from his cheeks. She found herself tempted to sweep aside the curtain, if only she could be sure she wouldn't get caught peeking.

Snapping the water off, she grabbed a towel and exited the shower stall impatiently.

"Let me know when you're through so I can brush my teeth." Sweeping out the door, she unwittingly slammed it behind her and winced as she imagined the big naked man behind it smiling. She hoped he smiled so hard he nicked his cheek with the razor.

But his cheeks looked as undamaged as ever when he emerged a short time later. He dressed quickly and then—right on time—they left the Carriage House, emerging into a courtyard bright with sunlight…where a visitor was waiting.

Louis Garceau.

He sat on a low wall beside their doorway, sipping elegantly from a china coffee cup. ''Lennon, so you and Josh are an item. I'm so happy for you.''

Lennon swallowed back a groan. She couldn't deny the obvious. Josh leaving with her meant only one thing—he'd been in her suite. As the sun had just made an appearance, the logical conclusion would be…

''Who could resist a lovely lady who believes that fantasy is better than reality?'' Josh wrapped an arm around her shoulders and drew her close, making it sound as though they were not only sleeping together, but as if they'd just met and started sleeping together *last night.*

By the glint in Louis's beady eyes, Lennon had no doubt that within the hour everyone on the guest list would hear the news.

Smiling gamely, she rested her head lightly on Josh's shoulder, refusing to give him the slightest hint that she had vengeance on her mind.

But there was an upside here. Lennon finally had the answer to her question about what to do with Josh. For all intents and purposes, her search for Mr. Right had just ended.

ANY THOUGHTS JOSH HAD about seducing Lennon during the gallery orientation died a premature death once they arrived at the museum and discovered another letter—the first of the letters that contained an actual threat.

Banish filth, along with those who put it in our museum.

Josh questioned the security guards and staff only to learn that the letter had been discovered in the café. As the museum had been open for business barely an hour yet, most of the café staff had been in the kitchen. Whoever had dropped off the letter had come and gone undetected.

To complicate matters, Josh had a difficult time staying close enough to Lennon to protect her as she assisted her great-aunt, along with several museum staff members and docents, in guiding the guests through the exhibits.

She discussed art and directed guests, looking gorgeous in a pale yellow suit that lent her a businesslike air, yet still managed to fix his attention on the slim curves beneath the linen.

But planting himself firmly at Lennon's side in the middle of the tour afforded him many opportunities to grill the guests and assess their motives, and review the gallery's vulnerable points. Logic dictated that the assailant had been waiting outside for Miss Q to emerge on the night of the flash-and-bang, which meant someone may have seen something. No street in the French Quarter escaped the festivities during Mardi Gras. Not even an alley.

Here was a situation where the police could help him investigate the incident, while keeping him free to protect Lennon. Josh debated the merits of involving them more than he already had. With the way the stalker seemed to come and go unobserved, museum security obviously didn't have enough staff to ensure protection against these threats, and with the opening under way, Miss Q's concerns about postponement were no longer an issue.

He decided to wait and see if the next letter contained a more explicit threat before filing a report with the police. Who knew? Maybe he'd get lucky, and all the guests swarming the museum this weekend would hinder the stalker from attempting another visit at all.

Josh certainly seemed to be having his share of luck today. The perfect opportunity to establish their cover had dropped right into his lap when they'd met Louis Garceau.

The man had done a damned good job at spreading the word, judging by the questions Josh had been fielding all morning.

Doc Linc caught him in the rococo art exhibit and grilled him. "Are you and Lennon involved?"

The man's polished looks seemed strained around the edges, as if his expensive suit was keeping his body temperature up despite the gallery's air-conditioning.

"Interested in her yourself, Doc?"

"Yes," the man replied honestly. "She's the main reason I'm here. Quinevere assured me she wasn't involved."

So Doc Linc had been grilling Miss Q about Lennon's personal life, too. Josh mentally filed the information and wondered if any of the other bachelors had also, because he wouldn't put it past Miss Q to encourage that kind of interest to get bachelors to sign up for the auction. It would certainly explain all their interest in Lennon at last night's reception.

"Not to worry," Josh said. "She's only involved for the weekend. She'll be available again on Wednesday."

Doc Linc scowled. "Don't you think that's in poor form, Eastman? Lennon McDarby isn't someone to toy with. She's a reputable woman with a standing in the community."

Yes, she was. Which was precisely why Josh shouldn't want her. And, yes, maybe he should feel bad about casting doubt on her reputation. But only a fool wouldn't take advantage of Louis Garceau's big mouth when he wanted Lennon for himself. Josh wanted Lennon and he was no fool.

"Listen, Doc, I don't see how Lennon's affairs are any of your business."

"You know, Eastman," Doc Linc growled, "your family's preoccupation with sex is no secret. But the fact that you haven't made it out of the gutter is coming as a big surprise.''

He opened his mouth to reply, but Doc Linc, in a show of bold hostility Josh hadn't expected, cut him down. ''Lennon's not stupid. She'll see right through you.'' Turning his back, the man made his way toward a crowd admiring an oil on canvas depicting a nude woman and a flying dwarf.

Josh mentally bumped up the name Lincoln Palmer, M.D., to the top of the suspect list. Although a flash-and-bang tossed at Miss Q couldn't be interpreted as an attempt to win over Lennon, Josh wouldn't put it past the man to frighten the McDarbys just so he could sail in to rescue them. His finances might not have yielded anything suspect, but the way he'd been sniffing after Lennon since the reception…

Not even the strong espresso Josh drank in the sculpture garden could wipe the bad taste from his mouth after the encounter. He didn't want to analyze too closely why a suspect's comments had stung. Josh had spent most of his adult life trying to create distance between himself and his family. It looked as if he'd achieved his goal.

On a more pleasing note, the plastic surgeon did steer clear of Lennon for the rest of the tour, which culminated in the auditorium, where Miss Q spoke about the gallery's mission statement of preserving, collecting and exhibiting erotic art.

She spoke about how Josh's grandfather had collected in the narrow field, which didn't mean his field of vision was narrow.

''His passion for discovery,'' she said, ''was focused and intensified because he was intimately acquainted with his subject. Each search became a grand adventure, with his

view of the world constantly challenged and refreshed by
finding things no one ever thought were there.''

Not even Josh, who'd known his grandfather his whole
life, could help but feel awed by the man and his accomplishments. He found the scope of the gallery very impressive. Especially Lennon's contribution.

She took the stage, confident and relaxed, to present the
more practical aspects of the gallery's public resources.
Josh sat in the wings, listening to her speak about curric-
ulums for educators and students, various online programs,
teacher workshops and school tours.

She'd also arranged a national lending program that
made the Joshua Eastman Gallery's art accessible to museums throughout the United States.

A polished, comfortable speaker, Lennon held her audience's attention by keeping to the point and promising
everyone that she'd soon let them get back to having fun.

He remembered the many business and charitable fund-
raising functions his grandmother had dragged their family
to during the years—most of which entailed sitting through
lengthy banquets and even lengthier speeches, and never
with a smile.

Focused solely on business and the bottom line, his
grandmother never mixed business with pleasure. In fact,
to Josh's knowledge she didn't know the meaning of the
word *fun*. If Eastman Antiquities or a charity organization
required a board meeting, it was conducted in a conference
room with no distractions. All fund-raising presentations
were focused on the horrible things that would happen if
enough money wasn't raised.

Hell, he would never forget the annual Christmas party
wars, as he'd dubbed them, when she would badger his
grandfather to give up throwing a party for his employees.
A waste of money, she'd always said, declaring the money

would be much better spent increasing the amount of the Christmas bonuses.

Josh wondered if his father had knuckled under to her wishes after his grandfather's death. Josh wouldn't venture to guess, not when he could be watching Lennon instead.

And as he watched her, he had to admit that Doc Linc did have a point. She'd make some man one hell of a wife. Damn shame he wasn't in the market for a society bride.

As the guests milled about the gallery before the luncheon, Josh found himself back in the rococo exhibit, facing another reminder that he'd put himself in the gutter, as Doc Linc had so aptly expressed it. As Joshua Eastman's grandson, he was expected to be an art authority.

"What do you think of this artist's use of aquatint?" a jewel-bedecked matron who sidled up to him asked.

Truth was, Josh hadn't even noticed the piece. He only stood beside it because it kept him close to Lennon.

"His soft tonal effects work well, don't you think, Josh?" Lennon turned to them, making it obvious that she was still paying close attention to him.

"Absolutely," he agreed.

"Oh, leave it to an Eastman to recognize talent," the matron enthused, earning a smile from Lennon before she moved on to the next piece in the exhibition.

"So you recognize talent, black sheep, is that right?" She arched a brow dubiously.

"It's what I live for. Take this painting here." Slipping his fingers around Lennon's elbow, he led her in the opposite direction from the matron. "The brush strokes and the attention to detail on that nude woman and flying dwarf—"

"Nude woman and flying dwarf?" Lennon drew the attention of several onlookers. "That's Venus and Cupid, black sheep. I take back what I said about your classical training. You've been slumming too long and it's showing.''

''Funny, that's the second time I've heard that today.''

She eyed him curiously. ''Oh, really. What happened?''

''Nothing noteworthy, trust me.'' He wasn't about to get into the Doc Linc story and his designs on Lennon. No opinion of plastic man's was worthy of repeating, no matter how close he'd managed to hit the bull's-eye.

To distract Lennon, Josh glanced up at the wall at a painting of a young woman sitting at a window with an older woman behind her. ''What's erotic about that? Looks like a mother and daughter. Or maybe a chaperon with her charge.''

Lennon gave him a slight smile. ''That may look like an innocent scene, but you've got to read between the lines. The title is *The Galician Women.* Anyone familiar with this period knows Galicia was a Spanish province where courtesans and prostitutes lived. See the low neckline and the red flower?'' She pointed to the portrait. ''That's a whore and her pimp.''

Sauntering away, she left him staring after her, seriously considering whether the time had come to crawl back out of the gutter.

8

LENNON FINALLY CORNERED Auntie Q in a private alcove before she disappeared into the sculpture garden, which was filled to overflowing with guests for the poetry reading.

Before Lennon could get a word out, though, Auntie Q wheeled on her and Josh, her gaze sweeping over them in delight. "So you're sleeping together, dears. How wonderful."

"That's all we're doing together, but you knew everyone would think otherwise when you blocked that last room so Josh and I would be forced to stay together in mine."

"Lisette hasn't decided if she's going to make an appearance this weekend. What else can I do? Olaf insisted. If there's even a chance to acquire *Tête-à-tête*... You know how much your great-uncle adored that piece." Spreading her hands in entreaty, Auntie Q looked like a fragile butterfly in her multi-hued pastel chiffon.

A very deceptive appearance.

Olaf shrugged, and Auntie Q apparently considered that reinforcement enough to support her case, because she said, "Josh Three needs to stay with you to protect you, don't you, dear?" She swung that feigned innocent look Josh's way.

"I do."

"Then I fail to see the trouble. Olaf's sharing my room to protect me."

This conversation was heading exactly where Lennon

didn't want to go, so she cut to the chase. "You've got a two-bedroom suite. No one thinks you're sleeping with him."

"If it bothers you, then say Josh Three's your, oh, I don't know…how about your assistant?" Auntie Q suggested. "You're a successful author. Don't authors have assistants?"

"*New York Times* bestselling authors, maybe."

"Well, it's not as if you'd starve without that pittance you eke out from those books, dear. Everyone knows you come from money and can afford an assistant."

Lennon's mouth popped open, but no words came out. She made a very good living with her writing. Okay, maybe not as much as if she'd gone to medical or law school, at least not yet, but as soon as she made the *New York Times* bestseller list… She'd already made the *USA Today* list.

Auntie Q quickly realized she'd bordered on hurtful with that remark, because she took Lennon's hands and held them. "Let people speculate about what you're doing. Especially with someone as handsome as Josh Three. Look at him, Lennon. Look at his ponytail. Makes him look like that swashbuckling pirate from your last romance novel, doesn't it?"

Lennon tried to hang on to her anger but failed miserably in the face of her great-aunt's heartfelt enthusiasm.

"The spy," she finally said.

Auntie Q darted her gaze back to Josh. "Not the pirate?"

"He had gray eyes."

"Oh, well, I haven't met your spy yet," Auntie Q conceded. "All the better. You need inspiration to write those spicy sex scenes, since you haven't had any inspiration yourself recently…." She waved a hand melodramatically. "Let people think you're sleeping with Josh Three. You are, aren't you?"

"Of course not," Lennon exclaimed, not bothering to keep her voice down, though she knew they were attracting attention.

Auntie Q shot Josh a glance that suggested he wasn't up to snuff. "You've got your work cut out for you."

Josh nodded. "I do."

"Your grandfather was man enough for the job when he courted me. Are you?"

From the way Josh's lips quivered, Lennon knew he was fighting back a smile. "I am."

"Good."

Auntie Q's blue eyes twinkled and Lennon tugged her hands away, leaving them to their lunacy. She was having no part of this craziness. Not when just the mention of sleeping with Josh started that insistent throb between her thighs. "You've all lost your minds."

Herself included.

Heading toward the sculpture garden, she plunged into the crowd of guests gathered for the reading of the first edition of Shakespeare's erotic poem, *Venus and Adonis.* Lennon greeted people, clearing her mind of Auntie Q's manipulations to get her to abandon the search for Mr. Right.

How ironic that her search had already ended now that everyone thought she was sleeping with Josh. Lennon couldn't lust after Josh *and* check out the bachelors—not and still look herself in the mirror. But she wouldn't let Auntie Q know that.

Or Josh either, for that matter.

She'd asked for his help and he'd refused it. That exempted him from any explanations.

Whether she decided to sleep with him or not.

Lennon settled herself on an unoccupied bench not far

from the piazza, where Auntie Q had set up a podium that displayed the priceless first edition.

Architecture in New Orleans wouldn't be complete without the requisite courtyard, and this thought had inspired the sculpture garden. With the benches positioned throughout the piazza to invite visitors to admire the ornate fountain and enjoy the wild songbirds that made their homes in the abundant foliage, Lennon thought the sculpture garden more resembled a tiny Eden.

The winter sun warmed the garden with its midafternoon heat, and Lennon thought the sunshine showed the garden to its best effect. The fountain's spray broke in a wide arc from the sculptured base, a haze of diamond chips that rippled on the surface, a gentle patter beneath the buzz of the guests' chatter.

The setting had been designed to be informal, encouraging visitors to enjoy a break outdoors, and Lennon did so—for all of two glorious seconds.

Inevitably someone would notice her sitting by herself in a crowd. Of course, that someone would be Josh, and she scooted toward the edge of the bench when he sat down.

"Are you done playing games with Auntie Q?" she asked. "If memory serves, you wouldn't let Louis Garceau voice opinions at my expense. Would you mind explaining the difference between him belittling my books and you trashing my reputation?"

"Happy to, *chère,*" he replied magnanimously, leaning against the back of the bench and hooking his hands behind his head, so his dress shirt stretched taut to accommodate the width of his chest.

Lennon forced her gaze up to his.

Mistake.

Those green eyes glinted with amusement, a reminder of

the intimacies they'd shared, of a night spent twined around each other, of naked bodies and slow hot kisses and revealing reactions to the edgy side of sex.

That ache between her legs throbbed a little harder.

"Well?" She lowered her voice, as Auntie Q had taken the podium and was encouraging guests to gather around.

"I'm not trashing your reputation. I'm establishing a cover to put a safe perimeter in place around you. I want every guest to know that they can't get near you without going through me. Not in public, not when you're asleep in bed." He paused for effect, his eyes flashing. "And I'm staking a claim, too, because I fully intend to make love to you."

Make love. She found his choice of words rather ironic— or would have had she been able to actually reason through the incongruities of having sex as opposed to making love.

As it was, just watching the possessive words form on his lips had scattered her thoughts so completely that she stared at him, not quite sure how to react. She heard the buzz of the PA system as background noise, but couldn't focus on anything but the desire so evident in Josh's expression.

Until his expression changed to a scowl before her eyes.

Suddenly Lennon noticed how quiet the garden had become. Peering around, she found every face turned to her and Josh.

Had everyone overheard their conversation?

The thought made her heart skip a beat, but before Lennon had a chance to say or do anything—like she could possibly say or do something to fix a faux pas of this magnitude—Auntie Q's voice rang out from the microphone.

"Well, come on, dears. Don't be shy. We're all looking forward to hearing you read our illustrious first edition. Aren't we, everyone?"

Enthusiastic applause followed.

"Of course, it's only right that they read from this treasure," she continued once the noise died down. "Josh Three to honor his grandfather, and, as most of you already know, Lennon writes romantic erotica. Maybe someday she'll pick up the story where Shakespeare left off...."

"How can she?" Olaf asked from the fringes of the crowd.

"Good question," Louis Garceau agreed from the front row. "Adonis died at the end of the poem."

Someone in the crowd laughed heartily. "Necrophilia!"

"Absolutely not." Auntie Q tutted. "Lennon likes happy endings, so she'll think of something. If Rhett and Scarlett can get back together..."

Josh was the first to come to his senses, pushing to his feet with a growl. He extended his hand and Lennon took it, walked toward the podium on legs gone stiff with her irritation.

Trapped.

She could only smile politely, when the last thing on earth she wanted to do was sit in front of this crowd and ape the erotic pleas of Venus as she vainly tried to persuade Adonis to abandon his hunt and take her to bed.

Auntie Q had always possessed a bizarre sense of humor, but this time she'd gone way too far.

On a more satisfying note, Lennon observed that Josh also looked as though this performance was on the bottom of his list of things he wanted to do. In fact, he looked downright out of sorts.

"Come here, dears." Auntie Q motioned them to a bench. "Sit here where everyone can see you."

Great. And of course they had to sit sandwiched together to read from the first edition. Lennon couldn't begin to say what distracted her more—Josh's hard thigh pressed against hers or the fact that fifty people gathered around, eagerly waiting to hear two supposedly real lovers act out a sexy power struggle between two mythical characters. With her on the losing end.

Arrgh. She gazed out at the sea of people gathered around and almost didn't have to fake her smile when Josh groaned by her side. After affixing the clip-on microphone Olaf provided to her jacket collar, Lennon inhaled deeply.

With unspoken agreement, they fell into a comfortable pattern of her reading Venus's words and Josh reading the narrative and Adonis's part. His voice was strong and rich, with just a hint of Southern drawl that made her forget the audience as the sound filtered through her senses.

She surprised herself by sounding reasonably normal, and it actually wasn't too bad until she reached the lines:

"'O, pity,' 'gan she cry, 'flint-hearted boy!
'Tis but a kiss I beg; why art thou coy?'"

Lennon spoke the words, remembering the way she'd begged Josh, by her actions if not her words, to kiss her last night. And she suspected he might have been remembering, too, when he started whispering racy asides that earned chuckles from the nearby guests. The whole affair became quite lively, with the audience enthusiastically interjecting comments into the pauses, such as, "Come on, Adonis, give her what she wants."

What had started out as a dignified poetry reading degenerated into raucous entertainment at Shakespeare's expense, and Auntie Q beamed in approval from a seat beside the podium. People were having fun. Her great-aunt thought there was no better pastime than that.

By the time she lamented the death of Adonis, Lennon

remembered Josh's comment about her getting to attend all the fun parties. Hadn't his family made time for fun?

That was a question she couldn't answer. After all, she'd never actually had to deal with the Eastmans.

But when Josh bowed to hearty applause from their audience, Lennon met his smile with one of her own, pleased he was here this weekend to be a part of this tribute to his grandfather and the recipient of Auntie Q's own unique brand of affection.

SHORTLY AFTER a museum staff member returned the first edition to its display case, Josh escorted Lennon from the sculpture garden with Miss Q and Olaf.

"We can ride back to the hotel together," Miss Q suggested.

Josh glanced at Lennon, who inclined her sleek blond head in consent. "Works for us," he said, not eager to tackle the midafternoon French Quarter in a suit and tie.

Olaf reached into a pocket, dug out a set of keys. "I'll get the car."

As he turned to leave, Miss Q wavered slightly, just a step backward that made Josh recognize she was unsteady on her feet. He reached for her the same time Lennon did.

"Sit here, Miss Q." He steered her toward a bench.

Lennon sank to her knees before her, searching her great-aunt's face with obvious concern. "Are you okay?"

Miss Q smiled gamely. "Lost my balance, that's all."

"Olaf, bring the car around to the emergency exit," Josh instructed the man who hovered over the bench like a mountain. "I'll call security and have them unlock the door."

Olaf took off toward the main museum, and Josh crossed the foyer to use the house phone. Spotting a watercooler, he filled a cup and brought it to Miss Q. "Here you go."

"Thank you." She took a sip.

"Are you sure you're all right?" Lennon touched a delicate hand to her great-aunt's wizened cheek. "You still look pale."

"I'm fine, dears. Just a bit weary." She returned the cup with a reassuring smile, then patted Lennon's hand. "I'll manage a nap before the masque."

"You'll manage a nap now, Auntie. We've got to head back to the hotel anyway, and no one will notice if you skip the musicale and slip upstairs. You've been running nonstop and you'll never make it through the night...*oh no.*" Lennon's smooth features twisted in abject horror. "We have a problem." She sliced her whiskey gaze toward Josh, eyeing him with an expression as sharp-edged as a knife. "The masque."

"What about it? Am I interfering with a date?"

"No. But I don't want to show up with the only man who's not in costume. Did you bring one?"

Josh's turn to frown. "No."

"Do you even own one?"

"No."

"Oh, dear," Auntie Q said, frowning at him as though living in New Orleans without owning some sort of costume was a crime. "I wonder if Olaf has anything at home?"

Josh immediately spotted a problem with that idea, but before he could point it out, Lennon shook her head and said, "I'm afraid I don't see how anything of Olaf's would fit him."

"I wish I'd waited before donating Joshua's costumes to the Krewe. He had some wonderful outfits, which would have fit."

"What about a costume shop?" Josh suggested.

They both peered at him as though he'd lost his mind.

"It's Mardi Gras," Miss Q said. "Even if you were lucky enough to find anything, I don't think you'll track down a costume of someone who contributed to the erotic art world."

Lennon rocked back on her heels and snapped her fingers. "I've got it. The Feminine Touch."

This didn't sound good. "What's the Feminine Touch?"

"A sweet little boutique right around the corner. I'm sure Toni can come up with something. We'll dress him in drag, and he can go as Lady Chablis."

It took Josh a minute to place the character from the wildly successful book *Midnight in the Garden of Good and Evil.*

"What do you say, Josh Three?" Though Miss Q sounded quite serious, Josh didn't miss the twinkle in those big blue eyes. "Lady Chablis wore the loveliest clothes. I saw a picture of her in this exquisite cream silk with a tiara and feathers—"

"I don't think so, ladies."

Miss Q shrugged. "Then you're right. We have a problem."

"Wait a sec. I've got another idea." Shooting to her feet, Lennon made a beeline toward the house phone. Just as quickly, she stopped and pirouetted back toward them. "Darn. I can't dial out and I don't have my cell with me."

"I'll give you mine if you swear to lose any and all thoughts of me wearing a dress."

"A tiara would be divine with that silky black ponytail," Miss Q said with a grin.

He scowled, wondering if there was a barbershop next to the boutique, because he was getting a damned haircut.

"I swear," Lennon said.

"I'm taking you at your word." Retrieving his cell phone from an inside jacket pocket, he handed it to her.

She dialed with impatient stabs of her slim fingers, then retreated out of earshot. Watching her, Josh sat beside Miss Q.

"She's not lying to me, is she?"

"Lennon doesn't lie. Remember that. It's a very good quality in a woman." Miss Q placed a fragile hand on his knee and squeezed. "You were wonderful today. Your grandfather would be very proud of the man you've grown up to be, Josh Three. Now he'd want to see you happy." She squeezed his leg again as Lennon whooped, attracting their attention. "Remember what I said about Lennon."

"What did you say about me?" Lennon asked, returning his cell phone with a satisfied smile.

"How proud Joshua and I are of you both today. You've handled yourselves beautifully."

"Especially since we've been maneuvered into some very awkward situations," she pointed out.

"I have no idea what you're talking about," Miss Q said.

Lennon bent over and kissed her great-aunt's fluffy white head fondly. "Right. And I'll believe that when they open an erotic art gallery in the Smithsonian." Before Miss Q could reply, Lennon said, "But I've solved our problem. Vittorio has a costume. He's going to drop it off at the hotel later."

"Vittorio?" Josh wasn't entirely sure what sort of costume a man named Vittorio might produce.

And apparently he wasn't the only one with questions. Miss Q asked, "Who's Vittorio?"

"He's the model my writers' organization hires to dress up as a hero when the national romance convention comes to town."

"Good idea, dear."

Josh could be a romance hero. It suited his mood, and

he knew no self-respecting hero would be caught dead in a dress.

The security guard arrived. Josh helped Miss Q up while the guard disabled the alarm on the emergency exit. Olaf had pulled the car up in the back alley, making the walk for Miss Q not as long as if they'd exited through the main museum entrance.

"Wait inside," Josh directed the ladies, scoping out the alley and the roof of the next building before he allowed them outside. Satisfied, he turned to Miss Q. "Shall we?"

She took his hand, and as he led her toward the waiting limo, his last image was of Lennon's smile. He'd barely settled Miss Q in the car and turned to assist that smiling beauty when three shots rang out.

9

LENNON JUMPED at the sharp blasts of sound, hadn't even comprehended what had happened before Josh spun around and thrust her back toward the museum entrance.

"Go," he yelled, reacting instantly.

He slammed the door shut just as the limo lurched into motion, tires screeching as it pitched down the alley, the cumbersome frame of the long vehicle rocking sharply as it sped toward the street.

The security guard yanked Lennon back into the doorway. She stumbled, but his strong hands held her, pulled her into the gallery, though her stunned gaze remained riveted on Josh, who sprang at them, clearing the door and—by a narrow margin—her and the security guard. Pulling the door shut behind him, he raked his green gaze over her so perfunctorily that it took a moment to realize he was checking her for damage.

"I'm okay." But she trembled, unsettled by the hard expression that had carved Josh's features into granite.

Swinging an arm around her shoulders, he pulled her close, held her tightly between his chest and the wall while barking orders at the security guard.

"Secure that door. I'll take her out the delivery entrance in the café. You go deal with security."

"Come to the security office while I call the police," the guard returned.

"For all we know those could have been fireworks. It's

Mardi Gras.'' Josh waved him off and guided her into motion, his arm tight around her shoulders. "Do what you need to do. I've got to get her back to the hotel, and I just sent her ride off."

The guard still looked skeptical, but Josh didn't give him a chance to argue as he swept her into the museum.

"Were they fireworks?" she asked.

"I don't know. You'd be surprised how similar a bottle rocket and a nine-millimeter sound. Either way, they were too close for comfort."

"Shouldn't we stay inside where it's safe?"

"Two choices, *chère*—stay trapped in this museum with a bunch of strangers, any one of whom could be after you, or hit the streets with a bunch of strangers who might be after you, but where you'll have a chance to run for it. Your call."

She didn't even dignify the question with a reply and dutifully followed as he whisked her toward the café, thrusting open the glass-paneled door with such force they drew attention from the patrons. Josh didn't seem to notice. Or care.

She wasn't the only one to perceive his no-nonsense expression. The young man working the cash register gaped openly as Josh swept her through the line of patrons and around the counter. His mouth slackened beneath a wispy mustache barely worthy of the name, and he yelled something, but Lennon didn't catch what, for Josh was hurrying her into the kitchen, clearly familiar with the café's layout.

Her heart thumped madly as he shot through the rows of preparation tables and startled cooks. His body was tense, and his movements radiated such coiled aggression that though protests and questions rang out from the white-aproned staff, no one made a move to stop them.

Suddenly they were bursting through the back door in

one of those startle-them-then-sweep-the-perimeter moves she'd seen a thousand times on television.

The French Quarter burst around them, noisy, bright and filled with meandering tourists, street vendors and locals.

Within seconds Josh had them moving away from the museum, secreted among the ranks of a group participating in a walking tour of haunted buildings in the French Quarter. Most of the tourists were cooling themselves with paper fans depicting the haunted tour's telephone number in creepy red letters. The tour guide kept up a steady flow of information as they walked—a man who should have drawn attention in his high boots, black leather pants and flowing chambray pirate's shirt, but as this was the French Quarter during Mardi Gras…

Lennon and Josh heard tales of vampires sealed in a convent's attic with a thousand blessed nails, and the details of one of the city's more gruesome historical homicides, before they ducked out of the tour and into a novelty store along Decatur Street.

Adjusting to the dim light after trekking through the sunny streets took a minute, and Lennon fell into place behind Josh as he snatched a hat from a rack, then grabbed sunglasses from a display.

With his profile silhouetted against the sunlight glaring through the open shopfront, he looked like a stranger, a man focused, intent, a man who reacted quickly to danger.

A man so unlike any she'd met before.

He possessed a hard edge beneath a civilized veneer, a tension that made him seem ready for action, a professional confidence that made Lennon feel safe. He obviously thought on his feet, didn't seem at all fazed by gunshots and getaways.

After tossing some bills on the counter in front of a startled clerk, he pulled on the cap and jammed the sunglasses on. Lennon put on her sunglasses and then followed him back into the street, blending in despite their business clothing.

"Why are we heading out of the Quarter?" she asked.

"We've got time to kill. If those were gunshots directed at you or Miss Q, the shooter might expect you to head straight to the hotel. I want to talk with museum security and hear what they've found out before we head back."

"Olaf knows to keep Auntie Q away, too?"

"He's driving across Lake Pontchartrain as we speak." A hint of a familiar grin took the edge off his expression. "We had a contingency plan. He'll contact me before he brings her back."

Lennon only nodded, relieved and so very appreciative that Josh had agreed to help them out this weekend. The idea of someone shooting at Auntie Q, or herself for that matter, scared her so much she wasn't sure how to deal with it. Lennon managed her fear because of the strong man who held her hand tightly.

He led her off the street and into the dim interior of a multistoried hotel parking lot. Attendants veered toward them, their protests echoing eerily against the vacuous walls of the parking garage. Indeed, Lennon read a sign in bold letters deterring pedestrians from entering the garage under threat of prosecution. Josh whipped a leather case from an inner jacket pocket and flashed some sort of official-looking badge to stem the protests, and they emerged a block south of where they'd entered, a neat little shortcut that sent them in another direction entirely.

Canal Street traffic on a Mardi Gras Saturday wasn't something Lennon would have normally cared to tackle, but she had no choice as Josh launched her into the street and the flow of oncoming traffic without even looking both ways. Enormously grateful she wore pumps that fit snugly on her feet, she hurried along beside him.

They dodged the cable car grinding into motion after stopping on the medium between the north-and southbound lanes of traffic, and after another breathless crossing against the pedestrian light, Josh steered her down Peters Street.

They barely got halfway down the block when he directed her across another street and up stairs circling a valet ramp.

"In here," he said.

Lennon recognized the low building with the multicolored domed roof. "Harrah's? Are we stopping to play the slots?"

"Those might have been gunshots, *chère.*" He pulled off his hat. "I don't think today's the day to try your luck."

Lennon had no chance to comment as he plunged them into the dim world of a legalized casino.

After their race through the French Quarter, Harrah's was like stepping into another world, with its life-size Mardi Gras floats, twinkling lights and perpetual hum of sound, complete with tourists and a real pirate ship.

Josh seemed to know his way around the casino as well as he'd known his way through the museum, nodding at costumed attendants as he led her through the place as if scoping out a winning slot machine.

"What are we doing?" she asked.

He cut her a distracted glance. "Casing the joint."

Oh. She supposed she should have known Josh would want to make sure they were safe here. With a little guidance, she could help, too. "What should I be looking for?"

"A machine ready to pay out the jackpot," he replied with a quicksilver grin that made her roll her eyes.

Okay, so he didn't want her help. Fine by her. Let him play big-hero man while she took in the sights.

"Oh, look at that, they host weddings here." She noticed a marquee listing amenities. "I didn't know that. I bet it's a spin-off of the Vegas thing."

She could only smile at the idea of hosting a wedding here. After the ceremony, the guests could run loose through the casino, eating, drinking and gambling to their hearts' content. A giant party. Polite society would think she'd lost her mind.

Auntie Q would book the room herself.

Two piano players dueled beneath a starry sky in the Jazz Court, filling the place with lively Dixieland above the beeps and clinks and buzzing of the slot machines. Lennon was more than ready when Josh steered her out of the action.

"We're clear," he said, drawing her to a stop in front of a wooden door with a gold plaque announcing the VIP Lounge. An attendant dressed in formal wear greeted them.

He swung the door wide, saying, "Good to see you again, Mr. Eastman."

"How are you, Nigel? Staying busy?"

"You know it, sir." Nigel flashed a grin that sparkled white against the polished ebony of his skin.

Josh preceded Lennon into the wood-paneled lounge, which hosted cozy arrangements of tables, and a buffet and bar. After checking out the room and greeting the bartender, who also addressed him by name, Josh led her to a table against the wall at the back, pulled out a chair and motioned for her to sit.

"Come here often, do you?" she asked.

He just inclined his head, but then again, what could he say? His VIP status pretty much said it all.

He shrugged off his jacket, laid it over the back of his chair and sat across from her. A waiter immediately appeared, but with her adrenaline pumping, Lennon couldn't conceive of eating, even if she'd been hungry. She asked for spring water. Josh ordered a double bourbon, straight.

Well, well, well. Even though she couldn't read a thing in his steely expression, Lennon would venture a guess his double bourbon summed up his emotional state quite clearly. And since he obviously didn't have a problem dodging bullets, was he bothered because he'd been dodging bullets with *her?*

Here was a question to consider.

"Why would someone shoot at us, Josh? To frighten us?"

"I can't be sure those were gunshots."

But she couldn't miss the way Josh's jaw clenched, throwing the firm lines of his face in sharp relief.

"They sounded like gunshots to me."

Josh didn't comment, only glanced up at the returning waiter and accepted his bourbon.

He lifted his glass in a toast of sorts. "Gunshots or Mardi Gras fireworks, you and Miss Q are safe."

So he had been worried about her. Lennon clinked the rim of her glass with his. "Thanks to you."

Josh only held her gaze with a stoic one of his own, as though saving damsels in distress was all part of a day's work. Lennon supposed it was. However, as a woman intimately acquainted with the minds of heroes, she knew he wasn't as unaffected as he tried to appear.

That double bourbon, straight, said it all.

A few deep swallows later, Josh asked, "Have you annoyed anyone lately?"

"Enough to try and kill me?" she asked dryly. "No."

"You're sure?" A hint of a grin lingered around his mouth.

"I'm sure."

"Tell me about your fan mail."

Lennon sat back in the chair, toyed with the edges of her moist napkin in an attempt to control the rush of adrenaline that was fading from pulse-pounding fright to a pulse pounding of an entirely different sort beneath Josh's steady gaze.

"What about it?" she asked. "Some readers like my books, others think I'm too emotional and chuck them against the wall. Normal stuff. Why?"

He drummed blunt-tipped fingers against the wood tabletop. "Just trying to assess all the angles. If those were gunshots today, the attempt wasn't random. I cleared that alley, which means if someone did pull a trigger they had to be lying on the roof waiting for someone to come out the Eastman Gallery back door. Given that Miss Q has a penchant for disabling the system and letting herself out..."

"*If* they were gunshots and not fireworks."

He nodded. "If."

Lennon wished they knew for sure, but the sudden image of Auntie Q with a bloody gunshot wound in her pretty pastel chiffon convinced her she'd much rather deal with at least the possibility of fireworks.

"So, what do you want to know?"

"Any threatening letters? What about posts on those reader boards? I logged on to a few of your fan sites last night."

"You did?" she asked, surprised.

"I did."

The roguish Josh she knew returned in one bold glance, and Lennon's anxiety melted away.

"I post onto the boards occasionally to say hi, but I can't keep up with all the threads. I'd never have time to write. I can't think of anything unusual. Most of the people seem like nice readers who are into romance."

"Any letters come from anywhere unusual? Someplace that sticks out in your mind?"

She shook her head. "Not really. I get letters from all over. I don't publish my post office box address, for security reasons, so my publisher filters all my reader mail before I get it. Most people don't write unless they have something good to say. Although I do get the occasional putdown. Oh, and then there are the prison letters."

Josh blinked and his double bourbon clanked down hard on the table. "The what?"

"Letters from prisoners. Romances are a big hit in prison." She smiled. "Most tell me how much they like my stories. I do get some telling me that I'm writing morally offensive stuff, but that's to be expected. I write sensual romance and it won't appeal to everyone."

"Like erotic art galleries."

Lennon nodded.

Josh sipped.

They didn't speak, enjoying a companionable silence that heightened Lennon's awareness of how quiet the VIP lounge was compared to the craziness of the casino beyond, of how cool the climate-controlled air was after their frenzied rush through the French Quarter.

When an insistent ringing interrupted the silence, Lennon nearly jumped out of her chair. Josh smiled and reached into his jacket for his cell phone.

"Eastman." He caught her gaze. "So she's okay. Good."

Lennon realized Olaf must be on the other end.

"We're clear. I haven't talked to museum security yet. They won't know anything until they're finished dealing with the police, and I want their spin on what happened. I'll give them a call before taking Lennon back to the hotel. Where are you?"

Whatever answer Josh received made him smile. "You made good time. Why don't you start back? We should arrive around the same time. Good work."

He ended the conversation and returned his phone to his jacket. "Miss Q and Olaf are fine."

"Thankfully." Lennon set her rumpled napkin back down on the table and picked up her glass. "So what are we going to do until you call museum security?"

"I think our luck's changed. Ever gambled, *chère?*" His grin flashed, nearly making Lennon choke on the sip of water she'd just taken.

She had tears in her eyes by the time she managed to catch her breath again, but she managed to gasp, "No."

"Come on, then. It's an experience every girl should have."

Lennon bet he said that to lots of women, but she followed him as he tipped the waiter and steered her out of the lounge.

Excitement filled the air along with the flashing lights and crowds of players on the gaming floor. "Want to try a table?" Josh glanced around at the action. "I'll find one where you'll fit comfortably."

But Lennon knew she'd never fit in comfortably with the guests leaning intently over tables where dealers dealt hands of what she recognized as poker.

She had no trouble envisioning Josh curled over any of the tables, though—self-assured and oh so handsome as he gambled big bucks to while away the hours. On the heels of that image came another—Josh wearing a black Stetson hat, a cheroot clenched between his teeth as he gambled on the deck of a Mississippi steamboat.

For the first time since she had begun writing romances, Lennon thought she just might want to try her hand at a story with an American setting.

With Josh as her hero.

"This is way too much for me," she said, turning on her heel and heading out of the Blue Dog Poker Room.

He caught up with her in three brisk strides. "Why don't we start with the machines, then. Less threatening."

"Threatening? As if."

But she knew he saw right through her. Aside from the fact that she'd run a fast few miles in dress pumps today, she found herself completely discombobulated. By him. Not that she'd ever let him know that.

"So, what do you do have to do in here to be on a first-name basis with the staff?"

"Spend a lot of money."

Did he usually come alone or was this his idea of a cool date? She could think of no subtle way to ask and decided not to speculate. Dates were for people who wanted to spend time getting to know each other. Dates weren't in the picture for her and Mr. Wrong here. If they were going to become better acquainted, they were going to do it horizontally.

"Sit here." Josh urged her toward a newly vacated machine in the middle of a row. "This'll be a good one. Looks like that guy had been here awhile."

She wasn't exactly sure why that would make this a good machine, and would have asked, but the woman sitting at a machine nearby cocked her head toward the chair. "Have a seat, babe. I need a change of scenery for luck."

Lennon wasn't exactly sure she'd fulfill that requirement, because the woman never actually took her eyes off her video screen. She worked the buttons in a blur of motion that Lennon could barely follow, and even managed to reach for a cigarette smoldering in the ashtray by her elbow.

"First time, babe?" she asked.

Lennon wondered what had given her away—her wide

eyes or the handsome man digging out his wallet beside her. Josh inclined his head in greeting, then fed a...

Hundred dollar bill?

"This machine eats hundred dollar bills?" she squeaked, drawing a glance from the distinguished gray-haired man seated beside the smoking woman.

"Mr. Cute's paying, babe," the woman said. "Spend big."

"Maybe Auntie Q's right," Lennon said weakly. "I earn a pittance compared to people who can afford to do this for fun."

"Like the lady said, *chère*. It's on me. You've got to play big to win big."

And with Josh leaning over her shoulder, Lennon learned to play video poker. She'd played real poker before and knew all the winning combinations, which clearly meant nothing once her neighbors joined Josh in coaching her on strategy.

"Personally, I never hold for a straight," the smoking woman, who introduced herself as Marguerite, said.

Her distinguished partner, Nick, agreed. "You're better off with a new deal. You might get something better."

Josh nodded, agreeing with their new acquaintances' strategy. Lennon pressed the button for new cards.

"See?" he said. "Now you've got two pairs and a win."

"Not much of a win," she complained. "I haven't won back what I lost on the last hand."

"That's why you have to keep playing," an older woman with white hair shouted from the far side of Nick, showing that she'd been listening to their conversation. When she shot them a twinkling glance, Lennon was reminded strongly of Auntie Q.

"My mother, Louise," Nick said, still managing to play his cards while performing introductions.

"Hi, Louise." Lennon waved and then proceeded to lose every red dime of Josh's money.

He generously pulled out his wallet, but before Lennon could tell him to save it, lights flashed on Marguerite's machine. She jumped from her chair, squealing with delight. Lennon caught her ashtray before it hit the floor and started a fire, while attendants rushed over.

Josh, Nick and Louise explained the proceedings of confirming a win, and when all was said and done, Marguerite handed Lennon a crisp new fifty and a deck of complimentary cards, and invited her to come again and bring more good luck. She, Nick and his mom all played the same machines every Wednesday and Saturday nights.

Lennon bid them goodbye before forcing the bill into Josh's hand. "Now I only owe you fifty."

"Ah, *chère,* I was hoping you'd work it off."

He sounded so disappointed that Lennon couldn't contain a laugh, but her amusement lasted only a split second before Josh planted a soft kiss on her forehead and said, "I still have the other fifty to look forward to."

Flashing lights and buzzing sounds faded beneath a wave of awareness that made her knees grow weak. Judging by the way he wound his hand around the back of her neck and pulled her close, Mr. Wrong knew just how welcome his touch would be.

She tried not to sigh, tried to maintain some semblance of control when this man worked his way down her temple with tiny kisses. And she just might have managed it if Josh hadn't chosen to lean back against the wall.

Lennon went with him, off balance, forced to press her hands against his chest and hang on. Silly her, though. She should have known he wouldn't let her fall. He braced her against him with his thigh wedged between hers, his hard muscles zeroing right in on the spot that made her ache.

A moan slipped unbidden from her lips, and Josh caught the sound with his kiss, leaving no doubt that the chances of surviving this weekend without making love weren't good. Especially when he trailed his hands along her back and waist as if he had every right in the world to touch her.

When a passerby made a laughing comment about finding a bed, Lennon dragged her mouth from his. "We're drawing a crowd."

"My reputation's already trashed, *chère,*" he said amiably.

"And you're doing quite a number on mine, thank you." Bracing both hands against his chest, she pushed out of his arms to the sound of his laughter.

"Come on, then." He led them to the valet station to get a cab. "I'll give the museum a call and we'll grab a taxi."

He made the call from inside the valet entrance. From his sober expression and the half of the conversation she overheard, Lennon guessed the police hadn't been able to determine if the blasts had been gunshots, either.

"No slugs or evidence of bottle rockets," Josh confirmed, snapping his phone shut and slipping it back into his pocket. "But the guard convinced the police he heard shots, so I told them to report the letters, too. They'll conduct an inquiry."

An inquiry sounded good, but Lennon didn't get a chance to comment before Josh herded her through the door.

One wave from a valet and a cab quickly pulled onto the ramp from the street. She preceded Josh inside, found herself quickly sandwiched against him on the vinyl seat. Just the feel of his hard body pressed close made her feel protected and safe.

Made her want Josh more than she'd ever wanted a man.

Lennon gazed up at his strong profile, admitted to herself that she'd gone and confused Mr. Wrong with Mr. Right and the only thing to do about it was have a fling to get herself straight on the differences.

A last wild fling with a one-night man.

But how should she tell him? Jump his bones when they arrived back in the Carriage House? Surprise him tonight with a mysterious seduction at the masque?

The endless possibilities left Lennon light-headed and keyed up on their return to the hotel, where they found Olaf parked at a back entrance. Josh assisted Auntie Q from the car and signaled Olaf to drive around to the valet station while he ushered her and Lennon inside.

Relieved to see Auntie Q's color had returned, Lennon nevertheless made her promise to rest. "I want you to turn off your phone and lie down until it's time to get dressed for tonight. You've still got plenty of time."

Before long Olaf returned, and after a brief consultation between him and Josh, they all headed off to their separate accommodations to rest before the night's events.

The minute they arrived in the Carriage House, Lennon noticed the message light blinking. "It's probably the front desk letting me know that Vittorio dropped off your costume," she said.

She heaved a sigh when the formal chocolate-colored frock coat and beige breeches arrived a short while later.

"Perfect. Now if it only fits." Whipping off the clear plastic garment bag, she handed the costume to Josh. "Try it on."

"Now?"

"If there's a problem, I'd rather not deal with it ten minutes before we're expected in the ballroom."

Without argument, he draped the costume on the bed and

began to undress. Lennon took the opportunity to check her own costume for any last-minute surprises.

The embroidered white "lingerie" dress with a green velvet Spencer jacket perfectly detailed Jane Austen's England, and when she'd had it made, Lennon had been delighted with the craftsmanship and her decision to attend the masque as Elizabeth Bennet of *Pride and Prejudice* fame.

Though playing the role of a romance heroine appealed, she couldn't help finding the dress too prim for a woman planning to live out her fantasy with Mr. Wrong.

She wanted something to spice up the costume, so that the sight of her would make Josh squirm throughout the masque tonight, let him know he was in for the fling of his life. She couldn't think of a thing.

Hanging the gown back up, she eyed the lace-edged petticoat with growing discontent. She wasn't in the mood to be prim, no matter how much Jane Austen had contributed to the romance genre of her day, paving the way for today's authors.

Then Lennon remembered something Josh had said, and inspiration struck.

I hope you're going as Lady Godiva.

Did she dare? Glancing over her shoulder at the man, she found him bare-chested and barefooted and unzipping his fly with a leisurely motion that had to be deliberate.

She did.

Lennon headed straight to the telephone in the other room, intent upon making a phone call before Josh finished dressing. And she'd no sooner replaced the receiver in the cradle when he reappeared, still bare-chested and wearing his slacks, though the button hung open to reveal that sliver of hair below his navel.

"Where is it?" she asked breathlessly, almost vibrating

with her own boldness. "Don't tell me it didn't fit. Vittorio's got to be close to your size."

"It fit," he said. "Well, almost."

"Then what's the problem?"

Disappearing into the bedroom again, he reappeared with the frock coat still on the hanger. "Lennon, look at this coat. Aside from the fact that it's so tight I won't be able to move my arms, this jacket has...*stuff* in it."

"What do you mean, stuff? Let me see it."

As soon as Josh handed her the frock coat Lennon recognized the trouble. "This isn't *stuff*. It's padding to make your waist look smaller. It was the rage during the Regency."

"It's not the rage now. I'm not wearing this."

Lennon frowned. "The padding only makes your shoulders and chest look larger—"

"It makes me look like a Saints' linebacker in drag."

For a moment Lennon could only stare as that image formed in her brain, then she leaned back against the desk, unable to stop chuckling. "Come on, Josh. I know it's a different look for you, but can't you just run with it for tonight? You'll have a mask on, so no one's likely to know it's you, anyway."

"No." He sounded resolute. "Who's this supposed to be?"

"The Marquis de Sade."

Technically, the costume was more English Regency than French fashion of the time, but she couldn't resist fueling the fire, and was rewarded by his scowl.

"Forget it, charity case. I'm not dressing up like a man who spent half his life in prison for torturing women."

She folded her arms over her chest, just as resolute. "He was a gifted writer. Dark, true, but gifted nevertheless."

"I've got an idea." Josh went back into the bedroom.

They were both just full of ideas today. She only hoped his was as inspired as hers. Unfortunately, when he reappeared she realized that she'd won the inspiration contest hands down.

He was dressed in jeans, a leather jacket and sunglasses. While he looked great—a hero from a redemption romance about a bad boy, no doubt—he didn't look like any character she could recognize. "Who are you supposed to be?"

He stared at her over the rim of his sunglasses, clearly affronted. "James Dean."

"And exactly what was his contribution to erotic culture?"

Josh flipped the sunglasses onto his head and peered at her with eyes wide with surprise. "You're kidding, right? The man made three films and women have lusted after him ever since."

"I'm missing something here. Women lusting after a dead actor translates into erotic culture how? I can see if he made racy movies or something—"

"It's the image, *chère*. Look at Casanova."

"Casanova kissed and told. He dated half the women in his time and then wrote extensive memoirs about his experiences."

Josh shrugged. "I don't do orgies and I'm not going to this party dressed like a man who did. I'll go as your hero. Milord Spy. We'll lose the jacket—"

"You won't look like my hero without the jacket. Besides, I hardly think Milord Spy signifies a person who has contributed significantly to the understanding of erotica through the ages."

"That's an opinion I'd expect from Louis Garceau."

Lennon wasn't going to waste her new and improved costume on him unless he played a real role, too. Of course, she couldn't actually tell him without spoiling her surprise. "No."

"If you won't compromise, James Dean is my final offer."

That cool green gaze told her he wasn't kidding.

One of them was going to have to bend, only Lennon didn't feel much like bending at the moment. She'd already bent enough this weekend. She'd bent by giving in to Auntie Q's coercion about sharing her suite with Mr. Wrong. She'd bent when she'd sacrificed her good reputation by letting everyone think she was having an affair with Josh Eastman. She'd bent by giving up her search for Mr. Right and deciding to have the raging affair—even though Josh didn't actually know about her plans just yet.

She wasn't bending any more today, thank you.

"All right, black sheep. I know how to settle this. You're a gambling man, right?"

His expression settled in wary lines. "I am."

"Well, then, how about a game of poker?" Reaching into her suit pocket, she plucked out the deck of cards Marguerite had given her for luck. "If you win, you go as James Dean. If I win, you wear the costume—with the jacket—and introduce yourself as the Marquis de Sade. Deal?"

Josh was a gambling man, all right. Fire leaped into those deep green eyes and he flashed her a grin that belonged on the cover of one of her novels. "Black Jack. One hand takes it."

"Strip poker." Lennon tossed the unopened deck at him, and to his credit, he caught it in midair. "I plan to take that so-called costume off you one piece at a time."

10

"I'M AFRAID WE DON'T HAVE another vacant room in the hotel, and I'll need Ms. McDarby's permission before I can release the last room in the art gallery's block," the desk clerk said nervously. "No one's picking up in her suite, but I've left a voice mail message. As soon as she gets back to me—"

"Send Vernon out to speak with me, young lady." Regina Penn-Eastman issued a curt nod, effectively dismissing the desk clerk, who paled considerably at the familiarity with which Regina mentioned her general manager.

This was the Château Royal, an exclusive hotel she'd done business with frequently through the years, whenever she'd been required to entertain in the French Quarter. If they could manage to find a room for her grandson to attend this art orgy, they could certainly find one for her.

"Mother, if they don't have room, what can the manager possibly do?" Davinia cast her a beseeching look Regina knew very well meant her daughter-in-law hoped to avoid a confrontation.

Davinia always hoped to avoid a confrontation, though, and Regina waved her aside impatiently. She would not move from this front desk, except to head up to the suite this hotel had better quickly provide for her.

"Why don't you have the manager just track Josh down? He's bound to be around here somewhere," Joshua suggested, giving his wife's hand a reassuring squeeze. "Then we can discuss this civilly. Unless, of course, you've forgotten to mention accepting an invitation to this event."

Regina met her son's gaze. He'd taken after the Penn side of the family with his light brown eyes and hair. A handsome man even in his mid-sixties, he was tall like his father had been, and balding slightly like Regina's father had once been.

Her grandson was the one who'd inherited her late husband's dark good looks. In fact, the last time she'd seen her grandson—at his grandfather's funeral two years ago—he'd matured so much that for a moment Regina had thought she was looking at her husband from fifty years before.

But her husband would never have been so rude or distant. She and her husband may not have shared a bed since conceiving their son, but they'd been friends—two people who'd faced life and their choices with respect for each other.

"You know very well I haven't received an invitation to this *event*. Nor would I be standing here crashing it if not for your son, who has apparently lost his mind. But I will not leave this hotel until I track him down and find out what he's doing here—besides making the family look ridiculous."

Joshua winced. Davinia twisted her hands. Their lack of control in their only son's life had been a source of distress for many years.

Regina had never been able to help mend that particular rift, though the good Lord knew she'd tried everything she could think of. But her grandson had chosen to keep his distance. When she'd heard through the societal grapevine that he was attending Quinevere McDarby's memorial gathering of eclectic weirdos, she was sure there'd been a mistake.

Her grandson didn't attend public family events if he could help it, and most of the time he could. Regina knew he wouldn't have surfaced without a reason. His appearance at this memorial art gallery opening was a completely unexpected move that made it appear as if the Eastmans actually endorsed this collection of expensive sex toys.

Just the thought stopped the proper flow of air to her brain, making Regina feel faint. She'd thought about calling her grandson and demanding that he come home and explain himself, but, quite simply, she feared he'd ignore her. And she couldn't bear to be ignored. No matter what her grandson thought of her efforts to steer him in the right direction during his formative years, Regina had always had his best interests at heart.

No, she wouldn't give him a chance to avoid her. She'd find out herself and in the process publicly disabuse any and all of the notion that the Eastman family proper sanctioned Quinevere McDarby's shrine.

"Mrs. Eastman." Vernon Carstairs, the impeccably groomed general manager of the Château Royal, swept into the front lobby from a door leading to the executive offices. "Jocelyn just informed me you were here. Please, please come into my office where we can talk privately."

She imagined he'd just love to tuck her away in his office, where the other guests wouldn't overhear his explanation of why he was refusing her service. Well, she wasn't about to start negotiations by making concessions.

"Thank you, but that's unnecessary. I'm sure we can sort this out quickly. I'm eager to get to my suite." She smiled, an imposing smile if Vernon's stiff back was any indication.

"What seems to be the trouble?"

"My family and I want to check into the hotel," she

said, her son and his wife flanking her in a show of support that immediately had the desired effect.

Vernon silently faced them, his usually stoic expression unable to hide his panic that the party confronting him had no intention of being reasonable. "My dear, dear, Mrs. Eastman," he murmured. "As much as we adore you and your family staying with us at the Château Royal, I'm afraid we do have a problem. It's Mardi Gras and I have no vacancies."

"None at all, Vernon?" Regina asked curiously. "That's odd. I recall James mentioning that management always reserves several suites for VIP guests during special events."

James Burgess was the distinguished owner of this property, and a personal friend, a spectacularly wealthy hotelier whose empire spanned three continents.

Vernon frowned. "That's quite true, but Mr. Burgess sent us several guests for the Mardi Gras festivities, and of course, I installed them in the reserved suites."

"I suppose that just leaves the available suite with the art gallery block, then," Joshua said.

Regina could tell by the way panic warred with annoyance in Vernon's beady eyes that he wished they didn't have this information about another guest's reservation. Lest he think his employees had been indiscreet, she said, "I learned through an acquaintance that the suite was being held, Vernon."

True enough. Annalise DesJardin, a highly respectable, if somewhat eccentric woman, had been eager to call Regina with the news that her grandson had made an appearance at the McDarby gala. Too eager, actually. While Annalise devoted her attention and money to good causes, she spent too much time concerned with her neighbors' business.

"Surely you understand that I'm unable to release that suite without the gallery coordinator's permission," Vernon said. "I couldn't possibly."

"Then why don't you call her?"

As a man who'd catered to New Orleans's high society for decades, Vernon Carstairs knew all about the history between the Eastmans and the McDarbys. He ran a nervous hand through his neatly combed hair.

"Couldn't we just stay with our son?" Davinia asked. "I'm sure he wouldn't mind."

Regina seriously doubted her grandson wouldn't mind returning to his room to find his parents and grandmother installed in it, but Davinia, the bleeding heart, just couldn't handle the pressure. She buckled under Vernon's obvious discomfort, when Regina was only getting warmed up.

"There you go, Vernon. An option. Why don't you look into it," Joshua said with a strained smile.

He didn't have to ask twice. Returning through the executive office door, Vernon quickly reappeared behind the front desk, where he brushed aside a desk clerk without a word of explanation and pounded so fiercely on the computer keyboard that Regina could hear his tapping fingers across the distance.

All at once Vernon's face positively blanched, and she watched, fascinated as he reached for a desk clerk, grabbing his uniformed arm so sharply that the young man winced.

Thus began a tense exchange that left Vernon paling further, to a shade of sickly white that made her son whisper, "Not good news, I'd say. What do you think?"

"Definitely not," she agreed. "Wonder what your son's playing at this weekend?"

Now it was Davinia's turn to grow pale.

Regina turned to her and smiled reassuringly. "We'll sort this all out, never fear."

Davinia managed to nod, but Regina guessed that was exactly what she was afraid of. A trim attractive woman who'd kept herself up through the years, she was a good wife to Joshua, even if she'd been a bit too softhearted and emotional as a mother. Still, Regina couldn't fault her for doting on her only son. After all, Regina still doted on hers.

She only wished that Davinia's efforts had yielded a similarly positive result. But her grandson had thwarted all their best attempts to guide him, and given that Regina currently stood in this hotel trying to crash a party she had absolutely no desire to attend, she'd say he was still up to his old tricks.

Vernon finally rallied the courage to leave the front desk, but Regina could tell by his waxen expression that it had been an effort of sheer will.

"Doesn't look good," Joshua said.

And it wasn't.

"Are you telling me that my grandson isn't staying in this hotel?" Regina inquired skeptically in response to Vernon's explanation. "There must be some sort of mistake."

"I didn't say he isn't staying here. I can't be sure, because there's no room registered in his name. His credit card is on file, though." Vernon cast a wild glance at the guests forced to sidestep the Eastman party, who were blocking access to the front desk.

"Whose room is he paying for?" Regina demanded, and for a second, she thought Vernon might actually swoon.

"Out with it, old fellow," Joshua said, and Regina braced herself for an answer Vernon's reaction strongly suggested she wouldn't want to hear. "Who is it?"

A breathless silence hung in the air, despite the activity in a lobby filled with people, despite the sounds of phones ringing and computer printers clicking from behind the front desk. By all rights, the manager's faint voice shouldn't have carried over all the other noise. But it did, loud and clear.

"Lennon McDarby."

Davinia gasped. Joshua chuckled, and Regina cast him a sidelong glance that quickly wiped the amusement from his face.

"Install us in the remaining art gallery room this instant, Vernon," Regina commanded.

"But the room block," he squeaked. "I can't release it without Ms. McDarby's consent."

"Send someone up to knock on her door," Joshua suggested.

"She's not answering," Vernon said, holding his ground.

Okay, time for some serious action, Regina decided.

"What's the name on your art gallery block?" she demanded, in a voice loud enough to halt the activity around the front desk as people turned to stare.

Vernon gaped at her, apparently not understanding the question.

"The name," she insisted. "The name of the event you've reserved all these suites and conference rooms for?"

She could tell the instant understanding dawned. Vernon's professional facade collapsed and he said in a weak voice, "The opening of the Joshua Eastman Gallery."

"And what's my family name, Vernon?" she intoned. "My son's name? My daughter-in-law's name?"

Eastman.

The man had the grace to blush before motioning them toward the front desk.

THREE BOOKS AGO, Lennon had written a story where her heroine had done a sexy Regency version of a striptease in an attempt to convince her rakish hero that she wasn't the virginal young debutante he believed her to be. Of course, her heroine *had* been a virgin—a condition remedied by the conclusion of the scene—but the young lady hadn't needed prior sexual experience to know how to entice her man. She'd just needed to watch his eyes and follow his signals.

That's exactly what Lennon did now.

Arousal flashed on Josh's face as he watched her prop her hose-clad feet—she'd already lost both shoes in a run of losing hands a few deals back—onto the back of the nearby sofa and toss her losing three-of-a-kind hand onto the table. His nostrils flared as he exhaled an audible breath. His chest heaved as he folded his arms across it and settled back to enjoy the show.

A slight smile played on her lips as she inched the hem of her fitted skirt up her thigh, and Josh's gaze swung to the area like a tourist spotting shelter from the rain.

This was power.

Lennon recognized the sensation, having fallen beneath its spell last night. Now she wove her own spell, created her fantasy, and Josh, bless his heart, played his part without direction.

After losing the last four hands running—five card draw, nothing wild—Josh made for a very attractive sight with his bared chest and feet, his jeans button still open.

Let him enjoy his moment, while Lennon enjoyed hers. He'd had the upper hand all last night, and again this morning when he'd walked around naked and intruded on her shower. Two could play this game. And though she'd planned to accept his invitation for a fling tonight at the masque, she'd bump up her timetable, since the opportunity had presented itself.

The poor guy didn't have a clue what he was in for.

Scooting forward on the chair, she hiked her skirt high

enough to reach the waist of her panty hose, giving him a glimpse of her silk-covered backside in profile. His sharp inhalation signaled the exact moment he realized she wasn't wearing panties.

Lennon's smile deepened.

She had his attention, all right. She could feel rather than see his gaze follow her hands as she rolled the hose down along her thighs. It was like the glancing heat of a lightning bolt. Leaning back just a bit, she lifted her leg to give him a better view.

Each new move in this performance was designed to entice and arouse, and it did—not just the man sitting across the table in rapt attention, but Lennon herself.

Power is the ultimate aphrodisiac.

She remembered the quote from a college political science class, but as she slid down her hose to the music of Josh's heavy breathing, Lennon decided it applied to sex, as well.

His gaze swallowed her when she leaned forward in an exaggerated motion, letting her hair swing over her shoulder and cover her face in what she hoped was a sexy move. Peeling away the last of the hose, she paused for dramatic effect, before sending them sailing in an arc toward him.

They landed on target, draping over his shoulder and arm.

The low growl that rumbled through the otherwise quiet room told Lennon he appreciated his win. And when he pulled them into his hands and audaciously lifted the crotch to his face, every nerve in Lennon's body prickled.

She swiveled on the chair. "Your turn to deal." She forced her voice to sound casual, and was gratified to note there was nothing casual whatsoever about Josh's expression.

His inky-black brows furrowed over smoldering eyes.

The hard lines of his jaw were clenched, his lips compressed in a face sharpened with wanting. Dropping her gaze to his bare chest, she found the rise and fall caused by his rapid breathing very satisfying, though she wouldn't have minded X-ray vision to see through the table to his crotch. Just to gauge *all* the effects of her striptease.

With studied motions, he grabbed the deck of cards and shuffled. "Cut."

His voice was a rough growl, one more husky reminder of sex in a moment filled with all sorts of sensual innuendo. From sitting half-naked across from each other to the deck of cards that symbolized the promise of more bare skin to come, Lennon found the pace of her own breathing mounting as she reached across the table and removed half the deck.

She watched him deal the cards with strong, blunt-tipped fingers that made her remember the feel of them stroking her flesh. More quivers in her tummy, when what she really needed to do was concentrate.

Dragging her gaze to the table, she picked up her cards and fanned them. She surveyed her hand, resisted the urge to smile, and wagered her skirt. If Josh could beat her straight flush, he deserved to see what was below.

Cards flipped.

No skirt for Josh. Not yet, anyway.

"Mmm. Now to solve the mystery of the black sheep." Lennon leaned back in her chair and settled in to enjoy the show. "Is he a briefs man or a boxers man?" she speculated. "Or does he wear nothing at all? Have I won this game already? There can't possibly be much left."

"Patience, *chère*," he admonished with a roguish grin while unfolding his lean body and rising to his bare feet.

He was powerful and oh so male, and standing so close. If Lennon breathed deeply, she could probably smell his unique scent, all Josh with a hint of healthy I-sprinted-through-the-French-Quarter sweat.

She didn't breathe, though, didn't even think her heart was beating at all as his strong fingers unfastened the zipper at his waist, that expanse of silkily furred chest and all those shifting muscles demanding her complete attention.

The fabric parted slowly, slowly....

She hadn't won the game. Not yet, anyway.

He grinned.

She inhaled a breath that sounded loud in the quiet suite and made his grin even wider.

So the man thought he had the upper hand, did he?

All Lennon could do was fold her arms over her chest and try to look bored as he wriggled his jeans down trim hips, revealing that he was indeed a briefs man. And, oh my, he did look fine with that snug white cotton hugging his rear.

"It ain't over till it's over, charity case." He shoved the jeans down his thighs, muscles rippling and angling with the motion. "You should know that."

"Looks to me like it won't be long now," she said boldly, only nothing about her voice sounded bold—bothered maybe, breathless absolutely, but nowhere near bold.

Okay, so their little power game had shifted sides again. He controlled the moment. But how could he not, when he kicked away his pants to reveal strong, masculine legs with a fine covering of silky black hair? The sight made her remember how it had felt to part her own thighs and ride against that hard length of muscle.

Her sex pulsed in response, and she shut her eyes to savor the sensation. He definitely had the control here, and judging by the way he bent to retrieve his jeans, gifting her with a prime view of the bulge between his hips, he knew it, too.

Taking a step forward, he draped the jeans across her lap.

Lennon's breath skittered, but her hands didn't tremble when she gathered up the jeans and buried her face in the crotch.

If his arrested intake of breath was any indication, the balance of power had shifted once again.

Lennon glanced up and found herself eye level with the length of impressive erection straining against white cotton. "It ain't over till it's over. *You* remember that."

Josh didn't—or couldn't—reply. He just spun on his heels, giving her a view of tight, white-cotton-covered butt that was so scrumptious she didn't think, she just grabbed.

He stopped dead in his tracks, and Lennon found herself blushing wildly as he cast a sidelong glance over his shoulder.

"You going to let go, *chère,* or would you rather I leave it with you for safekeeping?"

The heat in her cheeks prickled uncomfortably, but Lennon found herself positively inspired by the desire she saw in his gaze. "It would be anything but safe with me right now."

Her fingers lingered only a second more before she drew them away.

"You don't need permission to touch me. You've got full privileges." He sat back in his chair, leaving Lennon folding his jeans and placing them over the back of the sofa to the sound of his laughter.

She dealt the next hand.

The heat in her cheeks may have cooled before she'd said, "Hit me," but she could still hear the echo of his laughter when his four queens beat her two pairs.

Let him laugh. He may have won this hand, but unless

Josh had a sudden run of luck, he'd lost this game. One more loss and he was butt naked.

But he didn't look like a man who was about to lose. His gaze boldly captured hers, the silent challenge she saw there goading her to make the most of her win.

It ain't over till it's over.

Lennon had several ways to go here. She hadn't wagered any specific clothing this hand, so legitimately she could remove the beaded barrette holding one side of her hair behind an ear. Or she could remove her cream silk shell to reveal the lacy brassiere below. Or she could remove her skirt, beneath which nothing but moist throbbing skin resided.

Twirling on tiptoes, she cocked her right hip in his direction and accepted his challenge.

"Oh, yeah," he said, gratifying her with the catch in his voice. "I may get my wish and see you in nothing but hair yet."

Lennon smiled silkily. He had no idea.

Making a great show of parting her zipper, she shimmied the skirt over her hips, letting it slip down her legs with a whoosh that by all rights should have given Josh whiplash.

She twirled lightly on her toes, flashing him before she sat back down, her sex throbbing moistly against the cushion. Deciding to make the most of his undivided attention, she spread her legs just enough to reveal a nice view of neatly trimmed blond hair and moist folds of skin, with the hope of distracting him from concentrating properly on this next hand.

Of course, her boldness actually worked against her, because concentrating didn't seem possible when her head was filled with the inane thought that somewhere she'd heard people at nudist resorts always sat on towels for sanitary purposes, and sitting like this couldn't possibly be sanitary....

She picked up the deck, shuffled and asked him to cut.

He did.

She dealt.

One glimpse at her hand and Lennon knew she'd won the game. There was no way the man was beating a royal flush, and she knew he knew he'd lost, too, when she didn't trade in any cards.

"What have you got?" she asked.

"Nothing strong enough to beat whatever you're holding." He laid down two pairs—aces and fours.

She smiled and countered with her royal flush.

He whistled. "I suppose it was meant to be."

"You'll make a much more believable Marquis de Sade than James Dean with that ponytail, anyway."

"So you say." His smile flashed sexily.

"Yes, I do. And that's all that matters right now, isn't it?" she said boldly. "So lose 'em, black sheep. Unless you've got a money belt hidden inside those briefs."

Lennon leaned back in her chair, propped her bare feet on the table, giving him the mother of all crotch shots, and smiled in delight at the look of shocked lust he gave her.

"You weren't so modest about showing off the family jewels this morning," she reminded him.

Her words seemed to rattle Josh from his stupor. "You know what they say, *chère,* unlucky in cards, lucky in love."

"You wish."

He leveled a stoic glance across the table and said earnestly, "Yes, I do. Care to do the honors?"

She could tell by his amusement he expected her to decline. They were back to that power thing again.

Lennon glided to her feet so quickly the air swooshed

across her bare hips and bottom as if she'd stepped in front of an air-conditioning vent. "Don't mind if I do."

Surprise flared in Josh's expression and in the erection trying to burst free of its cottony prison.

Or maybe that wasn't surprise at all, but excitement.

Lennon stood so close she could feel Josh's male heat through his briefs. The blush rose again in her cheeks, but this time she wasn't so sure embarrassment had inspired it. More like need.

His skin was hot to the touch when she hooked her fingers inside the waistband and lifted. His erection rocketed out as though it were jet-propelled, thick, hard and staggeringly perfect in sheer proportion.

Somehow she managed to remain standing, despite the pulsing between her thighs, which had increased in rhythm to something akin to surf smashing a shoreline during a hurricane. All Lennon could think of was that if she were one of her romance heroines, she'd take full advantage of this moment.

That was all it took to gather her wits about her.

With a casual move, she eased her hand into his briefs and gently cupped his scrotum, protecting the warm velvet weight from the elastic as she tugged the briefs off his hips. A tremor rocked Josh from head to toe and he emitted a sort of gurgle that made her wonder if he was choking.

Keeping her head bowed, Lennon let her hair fall around her face to hide her triumphant smile. Bending before him, she dragged the briefs down those gorgeous thighs, past his knees and along the length of his strong calves.

"Lift up." When he didn't lift his foot so she could remove his briefs, she patted his ankle to coach him, then glanced up with a long, lingering look, letting him get his fill of seeing her on her knees, poised beneath his erect penis. And his low groan suggested that he enjoyed the view immensely.

And, of course, as she stood, she couldn't resist the opportunity to brush a silk-covered breast against that proud erection, making it bob wildly in reply....

Circling him slowly, Lennon took in the lean curves of muscle with an attentiveness she hadn't had time for this morning. His tan reached high up on his thighs before fading into his firm backside and resuming low on his hips, suggesting that he spent lots of time outdoors in shorts.

A dimple flashed in his pale buttock and a long groove indented the side of his thigh when he shifted to let her squeeze between him and the table. She felt her own bare bottom keenly while maneuvering the distance, her softly furred mound brushing his thigh on the way.

Coming to stand in front of him again, she ran a fingertip up the hot length of his erection. It jumped in instant reply and Josh sucked in a ragged gasp of air, his body swaying.

"I guess you were right, black sheep—you are lucky in love." She winked up at him, his bemused expression making that needy ache between her thighs throb hard, a reminder that Josh's good luck would be hers, too. "Or you're about to be."

11

"MY TURN, *chère*," Josh announced, a subject not up for debate.

He'd let her tease and torture him long enough, and was nearing the breaking point. He would play her power exchange game as long as he got another turn at wielding the power. One of the sexy scenes from her novels replayed vividly in his head, and he knew just how Lennon liked it.

She gasped as he wrapped his fingers around her waist and hiked her onto the table. Her sweet bottom slapped against the polished wooden surface, heightening the urgency of the moment, the demands of his mood.

And he had demands that made the blood course through his veins like high-octane fuel. The sight of glossy blond curls molding that soft swell between her thighs made him crazy. He could see a hint of tempting pink lips those curls *almost* concealed, and he wanted to take her with a fierceness he'd never guessed he possessed.

"I'm going to undress you, *chère*," he said, barely recognizing his own voice. "I'm going to touch every inch of your beautiful body until you ache for me."

With the swipe of a hand, he knocked his briefcase to the floor, then shoved aside portable computers to free up some room on a table crowded with equipment. She didn't resist as he urged her to lie back, then nudged her knees apart with his hips. Indeed, she arched toward him as he moved in, close enough to feel the heat of her sex scorch his erection, close enough to promise that once he removed her blouse, he could bend over her and catch a rosebud nipple with his teeth.

Lennon's hair flowed back from her face in tangled abandon. Her pouty lips were opened slightly, as if to sigh. And her eyes, whiskey smooth and sultry with wanting, met his with such passion that Josh knew what they shared was as unique to them as king cake was to Mardi Gras.

He'd never before needed to hear a woman moan in response to his touches, to see her arch greedily toward him with her own demand to be touched…by *him*.

The experience disoriented him, made him reckless, made him thrust his hands under her blouse and rake her sleek skin with his fingertips until she gasped.

And just hearing the throaty, excited sound whisper past her lips made him press his throbbing erection against her heat, to remind him he needed to savor the moment and bring her to the edge with him. He still had to dig out a condom from his wallet before he could sink inside her…and that would mean finding where he'd put it.

Josh wasn't going anywhere right now.

He ran his hands up her ribs, fingers grazing lace that blocked his way to the sweet swell of her breasts. Grabbing the hem of her blouse, he tugged awkwardly while Lennon arched back, raising her arms to let him pull the silky garment over her head.

Her beautiful body stretched before him, unexplored terrain so enticing, so reminiscent of how she'd looked last night with her wrists bound, that he could do nothing but drop her blouse to the floor and explore.

Josh caressed the slender length of her arms, brought his mouth to her lace-covered breasts. With his teeth, he dragged her bra up and away, permitting her breasts to tumble gloriously free. Lennon's breath skittered in her throat, a series of tiny excited sounds that brought a smile to his lips, a smile that lasted just long enough for him to draw a breath....

He caught one rosy peak with his teeth and tugged gently.

"Oh!"

Her gasp was pure pleasure. His erection strained against her sex like a heat-seeking missile, while that satisfied smile flitted across his lips again. Until he tasted her sweet skin, sucked that tightening bud inside to fill his mouth with warm satin.

He wanted to discover all Lennon's secrets, wanted to know what drove her wild, what made her blush and what made her sigh. He wanted to see how far he could push her before she lost all control. Before *he* lost control. He wanted to explore this attraction between them without hesitation, without boundaries. He wanted her to abandon herself, to surrender to his desire.

He wanted to surrender to hers.

Just the thought made his blood surge almost painfully, and he swirled his tongue around the peak of her nipple, seeking respite, seeking some diversion, because he was too close to the edge. She tried to lower her arms, perhaps to run her fingers through his hair or guide his mouth elsewhere....

He didn't let her.

Holding her arms braced over her head, he tested her nipple with his teeth again, then tried the other, beginning a game of taste and tug and lick that diverted him from his barely controlled need. She twisted hungrily against him.

Feeling this woman respond to him, writhe beneath him, abandon herself to him so willingly, so trustingly, stripped Josh of any and all pretense. His usual defenses were failing big time. His body vibrated with pleasure, and his need to make her vibrate in reply was drowning him, arousing him in places he hadn't acknowledged in so long he'd forgotten they existed.

No woman had ever affected him this way. Hunger spiked his need to such urgency that if she pulled away and told him to stop he might just die on the spot.

This was so much more than sex. Josh wanted to possess her. Be possessed by her.

He may have held Lennon's arms, may have had strength on his side in their exchange right now, but strength meant nothing when she controlled his body's responses to her.

And had no idea of the power she commanded.

I'm looking for Mr. Right, and you're Mr. Wrong in the flesh.

"Look at me." Josh ordered.

He raked his gaze upward along the smooth expanse of pale gold skin, over breasts glinting with dampness from his mouth, and nipples straining toward him in a silent plea for attention.

When he released her arms, she didn't move, only watched dazedly as he plucked at her nipples, not hard enough to hurt, but forceful enough to spark that fire in the whiskey depths of her eyes. He watched, fascinated, as her features sharpened and she lifted off the tabletop to press her breasts into his palms.

He tugged again, then skimmed a hand down her smooth belly, through the blond curls, targeting that core of nerves he intended to become very, very familiar with.

"Oh, Josh." Her breathy sigh might have been a power surge for the way it jolted his system, and her eyes fluttered closed, her lashes forming gold dust semicircles on her cheeks.

"Look at me."

He wouldn't miss a second of her response. Not when

he so enjoyed knowing he pleased her as much as she pleased him. And only when her lashes trembled and she met his gaze again, the amber lights in her warm eyes revealing how very, very pleased she was, did he reward her with a kiss....

Suddenly, her fingers speared into his hair, anchoring his head as she parted her lips and kissed him with a need that stole his breath. All demand, all possession, all urgency. Her tongue explored every recess of his mouth, engaged his in a tangle of frantic breaths and heated moans, and he responded with a finger circling that nub between her legs, the connection between his steady strokes and her frenzied kisses too blatant to ignore.

She finally let him go, only to slide her hands down his neck to his shoulders, urging him closer. But Josh wasn't getting any closer no matter how hard she dug those pointy nails into his skin.

He was nearly overwhelmed by the feel of her sex against his erection, hot, moist, each thrust of her hips a vain attempt to take him inside her. Backing away just enough to break contact, he gave himself the space he needed to bring his desire under control again, to hang on to the shreds of his reason.

"I intend to explore every inch of your sweet flesh until you want me more than you ever wanted before."

He heard the words as though someone whispered them into his memory, recalled Lennon's love story and the bold hero who'd vowed to make his lady breathe his name on the edge of sigh.

Sounded good to Josh. Right now he wanted to be this lady's hero more than he'd ever wanted anything in his life.

He sank a finger into her creamy flesh.

Lennon's gasp deepened into a low, velvety moan. Her hips rose off the table, only to settle back again, squirming against his hand, pressing against the thumb he held on that knot of nerves. He obliged her with slow, steady caresses, his finger driving deep into her heat, riding her with sleek strokes.

Her eyes fluttered closed once more. Josh didn't bother telling her to open them again, because somewhere in the back of his brain a plan was forming, and the first step was to watch her come.... Returning his attention to her breasts, he made her writhe and twist, made her smooth thighs work to ride his hand, to increase the friction.

His need flamed almost beyond control as pleasure burst upon her, a visible gathering of supple muscles and a moist clenching of her sex around his finger. Her hips arched and she clung to him, her low moans filling him with a sense of male triumph that she wanted him, *only* him.

"That's it, *chère*. Come for me," he whispered against her skin. "I want you."

Want?

Not in her wildest dreams had Lennon ever *wanted* like this. She couldn't force a sound from her mouth when Josh finally backed away from her, tight butt muscles flexing attractively when he reached for the wallet he'd tossed on an end table earlier.

When Lennon caught sight of a square foil package, she couldn't help but wonder what he was playing at. She couldn't possibly move right now, let alone feel anything more than she already had. She was as limp as a noodle and could barely think. He obviously didn't realize he'd annihilated her, because he whipped out the condom and rolled it onto that awesome erection.

"Josh, I'm gone." Her voice sounded as dazed and languid as she felt.

He flashed those even white teeth in a smile she recognized as masculine conquest personified. "Trust me, *chère.*"

Trust him?

She may have trusted the scoundrel with her body, but he couldn't be trusted with the tiniest smidgen of her heart. And somehow she had to remember that.

Mr. Wrong, Mr. Wrong, Mr. Wrong!

But the reminder flew straight out of her head when he towered above her, so tall and broad and oh so sexy. His grin flashed again, probably at the sight she presented, lying back on the table, legs parted, bra tangled up under her armpits, her head cushioned by a keyboard.

Lennon was too wiped to move even if she'd wanted to. However, the sight must be doing something for him because his erection was completely vertical.

"Ah, *chère.*" He shook his silky dark head. "I've got my work cut out for me."

"Only if you want me to participate. I can lie here just fine." She smiled weakly, a halfhearted attempt at a joke.

At his narrowed gaze, she infused her voice with more oomph and struggled to sit. "No, really, I'm fine. One good turn deserves another."

"Shh." He guided her back down on the table, his hands freeing her from the tangle of her lace bra. "I don't make love to unconscious women."

But he wore a condom.

And he must read minds, too, because suddenly he bent low, crowding out her view of the world with his broad, broad shoulders, and leaned close to her ear. His breath shimmered across her sensitive skin when he whispered, "Trust me."

Trust him to do what—kill her? She could see the coroner's report already: death by orgasm. Auntie Q would be thrilled. "If you had to choose a way to go, dear…"

With gentle strokes of his fingers, he smoothed away damp hairs from her temples, a gesture so thoughtful, so tender that Lennon could only watch him, fascinated by the play of expressions across his beautiful dark face.

Amusement, desire, challenge.

He skimmed his palms down her neck and along her shoulders, with a touch so light she could feel the heat radiating from his skin. Hairs along her arms lifted as he traced her breasts, her waist, her hips. All the while his expression revealed how beautiful he found the sight of her body, the play of light in his eyes shifting like a cut emerald held up to the sunlight.

Then he bent low over her belly, and his first kiss brushed her skin as softly as his hands had. She trembled, and he peered up at her from beneath the inky-black hair that had fallen over his brow.

"See? Life signs."

He was right. His second kiss emphasized the point, making her stomach muscles contract.

His third kiss, a delicious one in that sensitive space between her hip and her thigh, made her quiver.

"This won't be work, after all," he said, his throaty chuckle sending another zing of awareness jolting through her.

Guess not. She felt that last kiss straight down to her toes. And here Lennon would have sworn that her recent sleep deprivation had rendered her immune to mind-blowing orgasms. It showed how much she knew. Maybe Auntie Q was correct again—the right man *could* keep her awake.

Lennon managed to lift her hands to Josh's head, needing to feel the dark silk coolness of his hair beneath her fingertips, wanting to show him that his kisses were indeed bringing her back to life.

The sight of his darkly handsome face poised between her thighs started her insides humming, and when he skimmed his tongue over the fine curls, his breath gusting over the swollen and sensitized skin below, Lennon came off the table.

"Oh, no!" She couldn't handle this. His previous ministrations had left her so ultra-aware that his touch now felt too intense, far too potent.

"Oh, yes." He speared that wicked tongue a little lower.

Lennon's fingers tangled in his hair, and even though her brain was chanting, *No, no, no!* her hands were anchoring his face between her legs.

His rough velvety tongue stroked her most private place, exploring the hidden folds of flesh, learning how each stroke and breathy caress affected her, until she rocked against him in a steady rhythm that heightened the tension inside her, higher and higher....

Then he drew on that tiny knot of nerves, a tug so gentle, so exquisite that every bone in her body seemed to liquefy. She shouldn't have been able to move. The pleasure rolling through her was so intense she should have been paralyzed, but her knees drew up and her hands were suddenly on his shoulders, pulling her toward him as his name slipped from her mouth in a whimper.

Josh knew what she wanted and rose above her, and one glimpse of the stark planes of his face, the granite clench of his jaw, proved his need mirrored her own. His sooty lashes half shuttered his gaze as he glanced down to position himself at her moist entrance, stroking her, familiarizing her with his size, but not pushing in more than a few inches.

Lennon strained toward him, needing to feel the hot length of him inside her. That need energized her. Wrapping her legs around his waist, she wedged herself against him, until he had no choice but to slide his hand from between them and allow himself to be drawn inside. That one sleek thrust made her gasp and him groan, and proved that their bodies had been fashioned to fit together.

Lennon ground herself against him, and the corresponding wave of pleasure stole her breath, making her arch against him with a shudder.

Still Josh held back. Sunk to the hilt inside her, he didn't move, and the meaning of his shuttered gaze and rigid jaw finally penetrated her daze. He was on the edge.

But Lennon wanted him far too desperately to ride out his need for control. Locking her legs around him, she hoisted herself up in one inspired motion and scooted right off the table.

Surprise etched itself on his face for a split second, only to be wiped away by a reckless hunger that carved tight lines around his mouth and set his jaw. Forced to grip her bottom in both hands, Josh braced himself before they hit the floor.

But his hunger rendered him under her control, and with her legs locked around him, Lennon rose up, using her leg muscles to ride the length of his hard shaft and then to sink back down, a breathtaking stroke.

And one stroke was all it took for Josh to join her game. His strong fingers sank into her bottom, lifting her, plunging her back down in thrusts that made her ride against him, arms wrapped tightly around his neck, breasts rasping his damp chest.

Thankfully, the suite was small and the bedroom only a few halting steps away. Josh carried her, muscles flexing, and suddenly the bed loomed behind him. Lennon could tell by the way he glanced back and shifted his weight that he intended to turn and lower her to the mattress beneath him. Instead, she shifted, causing him to topple backward.

"Jeez, Lennon." He went down with a grunt, barely hanging on to her.

He scowled. She smiled.

Tucking her knees tight against his hips, she rode him until his scowl faded.

His green eyes glinted, hooded with desire as he reached up to stroke the undersides of her breasts, to thumb her nipples and prove she wasn't the only one with needs here, or the only one who could evoke a response.

She responded. And he responded.

Tension mounted, the combination of his thick erection filling her and his skillful hands caressing her kindling a blaze of sensation she was powerless to resist. Even the sight of him spread out beneath her engaged more than her body's responses: it singed her emotions.

He was Mr. Wrong, but in this moment, with their bodies joined and their passions exposed, wrong didn't seem to matter. Silky black hair escaped from his ponytail, clung to his face and neck, and she couldn't resist kissing those damp strands from his cheeks, melting inside when he leaned into her kisses, his passion-glazed expression hungry as she rode him.

He shifted beneath her, muscles tensing as he slid his hands down her back, her hips, her thighs. With a touch, he directed her to let her knees slide out from beneath her, and she did, lying across him, every inch of her hot skin melded decadently with his. He sank his fingers into her hips, guiding her, and suddenly long sleek strokes became powerful driving thrusts. Deeper, and deeper still.

Following his lead, she slipped her hands beneath him, sandwiched her fingers between his butt and the mattress, adding pressure to each thrust, meeting him stroke for heavenly stroke.

Burying her face in the crook of his neck, she kissed his

sweat-damp skin, inhaled his musky male scent. Sooty strands of hair clung to her lips, and Lennon reveled in the surge of pleasure, of completeness, of the sheer rightness of their bodies straining together.

And when she heard Josh groan, a gravelly sound that made his throat vibrate against her lips, she savored the feel of his quaking legs, rode out the sharp thrusts of his orgasm before her own world spun out of control.

12

IT WAS JUST SEX, Lennon told herself. *Incredible* sex. Grand passion was supposed to be this way, a feeling of being consumed, possessed and gloriously alive. Every sound echoed through her senses with a new clarity—their ragged breaths, the air-conditioner cycling on. Josh's pulse throbbed wildly beneath her lips, each beat timed with hers, mirroring the fading echo of her orgasm, which clenched his still-hard erection.

She was living the role of heroine in a scene from one of her novels—or at least that was the only coherent explanation her passion-soaked brain could come up with. What else could possibly explain what was happening here with Josh?

No sex in her experience had ever even come close to making her feel this intense, this incredible, this *right*.

Uh-oh. Even wrung out from the most incredible orgasms she'd ever had, Lennon recognized trouble when she saw it.

Fling, fling, fling, she chanted silently.

His hand slid up her back to cradle her against him, and it was the tenderness of the gesture, the gentle brush of his lips on her brow, that made Lennon finally face the fact that she was in trouble here.

Everything about this man fascinated her—from the line of his jaw, which had lost its granite hardness and seemed no more than stubbled skin over bone, to his determination not to lose control before making her climax with him yet again. Josh held her as though what had just happened between them was much more than sex.

But it wasn't, couldn't be. And Lennon wasn't going to ruin this fantasy moment with her fantasy man with analysis. She'd signed on for a fling, and that was exactly what she was going to have. No emotions except pleasure. She wouldn't allow herself to confuse fantasy with reality.

Josh wanted this weekend. She wanted this weekend. What was happening between them was about bodies and passion and sex. It was not about the heart or impossible futures.

"How'd you wind up with a name like Lennon?" he asked, turning his face to meet her gaze.

And she wasn't going to melt all over again just because he wanted to know something so simple about her. She had an unusual name. Curiosity got him, that was all.

"I was born during my mother's crush-on-a-rock-star phase." She infused as much laid-back distance in her voice as she could muster, given her sex was still giving the odd clench around his erection as her orgasm faded away. "I've got a collection of autographed memorabilia that rivals the Hard Rock Café's. I've thought about donating my stuff, but it would break my mother's heart. She ranks giving me that collection right up there with putting me through college and touring me through Europe."

He smoothed hair back from her face, traced the shell of her ear as if they'd been lovers for centuries and he knew every nook and cranny of her body. "It's different. It suits you."

"Are you saying I'm different?" She laughed, but didn't give him a chance to reply. "Auntie Q attaches all sorts of significance to names, you know. Her name's a variation of Guinevere, and she's convinced that explains her relationship with your grandfather. Unrequited love and all that. Although I don't suppose they were technically unrequited. She even brought up your name when we argued about needing a bodyguard.''

"Did she?''

''She said you were named after a line of strong men and would be perfect to protect me. I suppose she was right.'' Lennon was babbling. She knew it, but she couldn't seem to stop. Talk helped her put distance between herself and this man.

''If my name makes me a chip off the old block, I suppose that makes you a creative genius.''

She could tell by Josh's supremely satisfied grin that he knew she was babbling, too.

Good sex, good sex, good sex, Lennon chanted silently, wondering why she couldn't seem to remember such a fundamental, when she was wrapped around this naked, intensely handsome man who was still buried deep inside her.

''I hardly think I qualify as a creative genius.'' She tried to make a break for it.

Josh's arms were tight as whipcords around her and he didn't let go. He yanked the comforter from the corner of the bed instead, pulling it over them to cocoon their damp bodies together. She lay on top of him like a bare-skinned top sheet.

''You're quite the creative genius, *chère.* You've inspired some sexual variations I've never considered before.''

His so-green eyes smoldered hot with the reminder of their intimacies, and her body temperature jumped about ten degrees.

And her body heat wasn't the only thing to jump. His erection, which by all rights should have been depleted after *that* orgasm, jumped inside her with renewed vigor.

Her inspired sexual variations must have been a hit.

"So you're willing to postpone the wedding?"

Lennon thought the answer obvious, given the dynamics of their current positions. But if he needed to be reassured...reassurance was good. She could use some herself.

"I'm willing."

"For a fling?"

"Mm-hmm. A fling."

Some emotion flittered across his face, some expression Lennon couldn't begin to interpret. But she didn't have to, because Josh swept a strand of hair behind her ear and said, "We've got to come to a compromise on handling the rest of the weekend, then. I don't like you flirting when you're with me."

Lifting her head, she stared at him. "I don't flirt."

A disbelieving "humph" was his only reply.

Lennon wasn't sure what he was worrying about. Thanks to him and Louis Garceau and Auntie Q, she was reputed to be engaged in a hot affair, which wasn't exactly going to inspire any bachelor's interest.

Josh ran his hands possessively down her back, and to Lennon's amazement, tiny tingles ignited in the wake of his touch. Life signs.

"Listen, I'll make a deal with you," he said. "You stop scoping out bachelors when you're with me, and I'll share the information I uncover in their background checks."

Lennon opened her mouth to tell him that she'd abandoned her search for a husband the minute she'd kissed him, but there was something about his expression... something so utterly stoic and unreadable that she quickly shut her mouth again.

Was Josh offering to help her investigate the bachelors to remind her he was only interested in a fling? Did he think she needed reminding?

If he did, he'd be right. She needed reminding big time. *You want a husband and I can't be one of those.*

He had made that crystal clear. Lennon was the one getting romance hero and husband all mixed up in her head.

Letting Josh investigate the bachelors might be exactly the reminder she needed to focus on the fact that he was Mr. Wrong—even if she no longer needed the information. And if it would make him feel protected from expectations about the future…

"Agreed," she said with a forced smile. "I won't scope out bachelors if you help me investigate them."

"Agreed," Josh replied. "Give me your undivided attention this weekend and I'll help you."

He'd help her, all right. And Josh promised himself that when he was through investigating, lovely Lennon would have no questions about who was the right man for her.

Him. And only him.

He didn't want a weekend fling. Josh wasn't exactly sure what he wanted, but he damned sure wanted time to figure it out. He wanted time to know this woman who made him ache in a way he'd never ached before, who made him feel such a need to possess.

He'd never had sex like this and wouldn't give it up. Not until he was damned good and ready. He wouldn't be ready by Fat Tuesday. No question. And he didn't intend to stand by and watch her conduct a husband hunt when he wanted her so much that he couldn't even drag himself out of her body.

Running his hands over her hips, he cupped her smooth cheeks and pulled her closer. His erection surged and Lennon gasped. He definitely wouldn't give her up yet.

"We should probably start getting ready," she said, and he heard the breathlessness in her voice, knew she was looking to run because what they did together was so intense.

"No." He caught her whiskey gaze with his own. "I'm not in any hurry to dress in that getup."

Huffing, she twisted around to break his grip, and only succeeded in driving his erection deeper. "I've got someone coming to help me with my costume."

Not giving Lennon a chance to resist, he gripped her tight and rolled over, trapping her beneath him. Her hips sank into the mattress and he thrust into her to make his point, one hot stroke that made every muscle in his body clench tight. "Your someone isn't here yet."

Lennon's expression softened and her warm eyes grew dreamy. "That's true."

He lowered his mouth to hers, to taste her sweet sigh.

No, Josh wasn't ready to give up this woman yet. Not even close. He had a plan, and step two meant staying buried inside her until she came again.

She did. And he did. Only after they'd drained every ounce of passion from their bodies and risked being unable to walk without assistance did Josh let her shower and start dressing for the masque.

"Oh my gosh, we're going to be late," Lennon said, when she finally glanced at the clock. "Where's Joby?"

Joby, whoever he or she was, must have been standing outside their suite waiting for Lennon's cue, because a knock sounded on the door almost instantly.

Hooking his hands behind his head, Josh stretched to ease the languor that had claimed his strength, and watched Lennon sail across the suite in all her naked glory, nipples still rosy from his caresses and her chest still flushed from her orgasm.

"Hang on, Joby, I'm coming," she called out.

He enjoyed the show so much that when she reappeared

from the bathroom, dressed in a plush white robe, he still stood there.

Eyeing him with something close to panic, she said, "Do you want me to let her in so she can admire you, too?"

Joby was a she. "No."

"Then shoo." Rushing past him, she paused long enough to pat his backside and gaze at him with a dreamy expression, before heading to the bed to straighten out the tangle of sheets and comforter they'd made there. "Oh, and if you need anything out of the bathroom, grab it. I'll be in there for a while."

Josh attended to business, and when he reappeared, he was hastily introduced to an exotic-looking woman with cocoa-colored skin and loads of beaded hair extensions, who lugged two very large rolling suitcases behind her. "Have salon will travel," Joby said before disappearing inside the bathroom with Lennon.

Josh retrieved his borrowed costume, inspected the jacket to see if removing the padding without damaging the lining was a possibility. Damn, no luck. He considered ripping it out, anyway, and writing a check to cover the cost of a new costume, but didn't think he'd score any points with Lennon.

And tonight was all about scoring.

Marquis de Sade be damned. Milord Spy would be appearing, and he'd be staying close to protect—and seduce—his lady.

One look at the lady who emerged from the bathroom to the fanfare of Joby's applause convinced Josh that Lennon was going to need some serious protection. Not only from the alleged assailant, but from every man in the building.

"Damn, Lennon," was all he could say as he gaped at her, though by the glint in her eyes and Joby's dazzling white grin, he guessed his speechlessness was exactly the reaction they'd been going for with her getup. "Damn."

Poised in the doorway with a sexy smile on her face, Lennon wore nothing but a pair of clear-plastic high heels and a wig of long, chocolate-colored hair that reached almost to her knees. Otherwise, she was gloriously naked, every inch of her bare skin marbled from chin to toe in varying shades of flesh-toned body paint and some sort of shimmery glitter dust.

Lady Godiva.

His eyes nearly bulged from their sockets.

"Bye, kids," Joby said with a cheery wave, before wheeling her bags toward the door. "I'll see myself out. Have fun."

Have fun?

A surge of testosterone rendered him immobile.

Have fun?

Lennon expected him to let her walk out the door wearing nothing but hair and body paint? She actually expected to make it past the bed? Which meant she placed a lot more faith in his ability to control himself than he did.

SWITCHING COSTUMES from Elizabeth Bennet to Lady Godiva had been an outrageous move, but Josh's expression relieved any uncertainty Lennon had about appearing publicly in the buff.

"Do you have a free pocket?" she asked silkily, liking the sultry sound of her voice. "I have no place to put my mints."

His eyes looked ready to bug out, and she felt a tingle that made her breasts tighten.

"I'm not really nude, you know."

"No?"

That one word was nothing more than a strangled gurgle.

Lennon shook her head, sending a wave of heavy synthetic hair skimming along her sensitive skin.

"See?" Catching all the hair in her fists, she slowly spun, allowing him to view the full effect of the artwork Joby had just created on her body.

Joby was a local makeup artist and a personal friend, which was why Lennon had been able to coerce her into tackling this project on such short notice.

Josh moved in slow motion toward her, reminding Lennon of a moth drawn to a flame and not a man who'd spent the past hours satisfying his carnal appetite.

He lifted his hand to her, another slow motion effort, and brushed his fingertips across a breast where her nipple should have been. "Where are your—"

"This is liquid latex. Joby filled in all my gaps. Well, not exactly filled them, more like covered them."

Slowly circling her, Josh stroked a finger where the cleft between her cheeks had been, smoothed his fingers above her thighs where her silky hair should be.

His eyes blazed in appreciation for Joby's unique artwork. She'd used liquid latex to create a smooth surface on Lennon's body, then marbled varying shades of beige before sealing the effect with glittery gold dust.

Her artwork was exquisite and Lennon was pleased. By Joby's quick work, and Josh's reaction.

"Men are going to be all over you trying to decide if you're naked or not." He couldn't seem to drag his gaze away.

Lennon let the hair go, effectively shielding herself and making the choice for him.

"I'm not naked." But she wasn't exactly *not* naked, either. "You look handsome yourself. Not like a linebacker in drag."

That seemed to jerk him from his daze, and those deep

green eyes shot up to meet hers. "And the point of all this is…"

"To make you drool."

He grabbed her hand—a brief glance at it seemed to register that even her fingers had been painted—and brought it to his crotch. "Mission accomplished."

And so it was. His erection strained against the tight trousers. Lennon smiled. "Oh my, he's ready, already? I think this decision to have a fling with you is a winner."

Josh growled.

Lennon handed him her mints.

Before they could leave for the masque, though, he insisted on calling the museum to speak with security.

Lennon watched the time, not particularly caring that they were running late. She was far too excited about spending the next few hours building the erotic tension with Josh. Carefully, she affixed her mask on her face, a cocoa-velvet half mask that she'd stolen from the Elizabeth Bennet costume.

Let Auntie Q greet the guests. After all, she'd encouraged Lennon to include grand passion in her life, and grand passion made it hard to stick to a schedule.

"The police are still conducting their investigation," Josh said, turning toward her and stopping abruptly as if the sight of her had distracted him from his train of thought. "And another letter turned up."

"Are you concerned?" she prompted.

"You'll stay close to me tonight, so you'll be safe."

Josh covered the distance between them, caught her chin in his hand and tipped her face upward. "I'll be protecting you from men tonight, *chère*. Who's going to protect you from me?"

"Who says I want to be protected?"

He met her challenge with a sexy grin, but before she

had a chance to react, he'd grabbed her and pulled her against him. "Good thing, since I won't be able to keep my hands off you."

Suddenly his hands were everywhere, skimming down her back, cupping her backside and pulling her so close that despite the latex, Lennon could feel firm muscles capture all her soft spots and hug them tight.

"We're going to dance tonight," she said, captivated by the feel of him against her. "A lot."

He peered down at her, his gaze charged as he took in her mask and wig, before settling on her lips. "A lot."

"We might shock the other guests."

"They'll be jealous." Josh released her. "Let's go. The sooner we get down there, the sooner we get back."

"Be still my heart," Lennon said, and meant it.

Then they were hurrying into the courtyard toward the main hotel, their costumes drawing glances from the passersby. The night air rippled Lennon's wig and caressed her skin, making her hope Joby was right that the latex would hide little telltale signs of her nakedness, like nipple erections.

Entering the grand ballroom was like stepping into a street scene at Carnival. Walls were draped in swaths of purple and scarlet silk, showcasing elaborate grinning jesters, a gold-bangled gypsy, a laughing reveler masked in yellow feathers. The stunning decorations replicated Auntie Q's opulent sketches.

Music and laughter floated through the room, and the atmosphere seemed to have lured the guests into a partying mood. People mingled and danced in a multicolored blur of satin and silk garments from a mélange of eras, their identities hidden beneath both traditional and more fanciful masks.

Upholstered armchairs clustered along the fringes of the

ballroom in welcoming groups, circled curtained nooks where professional fortune tellers garbed as gypsies read palms and Tarot cards.

As Josh had predicted, his and Lennon's arrival didn't go unnoticed.

Searching glances and whispers of "Lady Godiva!" followed in their wake. Josh tucked Lennon close to his side.

"I'm not the only one drooling." His jaw clenched tight.

Lennon only smiled, fake bravado because she was suddenly very grateful for the mask and all the hair that protected her identity—at least until she met up with Auntie Q, and everyone guessed who she was.

Was it possible to avoid the hostess all night?

Not with Olaf standing head and shoulders above the crowd. He'd spot her in an instant—if he hadn't already—as easily as she'd noticed him in his powdered wig and *habit à la française* from Casanova's exiled years. His costume made him the perfect foil to Auntie Q's Madame de Pompadour.

Besides, feeling decadent was the whole point, Lennon reminded herself, plastering a smile on her face and giving herself permission to revel in the attention. With Josh holding her close and her body still tingling from the effects of their lovemaking, she felt very decadent indeed.

She'd once written about a brazen heroine, a woman whose every action had mirrored a confidence Lennon would have loved to possess in real life. She would be that heroine tonight.

The whole point was to entice Josh, and judging by the predatory gleam in his eyes as they meandered through the crowd, smiling and greeting guests on their way to find Auntie Q, she'd accomplished her objective big time.

As she'd guessed, Auntie Q was delighted with her costume. Beneath a pearl-studded mask, her blue eyes twinkled when she caught sight of them.

"Oh, my dears," she said, grabbing Lennon's hands and surveying her and Josh with a smile. "What happened to Elizabeth Bennet?"

"She's hanging in the closet."

"She was too blasé for this masque, anyway. Lady Godiva is perfect. I can't think of too many noblewomen who'd take off their clothes to support the arts. But why the change of heart?" She glanced sharply at Josh. "Did you manage the job?"

"Now, Miss Q, you know as well as I do it wouldn't be heroic to kiss and tell."

Auntie Q clearly interpreted that statement to mean he'd definitely kissed, whether he told or not, because she squeezed Lennon's hands tightly and actually giggled. "I'm so pleased. You look simply exquisite, dear. Joby?"

Lennon nodded, though she could tell Auntie Q was trying her level best to read her mind. "You look lovely yourself."

And she did. She'd dressed in an elaborate blue-and-rose creation with a pearl-studded mask, portraying Madame de Pompadour, King Louis XV's mistress, the art patroness who'd distributed such royal largesse to painters, sculptors and writers during her lifetime.

That Madame de Pompadour had remained on good terms with the royal family and lived with them all her adult life was a point Auntie Q couldn't resist making for anyone well versed in history enough to make the connection between Madame de Pompadour and herself.

"She has such a beautiful body, doesn't she, Josh Three?" Auntie Q was saying. "I've been telling her since she was sixteen to make the most of it. I'm just glad she's finally taken my advice before she's too old to enjoy it."

"Me, too." Josh swept his gaze from her head to her toes in one appreciative glance that didn't go unnoticed by her great-aunt, who was so pleased she actually reached up and pinched his cheek. "And who are you tonight?"

"The Marquis de Sade," Lennon said.

"Milord Spy." Josh ignored her.

"Oh, I don't believe I recognize that name."

"He's a hero from one of Lennon's books," he explained.

Olaf just rolled his eyes, but Auntie Q's gaze flitted between them, and Lennon could tell she was trying hard not to laugh. "So you want to be Lennon's hero, Josh Three. How romantic. You're so much like your grandfather." She fixed Lennon with a laser-blue stare. "Let him sweep you away. He'll inspire you, and you'll hit the *New York Times* bestseller list."

"Don't sweep her too far," Olaf warned. "Someone stuffed another letter under our suite door. I already called the hotel manager, and it wasn't delivered by any of the staff."

"I talked to hotel security," Josh said. "Was it a protest or a threat?"

"A threat." Olaf patted his waist, presumably alerting Josh to whatever weapon he had stuffed there.

"Oh, phoo. Enough with the threats already," Auntie Q said with a dramatic wave of her fan. "Ta-ta, dears, go dance and have fun. Oh, and have your fortunes read, too. Tell the fortune teller to take a break while you use the cubby to, er, get to know each other better."

Olaf shuffled from one foot to another, avoiding Lennon's glare, but Josh seemed to take the teasing in stride and bent down to kiss Auntie Q on her cheek. "It's no wonder my grandfather loved you, Miss Q. You're one of a kind."

''New Orleans couldn't possibly survive two of her.'' Lennon let Josh lead her away, still scowling.

''I don't doubt it, charity case, but trust me when I tell you that a little mischief never hurt anyone.''

Lennon opened her mouth to argue, but Josh swung her onto the dance floor and into his arms before she could get a word out, and all thoughts of families and society fled in the wake of his hard body against hers.

''Mmm, you're such a wonderful dancer.'' She followed easily as he whirled her among the dancing couples, their bodies pressed a little too close for propriety, his thigh intruding between hers just a little too forcibly to be a casual touch. ''Do you find much time to dance while you're tracking down bad guys or is all this skill left over from the days when you were forced to attend those boring parties you mentioned?''

Lennon wanted to know. She wasn't sure when or why knowing about Josh had become so important, but suddenly she was overwhelmed with the need to know about this man who could protect her from bodily harm one moment, then make love to her the next. He was such a contradiction. One minute he offered to find her a husband and the next he twirled her around the dance floor as though she was the only woman in the room.

''Scoping out bridegrooms?'' he asked conversationally.

''Excuse me?''

Lennon glanced up and saw nothing at all conversational about his tight expression. Josh really didn't like her looking at other men when she was with him, and his possessiveness sent a dark thrill through her.

''No, actually, I wasn't looking for bridegrooms. I was admiring that man's costume and trying to decide if he's dressed as Cupid or Eros.'' Which wasn't entirely true, as she'd been thinking about Josh. But she wouldn't admit that to him.

"What's the difference?" Josh snorted. "He's dressed in a sheet with puffy white wings."

Lennon found herself momentarily distracted when Josh abruptly changed direction, twirling her lightly away from the bare-chested bachelor with wings. She supposed, now that he mentioned it, the costume was rather feminine....

"His name's Jake Hanlon," he informed her tersely.

"Oh, the bachelor from the dot-com sector. How can you tell? His mask covers his entire face."

"The shiny skin around his upper arm."

"Oh, Jake Hanlon has shiny skin around his upper arm? I don't remember reading that in his bio."

"You didn't." His gaze pierced through the black velvet mask covering half his face. "One of his credit cards recorded a transaction for a tattoo removal at Doc Linc's office."

"Doc Linc, hmm?" Lennon was more impressed with Josh's powers of observation than she was with the information. Women who were looking for husbands didn't wear liquid latex instead of clothes in public, and if Josh had *really* been paying attention, he might have noticed.

While she didn't want to hear about another man while wrapped in Josh's arms, she felt it only right to rally a decent response, since he was making such an obvious effort to help her. "Jake Hanlon, huh? He's big bucks."

"Yeah, but it's a mystery what he does with it all."

"A mystery?"

"He's the CEO of a very lucrative company, but doesn't have two nickels to rub together."

"Really? What's he doing with all his money?"

Josh maneuvered her even farther away from the winged bachelor in question. "My guess is that money burns a hole in his pocket. His portfolio's pathetic for a man raking in the kind of numbers he does annually. From what I've gleaned from his profile, he's an erratic spender—expensive trips, fancy cars, in and out of houses at whim, tattoos—nothing sinister.''

''Well, I won't marry a man who can't handle his money,'' Lennon said decidedly. ''Financial responsibility is important.''

''Given his family connections, I don't think you or the kids would starve. That is, of course, provided he's not trying to hurt you or Miss Q.''

''Do you think he's the one?''

Josh shrugged. ''Money can be a powerful motive.''

''But what could he possibly hope to gain?''

''Maybe he wants to marry into your family.''

''Throwing a grenade at my great-aunt sounds like a surefire way to attract me.'' The man couldn't be serious. One glance at his deadpan expression clued Lennon in on his game. A game two could play. ''You'll just have to catch him and send him to jail then, because financial pressure can put too much stress on a marriage. I'll keep looking, thank you.''

Josh appeared satisfied by her announcement, but before Lennon had a chance to dwell on why this silly game should please him, raised voices from the nearby ballroom entrance caught her attention.

She peered around him to check out the commotion, and judging by the crush of tuxedoed shoulders barring the entrance, guessed exactly what the trouble was.

''Gate-crashers.'' She stepped out of the circle of Josh's arms. ''I don't see Auntie Q and Olaf. Let's deal with it.''

Josh led her toward the entrance just as one of the bouncers he'd arranged to have posted at the entrance moved to shut the door.

"What's the problem?" Josh asked, stepping neatly in front of Lennon, blocking the door from closing and shielding her bodily.

"No invitations," the burly bouncer said, motioning for Josh to either come through the door or to back up so he could close it. "Don't want to disturb the guests."

"My name is on that guest list, young man," an authoritative voice declared.

Lennon didn't recognize the voice, but she recognized Josh's reaction. His body tightened to full alert, with that same wariness she recognized from their flight through the Quarter earlier.

Glancing up at him, she watched the color drain from his face below the edge of his mask, and concerned, she stepped out from behind him—to find herself staring at a steely-haired, scowling woman she'd seen only in pictures.

Josh's grandmother.

13

"CLOSE THAT DOOR," Josh ordered the bouncer, while he braced an arm around Lennon, pulling her near before she unwittingly stepped into the line of fire.

Only one thing would have brought his grandmother, and his parents, too, he quickly noted, into the French Quarter during Mardi Gras—his involvement with the gallery opening. And he didn't need to see his grandmother's scowl to know she wasn't happy about making the trip.

"Our invitation to this…*event* seems to have gotten lost in the mail," his grandmother informed them haughtily.

"Mom, Dad, Grandmother…" He ground out the civilities between clenched teeth. "You know as well as I do there wasn't an invitation, so what brings you here tonight?"

His father extended a hand and issued a gruff greeting, while his mother reached up to press a kiss to his cheek. She tugged lightly on his ponytail, clearly amused by his new style. Then he noticed both his parents were costumed in some European fashion he vaguely remembered seeing in school history books.

He tugged off his mask. "You came to attend the masque?"

Before either could reply, his grandmother speared Lennon with a lethal stare. "Are you naked, young lady?"

"Ah, not exactly, ma'am."

Josh didn't miss the flash of embarrassment behind Lennon's mask before she hid it with a light laugh.

"Not *exactly?*" his grandmother demanded, as if there could possibly be some doubt.

Pulling Lennon closer Josh gave her what he hoped was a reassuring smile, and assumed control of the situation. "Lennon, these are my parents, Joshua and Davinia Eastman, and this is my grandmother, Regina. Folks," he said, spearing them with his own warning stare, "I don't believe you've ever been formally introduced to Lennon Mc-Darby."

"No, we haven't." Following his cue, his father extended his hand. Josh didn't miss his look of surprise, though, when he noticed that her unusual costume extended right down to her fingertips. "A pleasure, Ms. McDarby."

"Lennon, please." She smiled pleasantly, impressing Josh with her rapid recovery. She took a step away, subtly putting distance between them.

"If you're not exactly naked, what are you supposed to be?"

Lennon met her gaze and said evenly, "Lady Godiva."

The dowager swung a scowl at Josh. "And you are?"

"The Marquis de Sade," Lennon said.

His father shot him an amused look, but his mom winced.

"*Not* the Marquis de Sade," he assured them. "I'm the hero from Lennon's latest book."

His mom smiled uncertainly, then motioned to her own costume. "We thought we might need to dress up to get inside the masque to find you."

His grandmother frowned, and he observed that she wasn't wearing a costume, but had dressed in one of her usual neutral silk suits.

"No need. I'm here now," he said. "So what's up?"

"There is a need, young man." His grandmother leveled an imposing glare at him. "Since you've taken it upon yourself to endorse this event on our family's behalf."

"Joshua," his dad said, motioning for them to move away from the bouncers. "What possessed you—"

But Regina interrupted him. "If the family is going to endorse this—this…" She floundered, obviously searching for an appropriate definition.

"Memorial art gallery," Lennon supplied.

"Sexual shrine," the older woman corrected, "shouldn't you have sent invitations to us all?"

"I'm not endorsing the gallery on the family's behalf." Josh struggled to keep his tone level, knowing that getting defensive would only put his grandmother into attack mode. He wanted this misunderstanding resolved quickly, without any unpleasant repercussions, so he could get back to the ball to dance with Lennon.

But Lennon didn't give him a chance to finish the thought. She swept her gaze between his parents and grandmother, any embarrassment she may have felt for her outrageous costume well hidden beneath her proud stance and welcoming smile. "Please accept my apology for the oversight. Of course you're all welcome. I'm sure Great-uncle Joshua would be delighted that we're all together to celebrate his memorial."

From where Josh was standing, her use of "great-uncle" had a remarkable effect as his family witnessed firsthand how his grandfather had made himself a part of Lennon's family. All three of the elder Eastmans stared, Lennon's invitation clearly taking everyone aback. But like it or not, their families were connected, and Lennon spoke of that connection easily and with a great deal of pride. She'd obviously cared for his grandfather and wasn't shy about letting everyone know it.

The effect was twofold. Her invitation forced his family to reevaluate their position. Whatever they had meant to accomplish by coming here tonight, Josh could tell they hadn't expected to be warmly welcomed into the fold. It threw them. Especially his grandmother, who stared at Lennon as if she was a visitor from another galaxy.

And his family's surprise also served to pitch the balance of control into Lennon's favor. She ran with it. She apparently didn't want him running interference for her with his family, so he stood back and let her take control.

"You're dressed perfectly for the masque." Lennon touched his mom's burgundy sleeve. "What fabulous costumes. Dutch?"

"Yes. Seventeenth century." His mom beamed, pleased Lennon had recognized the style. "Jan and Margaretha Steen."

"An exceptional choice. You'll fit right in tonight, and I do believe you'll be the only Steens. We have quite a number of Cupids, I'm afraid." She shot Josh a smile that made his blood flow increase its pace, before she rushed on. "I adore the subtle sensuality of Jan Steen's paintings. I had the pleasure of admiring his *Dancing Couple* when I was in D.C. at a conference recently. Have you had a chance to see it?"

"Joshua and I..." She gazed lovingly up at the man by her side. "My *husband* Joshua and I visited the exhibition there just before Christmas."

"Are you of the school that interprets the painting as a wedding feast of a rich girl and a country boy? Or do think it's an everyday life scene like so many of Steen's others?"

Lennon was obviously trying to defuse the situation, and had wisely zeroed in on his mother as the prime candidate to accomplish the task. Josh was pleased to see his mother lend her efforts to the cause.

"The wedding feast, absolutely." Her face lit up with her enthusiasm. "Just look at the symbolism. The caged birds stand for virginity and the broken eggshells refer to losing it."

"The cut flowers and soap bubbles, too. Both fragile and short-lived. I think they suggest fleeting time or love, which would be especially poignant, given the obvious differences in the couple's social classes."

One thing became obvious as Josh listened to their chatter—their families were connected in their love of art. The Eastman empire may have been built around more conventional antiquities, while the McDarbys favored the more outrageous, but there was definitely a connection here that couldn't be ignored.

Given his grandmother's frown, he guessed she'd noticed.

"Josh, would you please ask one of the ushers to go find Auntie Q? She'll want to greet your family personally." Lennon glanced at him, whiskey eyes twinkling. "Tell them to look for the giant in the powdered wig. Olaf shouldn't be hard to spot."

"My grandmother's not wearing a costume," he pointed out.

"Technically, she gave us Great-uncle Joshua," Lennon said. "As far as I'm concerned, that's the best contribution of all."

Her generous and respectful acknowledgment of his grandmother's connection to the gallery sealed the deal. There was no graceful way of declining this invitation, and Regina Penn-Eastman was nothing if not socially graceful. His grandmother was soundly caught, and her deepening scowl meant she knew it. Josh would bet money she'd gotten more than she'd bargained for with Lennon McDarby tonight. A courteous, caring person, Lennon had met vinegar with honey and won this round.

"I'll handle it," Josh said.

"So Olaf's working for your great-aunt now?" Josh heard his father ask as he headed toward the bouncers. "He's been sorely missed at Eastman Antiquities, I can tell you...."

Before Josh made it to the entrance, though, the door swung wide and the couple in question burst from the ballroom.

"What's going on, dear?" Miss Q asked, catching sight of Josh. "Olaf said he saw you and Lennon leaving—"

She obviously recognized his family, because she stopped short, a smile curving her mouth below the pearl-studded mask.

"Well, well, well, Regina," she said. "What brings you here tonight?"

"To find out why you've involved my grandson in this—this..."

"Memorial art gallery," Lennon supplied helpfully.

"Sexual shrine to my late husband," his grandmother corrected.

On immediate alert, Josh motioned the bouncer to shut the door. "Don't let anyone out until I give the word," he murmured.

"Sexual shrine?" Miss Q laughed as she swept by, glancing askance at him and whispering in a voice only he could hear, "Regina rhymes with vagina. It's no wonder she has issues."

Josh blinked, too surprised to react before he was staring at the back of her elaborately coiffed head. He wouldn't stand by and allow Lennon or Miss Q to be insulted, especially not by his grandmother, but there was another part of him—a morbidly curious part—that made him want to hang back to watch the show.

If he'd learned anything about the McDarby women these past few days, he'd learned they could hold their own.

"I'm not memorializing *your* late husband with a sexual shrine, Regina. I'm immortalizing *my* late lover by sharing his life's dream with the world."

Miss Q came to a halt in front of his grandmother, satin swishing and coiffed head high. Seeing them brought to mind a brightly colored butterfly taking on a brooding bird of prey.

"Josh Three isn't here to endorse the gallery," Miss Q added. "He's here at my request to protect Lennon."

"Protect her?" His dad glanced askance at Lennon, as though her provocative costume might have something to do with her need for protection. "From what?"

Josh went back to Lennon's side. "Miss Q has been receiving threatening letters, and there have been a few incidents that made us feel it was best to take precautions."

"Josh Three has been simply wonderful. You would be so proud of him," Miss Q said rapturously. "He's been coordinating security between the museum and the hotel. You should have seen him today. He was so heroic the way he protected us during the shootout."

"Shootout?" Davinia squeaked, staring at him as though searching for gunshot wounds.

"The police couldn't determine if it was actually gunfire," Josh said. "Nevertheless, there has been some protest about the opening, so to be on the safe side—"

"I'm not surprised there's protest." His grandmother eyed Miss Q's elaborate costume haughtily. "Schoolchildren visit this art museum."

Miss Q rolled her eyes at Josh as if to say, "I told you she had issues." Then she smiled in exaggerated reassurance. "I promise you, Regina, we won't be touring any elementary schools through the Eastman Gallery."

"Of course not," Lennon interjected. "I've put together the public resources. The Eastman Gallery will be working with colleges and universities all over Louisiana, and we've had some national interest, too."

Josh could tell by his father's sharpening expression that Lennon had caught his attention. "National interest? Impressive. Perhaps you'd be gracious enough to tell me more about the sort of programs you're running here. Involving Eastman Antiquities in the art education arena has long been an interest of mine."

An interest Josh knew his father hadn't been able to indulge much. His grandmother's focus on markets that yielded more lucrative financial gains had curtailed many of her son's interests, and Josh's father had never been as strong as Josh's grandfather in dealing with their formidable matriarch.

"I'll be happy to." Lennon gifted him with a smile Josh could tell went a long way toward winning his father over. "We'll make time to talk. If not tonight, perhaps tomorrow." Then she turned to her great-aunt and said, "I've invited the Eastmans to attend the opening."

"Wonderful." Miss Q didn't miss a beat. She smiled amiably and patted Olaf's huge brown hand. "Please attend to the details, dear. Put the Eastmans down on the guest list and arrange for a schedule to be sent to them." She glanced back at Regina. "Where are you staying?"

"I have the remaining room in your block."

Score one for the Eastmans.

Miss Q didn't give his grandmother the satisfaction of a reaction. She turned to Lennon instead. "See, dear, there was a reason I wouldn't release that extra room to you and Josh Three. I thought I was accommodating Lisette, but apparently Joshua wanted to make sure I had a room for his family.''

Josh's grandmother and parents all fixed wide-eyed stares on Miss Q, but Lennon didn't seem to think anything at all strange about her great-aunt's statement.

She simply smiled and said, ''Well, he was right about the color of the decorative arts exhibition hall, too. Shall we?''

Turning on her see-through high heels, Lennon motioned them all toward the ballroom. Josh watched his grandmother's dark gaze take in the flashes of her glittery painted skin.

''Young lady!'' Her voice rang out. ''Is my grandson staying with you as a bodyguard or are you sleeping with him?''

The entire group stopped dead in their tracks, their temporary truce shattered. Josh took hold of his grandmother by the arm and steered her away from the group. They were about to have a serious discussion about what he would tolerate as acceptable behavior.

Before he managed to get far, Lennon said, ''Mrs. Eastman.''

They both turned back to her to find a slow smile curving her pouty lips, a smile that turned his blood into lava on the spot. ''It wouldn't be very heroic of me to kiss and tell.''

Miss Q exploded in laughter, clapping her hands in obvious delight. ''What a pair!'' Her smile widened when she saw his grandmother's arrested expression. ''Your grandson told me exactly the same thing a while ago when I asked him that very question.''

"Which I interpret to mean we should all stay out of Josh and Lennon's business," Davinia said.

Meeting his mother's amused gaze, Josh inclined his head in silent thanks. "Agreed."

LENNON'S STOMACH fluttered wildly when Auntie Q headed toward the stage, stopped the band in midmelody and commandeered the singer's microphone.

"Esteemed guests," she said, once the last strains of music had died away and all eyes were riveted on the stage. "Are you enjoying yourselves?"

The roar that ripped through the crowd made Lennon smile. Never let it be said that Auntie Q couldn't throw a party.

"Wonderful, wonderful." She laughed, then waited for the tumult to die away. "Please forgive my interruption, but I simply must share the arrival of some very special guests, whose presence tonight signifies the goodwill and generous spirit with which the Joshua Eastman Gallery is embraced by the art community. Everyone please join me in welcoming our beloved Joshua's family." She motioned them onto the stage. "His late wife, Regina, his son, Joshua II, and his daughter-in-law, Davinia."

If the guests had been surprised by Josh's appearance at the welcome reception, it was nothing compared to their reactions now. There was a moment of total silence, during which, Lennon guessed, most every person in that ballroom was registering the incredible fact that Great-uncle Joshua's family was actually standing in the same room with Auntie Q.

But the guests didn't disappoint. The applause rang out, solid, welcoming, and Lennon heard Mr. Eastman hiss, "Just smile," as he and Davinia each grabbed one of Regina's arms and herded her onto the stage.

"Score one for the McDarbys," Josh whispered in her ear, his warm breath transforming her nervous flutters into tingly flutters of awareness. "My grandmother would never publicly humiliate herself by saying anything unkind about the gallery. She'll have to play along."

"I do hope she plans to stay until Tuesday. I don't think this crowd is going to let her go."

"Serves her right." Josh laughed, and Lennon gazed up into his handsome face with a smile.

"Shh. We've dealt with the immediate crisis. Let's get them all settled so we can dance again."

"Good idea."

As soon as Auntie Q relinquished the stage to the band, she and Olaf hustled Mr. and Mrs. Eastman off to mingle, while Lennon and Josh saw Regina firmly ensconced in a nook beside a fortune teller, where she sipped champagne and held court with the many people who wanted to hear her views on her late husband's collection.

Then Lennon followed Josh back onto the dance floor.

"She came to make trouble, you know." He was frowning, his expression dark and forbidding as he gazed at his grandmother.

"Hmm." All Lennon could manage was a murmur, preoccupied as she was with the feel of his hard thigh nudging its way between hers.

"You were gracious."

Apparently he wanted to talk. "They're your family," she answered.

"They're not easy to deal with."

"Families often aren't," she mused, thinking about her own mother. "But they're family. You deal with them. I like your mother."

"I'd venture to say my mother likes you."

For some reason Lennon didn't care to analyze too closely, earning Mrs. Eastman's approval was important to her. She only wished she'd worn the Elizabeth Bennet costume. Meeting Josh's parents in the buff wasn't exactly the first impression she'd have gone for, given advance warning of their arrival.

Good thing she wasn't hoping to have them as in-laws.

But she was pleased that Josh seemed reconciled to having them there. When he'd set eyes on his grandmother, Lennon had thought he was going to explode. She hadn't wanted to overstep her bounds and upset him, but no matter how difficult, they were his only family, and she didn't like the thought of him isolating himself from everyone who loved him.

And his family did love him. She needed only to see his parents' faces to know they were starved to see him, and the longing in his mother's eyes had been heartbreaking.

"Your parents seem to be enjoying themselves," Lennon said, spotting the Eastmans across the floor, wrapped around each other almost as tightly as she and Josh were.

Josh maneuvered her around gracefully, using the opportunity to slip his hand a little lower on her waist and pull her even more tightly against him.

"Good for them," he said, though Lennon couldn't be sure whether his smile meant he was happy for his parents or he was enjoying pressing his growing erection against her tummy. "They haven't pursued many of their own interests because they've spent so much time catering to my grandmother's fixation with social obligations and business. But I haven't been around them much for a long time. Maybe they've finally learned to please themselves and still keep my grandmother happy."

Lennon didn't miss the note of hope in his voice, and she wondered if being with his family tonight would be good for Josh. She could hope, anyway.

"Your grandmother strikes me as someone who doesn't know how to include herself in the fun." Lennon spotted

Regina sitting on an overstuffed armchair, a queen among guests who clamored at her feet. "Your family never made much time for fun, did they?"

"Not when my grandmother was around. She doesn't operate in the fun mode. I don't think the word's even in her vocabulary." Catching sight of Lennon's frown, he smiled. "I'm not harboring ill-will against my grandmother, charity case. I just got tired of being strong-armed into her idea of how to live my life. She was pushing me toward a business degree and grooming me to take over Eastman Antiquities, and that wasn't what I wanted. The power struggle and disapproval got old."

In his strong face, Lennon could still see the boy who'd often shown up at their doorstep looking for his grandfather.

Or had he been looking for acceptance?

"Did you know that Eastman Antiquities actually began as my grandmother's family business?" Josh asked.

"No, I didn't."

"Her family had lost everything in the Depression. That's how her marriage to my grandfather came about. He was up and coming in the import-export industry and was the best chance to reestablish the business. With my grandmother's name and connections, it was a good opportunity for him, too."

"What went wrong?"

"My grandmother never felt secure. She spent her life safeguarding herself against another financial disaster, even though my grandfather had rebuilt the business and made it stronger than it had ever been. After my father was born, my grandfather wanted other things in their life besides work. He wanted to enjoy his son, take vacations and have a big family. My grandmother resented any time spent away from the business. She still does."

"It's sad she was never able to move beyond that."

But maybe there was hope yet, Lennon thought. For as cantankerous as his grandmother was, she'd obviously been delighted to have the chance to argue with her grandson.

Apparently Josh hadn't noticed. He operated with a lot of distance in his life. Distancing himself from his family. Investigating the bachelors for her, to make sure he had an "out" regarding their relationship. She wondered if he ever got lonely. Snuggling up against him, Lennon decided he wouldn't get a chance to this weekend.

"There is a balance, you know. Your grandfather found his. He made his choices and managed the best of both worlds. It wasn't without sacrifice and compromise, but it seems to me that everyone got what they wanted from the situation."

He dipped her over his arm, and she went with the motion, unable to swallow back a sigh when his thigh pressed between hers, creating friction through her skimpy latex covering.

"Looking for a happily ever after for me and my family?"

Lennon huffed as he swung her out of the dip. "I've got enough trouble trying to find my own, thank you."

Josh's amused gaze told her he wasn't buying it. "Speaking of happily ever afters, *chère,* there's Gray Talbot."

She followed his gaze to a nearby couple. The woman was costumed in a chic twentieth-century style—Anaïs Nin or Colette, perhaps. But the man she was dancing with, judging from his wonderful medieval outfit, could only be Chrétien de Troyes.

"I've met him before. He's an investment banker with his family's bank. No doubt he can handle his finances."

"Probably, but he's been engaged four times. Hasn't made it down the aisle once."

"Oh. Commitment issues, do you think?"

Josh nodded. "Not a good quality in a husband."

"Definitely not. Where's he on the suspect list?"

"I'm looking into revenge as a motive. Your great-aunt recently stopped doing business with his bank. Losing her came as a definite blow. I overheard him talking to someone on the tour today about how he almost didn't come this weekend."

"Oh." Lennon didn't like the sound of that, and a glimpse of a couple beside them caused her to ask, "What about Mark Martin? Does he have a motive?"

"He's the personal injury lawyer—an ambulance chaser. He could have arranged the incidents with the hopes of talking you into suing the museum. It's weak but worth considering. Given what I've read about his cases, the guy's morally impaired."

"And Dan Wallace? He runs his family's country club."

"No motive I can determine, but a lousy candidate for a husband. He's been accused of sexually harassing several female employees. I read the reports and think his family's money and connections are the only reasons the charges were dropped."

Though everything about Josh was serious, his tone, his expression, certainly his news, Lennon knew he was enjoying eliminating her potential bridegrooms.

"What about Linc Palmer?"

"Good old Doc Linc," Josh said, grimacing. "That man is so fixated on how people look that he stalks women like a gambler looking for a winning slot machine. Makes me wonder if he's frightening you and Miss Q so he can charge in to save you."

"That's not a motive."

Josh shrugged. "The man practically threatened me when he heard about our affair. I had to tell him to move on because you were mine."

"You did?"

Josh nodded.

Linc's interest didn't impress her nearly as much as Josh driving off the competition. From their first night together he'd objected to her talking with the bachelors. His possessiveness seemed so at odds with the premise of a fling.

While wrestling down the absurd hope that something more might be happening between them, she found herself completely distracted when Mr. Eastman appeared.

"Switch partners with me, Josh. You're mother's dying to dance with you and I'd like a chance to speak with Lennon."

Given the sudden flash of annoyance in Josh's expression, Lennon guessed he wasn't thrilled with letting anyone touch his almost-naked lover—no matter who that someone might be.

Lennon had to admit to being very grateful for the sheer volume of her synthetic wig, although to Mr. Eastman's credit, he proved solicitous about where he actually placed his hands.

"It's nice to have the chance to meet you, Mr. Eastman," she said, when he whisked her away, with all the strong grace his son displayed on the dance floor.

"Joshua, please." He smiled. "Although your great-aunt has taken to calling me Joshua Two."

"Auntie Q's into names. You'll have to ask her to share her theories on where Olaf picked up his Scandinavian name in a South American jungle. It's rather entertaining."

"I'll keep that in mind."

He smiled warmly, and Lennon saw glimpses of Josh and his grandfather in that smile, though this Joshua definitely favored his mother with his gray-flecked brown hair and brown eyes. Still, he was a handsome man, and the fact that he was not ill at ease given the fact he was waltzing his son's almost-naked lover over the dance floor endeared him to her.

"Now, tell me all about the gallery's public resources."

Lennon did. The song ended and another began, but Mr. Eastman asked her to dance the next and the next, and Lennon suspected he was having a grand time steering her away from his wife and son. She caught glimpses of Josh scowling at them from among the other couples, and wondered what the deal was. Her bewilderment must have been evident, because Mr. Eastman chuckled and said, "We seem to have a phenomenon on our hands."

"A phenomenon?"

He gave a decided nod. "My son is positively prowling the dance floor. He won't let us out of his sight."

"That's why you're whipping me around like this. You're making Josh chase us." Mr. Eastman's grin confirmed her suspicions, and Lennon was strongly reminded of Great-uncle Joshua. "Your son is my bodyguard this weekend." *Among other things,* she silently added, and experienced a warm glow at the thought. "He can't let me out of his sight."

Mr. Eastman considered her thoughtfully. "Lennon, it just occurred to me that I haven't seen my son in well over a year." Judging by the furrow creasing his brow, she knew that realization didn't please him. "Even so, trust me when I say I can tell the difference between protection and prowling." He gave a surprised laugh. "He's prowling, and I suppose I'd better let him catch us before he gives his mother whiplash."

Lennon giggled as, sure enough, Josh promptly caught up to them.

"As enjoyable as my dance partner has been, I need Lennon back." His tone left no room for argument.

Kissing his mother's cheek, he told his parents to enjoy themselves, and pulled Lennon into his arms. His dad actually winked as he waltzed his wife off into the crowd.

Prowling, hmm?

Lennon couldn't read Josh's poker-faced expression. But he held her tightly against him and didn't let go. When one song segued into the next, he made no move to leave the dance floor. And when she finally begged for champagne and a break, he looped his arm through hers and led her to a nook, where he regaled her with more horror stories about the bachelors.

And Lennon responded with a crazy swell of excitement in her chest, a growing hope that perhaps Mr. Eastman had been right. Maybe Josh had been prowling. Maybe he'd decided he wanted more than just a weekend fling.

She recognized the feeling, this wild sense of anticipation, as the upside of grand passion, where her mood directly reflected the state of their affair.

Of course, every upside had a downside. The downside here was that she didn't know what Josh wanted. Why had he offered to share what he knew about the bachelors, only to methodically knock each one out of the running?

Prowling, hmm?

Lennon couldn't say. But one thing was clear. They'd only been together a few days, and just the thought of leaving the hotel and never seeing him again left her feeling so empty that she had to ask whether she really wanted a marriage with a companionable man—with *any* man besides Josh Eastman.

He was already making her crazy.

HER ELABORATE and very top-heavy wig bobbled precariously as Quinevere craned to see around Olaf's girth, wishing not for the first time in her life she'd grown taller than her present five feet three inches. Not too much taller, of course, as she'd always enjoyed feeling delicate and feminine beside a much taller Joshua, but tall enough so she could see actually over all the heads on this dance floor to spy on Lennon and Josh Three.

As it was, she barely reached the middle of Olaf's wide chest, and seeing around him proved a bothersome business indeed.

"You're worried," Olaf said, weaving her past couples so she could view the row of fortune tellers' tents unobstructed.

"Everything was going so well," she lamented. "Now Regina's here muddying the waters with her disapproval and frowns. Josh Three simply won't tolerate it. He'll leave."

Olaf gazed at some point over her wig and then shook his dark head emphatically. "He won't leave Lennon unprotected."

"I wish I could be so sure of that." Quinevere had known Josh Three since the day he'd been born. She'd watched him grow into the man he'd become—a wonderful man who would make her great-niece very happy. But a man, nevertheless, who hadn't learned to balance life on his own terms with the often trying demands of his grandmother. "But he's not really protecting Lennon, because she hasn't been threatened. I've been threatened."

"What about today?"

"Those fireworks went off when Josh Three was helping me into the car."

"You sound certain they were fireworks."

"Of course they were." She waved her hand impatiently,

allowed him to steer her back into the crowd with strong smooth glides that were amazing for a man so large. "Joshua was far too responsible to have gunfire whizzing around our heads, no matter how noble the cause."

"So those fireworks were Mr. Joshua's doing, hmm?"

She thought she saw a twinkle deep in those beetle-black eyes. "What else could it have been?"

"A timely coincidence?"

"Oh, phoo, Olaf, I'm surprised at you. Coincidence? I don't think so. Joshua's helping us out and doing a fine job, I might add. Did you see how quickly Josh Three got Lennon back into the gallery? Danger can be such a wonderful aphrodisiac."

"Apparently." He gazed down his nose at her in a look of undisguised amusement. "Then what's the problem?"

"Lennon and Josh haven't had enough time together to withstand a full frontal assault from Regina Eastman. I'm afraid Josh Three is going to bolt. He always has. I'm afraid he always will. And I won't ask the Eastmans to leave. I'm glad they're here to honor Joshua. We can all manage to get along for the weekend."

"Except for Josh Three."

She nodded. "Except for Josh Three. There's no question that Regina's the matriarch from hell. She tries to impose her will on everyone. Josh Three got frustrated and washed his hands of the whole situation before he learned to placate her and do what he wants anyway. If only he'd have given his grandfather and parents a chance, I know he'd have found them supportive of whatever he chose to do with his life."

Olaf considered her thoughtfully for a few turns on the

dance floor and then said, "Maybe we should up the stakes. Maybe it's time for Josh Three to protect Lennon."

Quinevere tipped her top-heavy wig back and peered into Olaf's smiling face. "Joshua always said that of all his acquisitions you were his greatest find. I completely agree."

14

PULLING LENNON BENEATH the showerhead, Josh coaxed the hot spray over her soapy skin, washing away all remnants of Lady Godiva. She'd been a temptation all night, but he wanted Lennon back, wanted the freedom to run his hands over her slick curves, wanted to taste her smooth skin liberated of latex and paint.

As the last of her costume swirled down the drain, she glanced down at herself, then sighed almost sadly.

"I'm just me again."

He wasn't remotely sad and skimmed his hands over the sweet swell of her breasts to prove it. "I want you."

She grinned up at him, blinking away the water that spangled her lashes, and arched her breasts into his hands. "But there's nothing exciting about plain old Lennon."

He would have disagreed, but her sulky voice and pouty lips sent blood spearing straight to his crotch, making him ache with a razor-sharp need that came damn close to killing him.

A night spent swaying against her near-naked curves on a crowded dance floor in full view of his family and half of New Orleans's high society had spiked his urgency to the breaking point. If she kept teasing him…

She did.

Shimmying her slippery body downward, she nibbled at his chest along the way, tortuous little nips that forced him to lean back against the shower wall to remain standing.

He could only stare as the water streamed over her, plastering her hair on her shoulders in wild strands, and brace himself as she sank to her knees before him, body coiling into a naked curl of pale gold skin. All plans to make love to her until dawn took a detour.

Damn, he was a goner.

He would never withstand this kind of assault on his senses, not when he'd already been tempted beyond endurance. But he couldn't steer Lennon away or utter one syllable of protest when she brushed her soft mouth along the underside of his erection.

The guttural sound that erupted from him made her smile, but that was the last Josh saw of her mouth, because he could only close his eyes when her tongue darted out from between those pouty lips, circling his shaft in a long slow stroke.

Damn, he was *really* a goner.

His body jumped in response to her touch and his head filled with the memory of the sexy scene he'd read on her laptop. Here was another glimpse of the way Lennon liked it, and she clearly wanted control tonight.

Exhaling sharply, he tried to dispel the tension that had taken possession of his muscles and locked him above her, subject to every sweeping caress of her skilled tongue, every spiraling swirl she lavished over his responsive skin.

Then she sucked him into her mouth with one hot swallow. Bucking hard, Josh almost lost control right there, but some barely functioning part of his brain warned that if he gave in now this exquisite torture would end.

Each moment he managed to stand, immobilized, suspended right on the brink of giving way to the most explosive buildup of lust he'd ever known, became another moment of victory, a moment of triumph that she rewarded with the passionate attention of her sultry mouth.

And then she touched him with her hand. Not around his erection, though he craved the contact, but lightly cupping his testicles, fondling their heaviness in her wet palm, squeezing gently, until his heart hammered in his chest and the sound of running water faded beneath that of the blood pounding in his ears.

The moment became charged, a battle of wills, his resolve to savor this excruciating pleasure against Lennon's determination to make him lose control. His tenacity against long sucking pulls of that hot velvet mouth. His ability to resist the fingertips that skimmed between his legs, back where they had no business skimming....

Damn, he was done.

All he could do was spear his fingers into her wet hair and hang on as his body exploded.

Lennon gently guided him out of the shower, his weak legs only just holding him upright. He was barely aware of collapsing in bed beside her, still dripping wet, but as he came to his senses again much later, Josh clearly remembered the smug smile on her beautiful face as she'd fallen asleep curled tightly around him.

Propping himself on an elbow, he gazed down at her. Her hair streamed over the pillows, the moonlight shining through the window casting the tangled mass in a haze of silver and shadow. Even in the pale glow of night, her mouth looked soft and bruised from his kisses. Each whispery breath marked a beat of his heart, and Josh knew he wouldn't sleep again tonight, though only a few hours remained before they were due at the museum for the start of another action-packed day of erotic events.

Thoughts crowded inside his head, forcing him to deal with things he'd spent so long avoiding. His family. What he wanted for his future.

When he thought about the future, he thought about Lennon.

Instead of panicking tonight at his family's unexpected arrival, she'd breached a wide gap and, with dignity, established her place in his grandfather's life.

There is a balance, you know, black sheep.

She was right. Family was family, the good right along with the bad. Otherwise, what did he have? A life that strung from case to case, affair to affair, none of which had ever left him feeling this hot sexual glow, this smug satisfaction that he could make this amazing woman come apart in his arms.

That she could make him come apart in hers.

He couldn't deny that seeing his family had meant something, too. In just a few dances, his mother had filled him in on Eastman Antiquities and all her social endeavors, while finding out all she could about his work and mental health.

She'd breathlessly managed to cover months in that short time—unwittingly making him feel selfish and stingy for never talking to her except when she called him.

Judging by the way his dad had monopolized Lennon, Josh guessed his own taste in women had met with approval, too. That was something. And remembering his grandmother battling wits with both McDarbys brought a smile to his lips.

But perhaps the greatest revelation of the night had come when he'd realized his parents were getting older. When he'd shown up on the night of the flash-and-bang attack, he'd been shocked by how frail Miss Q's hand had felt in his, her arm so shrunken he feared he might accidentally break her bones if he didn't handle her gently. She'd gotten old, and he wondered if his grandfather had seemed as old before his death, too.

Josh didn't know, and that bothered him. While he couldn't change the decisions he'd made so long ago, did he really want to make the same choices again?

At seventeen, leaving home to establish himself as independent from his family had seemed necessary. Josh wasn't seventeen anymore. Choosing his own career, his own interests, *his own woman,* was no longer a battle of wills.

The distance he'd placed between himself and his family seemed a mere formality now. Their presence tonight—no matter what their motivation for coming—proved they were willing to accept his decisions. They may not agree with them, but they would respect them. If his family could bridge the Eastman-McDarby connection for his benefit, then the time had come to put the past in the past and move on.

So what did he want for his future?

Gazing down at the beauty sleeping beside him, Josh smoothed away silky strands of hair from her cheek and knew that what he wanted was to feel like he did when he was with Lennon. Sated, challenged, tensely expecting the unexpected—because there was no way in hell he could have anticipated her marching out of that bathroom *un*dressed as Lady Godiva tonight. As stupid as it sounded, he liked the way he felt when she looked at him—like he was her hero.

If only being a hero was a good thing. Lennon believed heroes were only good for love affairs.

When she sighed deeply and rolled to her side, Josh used the opportunity to slip out of bed. Sleep simply wasn't part of the equation tonight, not when he had suspects to investigate, dirt to dig up on more bachelors, and some reading to do—to find out how *Milord Spy* might convince his lady to take a chance.

THREE HOURS OF SLEEP wasn't nearly enough to hit the ground running, especially after dancing and making love most of the night. But Lennon put on a good face—especially since she suspected Josh hadn't slept at all.

"What happened to you last night?" she asked when he emerged from the bathroom still dripping from a shower.

Standing framed in the doorway, he toweled his hair dry, giving her an eye-opening show of tanned, gleaming muscles and sexy, long wet hair.

"There didn't seem to be much point, *chère*. And I had to get some work done. As it turns out, we've had a development."

"What?" she asked, bracing herself.

"Spoke with Olaf just a few minutes ago and your aunt hasn't received any letters. According to my calculations, one should have arrived after the masque and another this morning."

"What do you make of it?"

"I'm not sure yet. It may just be a lapse. We'll have to wait and see if any more arrive today. I find it strange that they would just stop."

Strange, indeed, but hopefully this would prove to signify the end to the harassment. Though they couldn't be positive someone had shot at them in the alley yesterday... Well, she could lie in bed and hope for the best anyway, and watch Josh rub that plush towel across the corded muscles of his arms, his torso, his chest.

Mmm... She could get used to waking up like this every morning. Opening her eyes to the sight of a gorgeous naked man, all her senses titillated before she'd even had a swallow of caffeine. All her drowsy thoughts focused on how to lure him back between the sheets.

Of course, if this were a normal part of her life, she'd probably never make it to her computer, because she'd never get out of bed. Then her books wouldn't get written, which meant she'd lose her readership and have to live off her trust fund. And when that ran out she'd be forced to use her degree to get a practical job as an English teacher or a newspaper columnist.

Just about the time she decided to get out of bed to avoid the dire consequences of lounging around admiring Josh, the man himself showed up at her side, looming tall and breathtakingly naked. With one quick motion, he whipped the sheet back, exposing her to the cool air and his heated gaze.

"I know what I want to do today, and it involves you naked." He grinned devilishly.

Lennon's insides quivered in response to his throaty declaration, tiny ribbons of heat uncurling low in her belly.

"I'm afraid we've got a full slate of events scheduled." She tried to sound casual, though a slow, steady heat flushed her skin.

He must have noticed, because suddenly, in one fluid motion of contracting muscle, he was on his knees beside the bed, reaching out to thumb her nipple.

"Erotic events, *chère.*"

As if she could forget. All she could do was catch a breath as he fingered the underside of her breast, as if it was his privilege and right to touch her at whim.

Arrogant man. But she leaned into his touch, eyes fluttering closed when his tousled dark head descended and his hot mouth fastened on one wanting nipple, a long gentle pull that made desire pool between her thighs.

Oh, she could definitely get used to waking up like this.

Another slow pull with his talented mouth and she sighed aloud. "I want you."

"Not enough." His breath gusted warmly against her skin.

Not enough? Was there some sort of passion barometer she'd missed in her research? How much more could she possibly want him? Her thighs had parted of their own accord, and she could feel the cool air brush her sex, vividly exposing just how moist and ready she was for his attention.

And the man must have radar, because his free hand hovered above her thighs, his fingertips dipping into the juncture there, over silken hairs, zeroing in on the core of nerve endings with a precision that made her suck in a gasping breath.

"Definitely enough," she told him, her words echoing through the morning quiet.

Josh's gravelly laughter mocked her claim, and a finger probed her slick opening, stroked her moisture up to that tiny core, made her sex contract hungrily. Squirming against his hand, she forced her eyes open. Sooty damp hair framed a face potent with hunger and male satisfaction. He liked that she yielded to his slightest touch.

"Not nearly enough, *chère*. I want more."

She got the impression that he alluded to some deeper meaning, one that completely escaped her in this still-sleepy, passion-soaked haze.

But she tried to accommodate him anyway, spread her thighs to increase the pressure of his touch, though he stroked her with the same steady, dizzying caresses.

"You promised I could tie you up again." Gazing up from beneath the tousled hair that had fallen over his brow, his green eyes glinted wickedly.

"Oh."

Another hot pull of his warm velvet mouth and she felt the tension inside her welling up like a silky wave.

"Will you let me?"

Let him? How could she possibly deny him, when his

finger stroked her wet opening again, probing the most tantalizing inches, then glazing across her skin, in a sheen of her own moisture? And all the while his thumb circled steadily, and his mouth pulled and teased.

Lennon could do nothing more than lie spread before him, drugged by the hot tide inside her that ebbed and then rushed back, stronger with his every caress. He wove magic around her, lifted her in a swell of sensation that made her gasp when it finally surged and broke over her in a languid torrent.

He gave a final flick of his tongue and grinned at her. "Feel better now, *chère?* Ready to start the day?"

"Definitely ready," she managed to say, though the words rasped out in a raw groan that made his smile widen.

She tried not to think about the sight she must present, naked and spread for his pleasure—and hers—with his hand wedged between her thighs, her hips still squirming as she rode out the fading breakers of an exquisite orgasm.

But if his smile was any indication, he was enjoying the sight immensely. Suddenly, he rose above her, all flexing muscle and fluid grace, and extended a hand to help her stand.

Uh-oh. Lennon was in way over her head. No more denying it. And that thought propelled her from her daze, gave her the strength to take his hand and launch herself from the bed.

Fling, fling, fling!

She wanted to get married, have a normal home, make babies. Just looking at this man made even the fading pulses of her orgasm clench with renewed intensity. This feeling wasn't normal. Josh Eastman wasn't normal. He was a romance hero with his too-long hair and bedroom eyes, a rogue who used sex to titillate her, to confuse her, to make her crazy.

She didn't want crazy.

Did she?

No, no, no!

And what she wanted didn't matter anyway, because Josh didn't want marriage, a normal home or babies.

Lennon was still reminding herself of that fact a short time later as she sipped coffee on the balcony, letting the cool dawn air clear her head while Josh made telephone calls to the police and museum security.

The sun rose in pastel streaks above the rooftops, washed the dewy courtyard with a soft-focus sheen, made the geraniums in the window boxes glow vibrantly against misty brick walls. Water dripped from a nearby gutter and leaves rustled as a tiny songbird hopped through the branches of a tree. The morning seemed to glow with the freshness of a new day, and Lennon sipped her coffee, enjoying the sight, even while realizing caffeine wasn't going to do much except wake her up.

Getting control of her overactive emotions didn't seem to be in the cards today. She just didn't have the brain cells for it. Her mood was too dreamy, her thoughts too dazed, her body too languid. Josh had done this to her. She wanted to view her feelings for him with the same freshness of the sunrise, the same eager dawning of a new day. But she would be a fool to give in to the urge. There was no new day for a woman who wanted a normal marriage and a man who didn't want marriage at all. There was only this moment.

Lennon turned to head back inside at the exact moment when a terra-cotta flowerpot exploded a foot from her head. The sharp blast of sound made her yelp in surprise, and the cup slipped from her hands and crashed on the balcony, raining hot coffee over her shoes and ankles.

Josh burst through the French doors before the broken

shards of terra-cotta and shattered ceramic mug had even settled at her feet, and he shoved her back through the doors with a harsh, "Get away from the doors."

Her heart knocked hard as she grabbed the back of an armchair to steady herself, before moving away from the doorway just enough to keep an eye on Josh, who was still at risk outside. She could see him bent over the balcony rail as though straining to see down the alley, and was grateful she didn't have to wait long before he strode back inside.

"Are you okay?" His gaze raked over her perfunctorily, taking in the splashed coffee on her hose and shoes.

"Fine. What was—"

"This." His expression was grim as he held up a palm-size stone for her perusal. "Someone threw this and broke the flowerpot. Did you see anyone?"

"No." She wouldn't admit that she'd been so wrapped up in her daydreaming about him that she'd have missed a Mardi Gras float parked in the courtyard. "Did you?"

He frowned, pulled the door shut behind him. "I saw someone tearing down the alley. Male, I believe."

"Do you think he was aiming for me and missed?"

Josh covered the distance between them in two long strides. Wrapping his arms around her, he pulled her close, so close she could feel his heart pounding as hard as her own. "I think he meant to scare you."

"He did."

Josh pressed his lips to her brow, a gesture of reassurance that brought Lennon's whirlwind of tender emotions right back to the surface again. "It's okay. We'll lie low this morning and have Olaf do the same with Miss Q."

Then the moment was over and Josh stepped away. "I've got calls to make. The police, hotel and museum security. Why don't you go change? I'll only be a few minutes."

Lennon did, and by the time they arrived at the museum, Auntie Q had already breakfasted with the Eastmans. Lennon grabbed another cup of coffee—feeling too unsettled to eat—while Josh pulled Olaf aside to tell him about the morning's events.

"Lennon and I aren't participating in the sex toy scavenger hunt. We're heading to the art studios," he informed them when he rejoined their group. This was definitely news to Lennon.

Auntie Q seemed delighted, though, bobbling on her delicate heels excitedly. "I've set up all the studios for boudoir photography, sketching and sculpting—whatever you'd like to try your hand at." And the look she gave Lennon revealed that she knew exactly what he'd want to handle.

His dad gave him one of those chip-off-the-old-block sorts of smiles, but Davinia actually blushed to the roots of her sleek brunette bob.

If Lennon had felt more comfortable with his family today, suitably dressed in a flowing linen dress that covered her all the way down to her ankles, the feeling evaporated beneath their speechless reactions to the news that their son was going to take his grandfather's mistress's great-niece to an isolated art studio to photograph, sketch or sculpt her.

Conversely, his grandmother hadn't at all lost her ability to speak. She issued a loud snort of obvious disgust and said, "You all play your sex games. I'm going to spend my morning listening to the lecture on Georgia Devine's work."

Lennon's gaze shot to the massive erection and open mouth displayed below Great-uncle Joshua's portrait, and guessed Mrs. Eastman had no idea what she was letting herself in for.

"You enjoy yourself, Regina." Auntie Q's cheery tone

told Lennon a similar thought had crossed her own mind. "And, we'll have fun anyway, won't we, dears?"

Mr. Eastman smiled gamely, took his wife's hand and said, "I'm sure this will be an experience."

"It will be." Josh raked Lennon with a scorching gaze that made her entire world tilt crazily.

When Josh pulled Olaf aside in quiet conversation, Auntie Q pecked Lennon's cheek and gave her hand a reassuring squeeze.

"Any more letters, Auntie?" she asked.

"Not a one, dear, so no more worrying. Go have *fun* with your handsome young man."

Auntie Q was still giggling when Josh led Lennon into the main museum toward the hall of conference rooms that had been temporarily commandeered into erotic art studios.

She had to give Auntie Q credit—her great-aunt didn't know the meaning of halfway. She'd designed the studios with fun in mind, and this set resembled a lush Victorian boudoir. One wall housed a rack of sexy costumes, and along another, shelves held everything from canvas to clay to top-of-the-line digital photography equipment. It was a voyeur's playroom, and Josh gave a laugh as he locked them securely inside.

"She wanted to make sure no one got in or out, huh?"

Lennon shrugged, suppressing a tiny tremor of anticipation as Josh turned to face her, his expression transforming from amused to predatory before her eyes. "She wanted people to feel safe so they could explore their fantasies."

But safe wasn't what she felt as he covered the distance between them in two long strides, crowding her back against the rack of costumes, so close he seemed to suck up all the air.

His gaze was purely sexual. "You said I could tie you up."

"So I don't get to take pictures?" she asked lightly, a show of bravado when adrenaline enhanced all of her senses.

"No pictures." Circling a hand around her neck, he lifted her hair from her shoulders. "I want to see you naked."

Lennon hesitated, debating whether to let him call the shots. He must have recognized her uncertainty because he said in a silky voice, "I've got an image of you I want to recreate."

"I thought you said no pictures."

He thumbed her lower lip, his mouth tilting upward in a mysterious smile. "Do you trust me, Lennon?"

His hunger was so obvious, so potent, that goose bumps chased along her skin. She didn't have to consider the question. "Yes."

He pressed a kiss to her lips, a gentle kiss that sealed the deal and thanked her for gifting him with her trust. Then he unzipped her dress and slid it down her arms.

"Naked?" she asked, eyeing the variety of sexy costumes with a pang of regret.

"Naked."

The dimensions of the studio seemed to shrink with her every excited breath, with each piece of clothing he removed. He peeled her hose down her legs with great care, clearly in no hurry. Neither was Lennon. Seeing him kneeling before her, fully clothed, his dark head level with her bare stomach, was an experience to savor.

Then he stood, brushing against her in a tantalizing move as he reached past her shoulder to select two diaphanous scarves from a rack. "We're going to act out a fantasy here, *chère*."

"When have you had time to think up fantasies about me?"

"When I'm not touching your beautiful body, I'm thinking about touching it."

Something about such a simple, bold admission moved Lennon deeply, but she squelched the feeling. She wouldn't clutter the moment with emotions. Not when Josh wanted to blaze new trails.

She nuzzled his neck, brushed a kiss above his collar. "I like being your fantasy."

His arms lashed around her and he scooped her up and carried her to the chaise. He settled her upon it and she arched against the curved back in an artful pose. Lennon knew she must look like something out of a gentleman's entertainment magazine, and felt vulnerable and trembly as he watched her.

His expression smoldered with passion and…something else, something intense, unreadable. And when he reached into his pocket, extracting a pair of shiny metal handcuffs, her breath hitched in surprise.

"Handcuffs and scarves? Are you afraid I'll leave?"

"No." That one bold word epitomized how much power she was giving him, how much control he would take. "I wouldn't let you."

His admission sent a tremor of awareness through her, and her breaths grew tight as he guided her hands over her head, forced her to arch her back and thrust her breasts forward.

With the clink of metal, the cool bands circled her wrists.

Josh was a man who knew what he wanted, and right now he clearly wanted more than restraint. Threading the silk scarves through the handcuffs, he tied her to the chaise's mahogany finials, a position so reminiscent of their first night in the Carriage House that Lennon realized just how much Josh had been thinking about her.

She gave a token tug and found her wrists securely

bound. He didn't say a word as he sat beside her, swept her hair back from her temples and arranged it on the pale pink leather. Then his face descended and he kissed her, a hard, hungry, devouring kiss that Lennon fell into with a longing sigh.

He nipped at her lower lip with his teeth, making her moan as a spark burst into flame at his touch.

Then Josh shifted his attention downward. He cupped her breasts, fingers kneading her nipples until they strained toward his touch, and she recognized the passion in his face, not just passion for sex, but as an artist shaping his creation, bringing his vision to life.

She was his vision, the way she looked aroused by his touch. And the intensity, the honesty of the moment exposed such an unexpected side of Josh, a man affected by her and unafraid to show it.

"Close your eyes and don't open them until I tell you," he said, and she didn't pause to consider, didn't need to. Seduced by the moment, she cast a final glimpse at the concentration carving his dark features into stark lines, then let her eyes flutter closed.

"I want you to lie there, knowing I'm watching you." His rich voice filtered through her, and he kissed her mouth again, a kiss of reassurance. Then the cool air caressed her where he'd been, and she heard him move toward the shelves of equipment.

He dragged something across the floor, heard the clinking of metal joints as he unfolded or adjusted some piece of equipment. A tripod? Lennon waited, half expecting to hear the electronic clicking of a digital camera, though he'd said he wouldn't take pictures.

Anticipation took on an edgy thrill, the moment suddenly so titillating, so tense, that suddenly a simple little thing like keeping her eyes closed became an effort. She breathed deeply to curtail the urge to shoot up off the chaise and shake off this feeling of vulnerability.

Yet vulnerability had a double edge, because she found power in the feeling, in the connection between them, a connection built on Josh revealing how much he wanted her and how much she had to trust him to do as he asked.

Then she felt warmth brush her bare skin and guessed he'd positioned a photographer's lamp to highlight her body. With her arms bound high above her head, her body stretched naked across a pink chaise, her skin flushed with desire, her nipples peaked for his touch, Lennon had never felt more beautiful than she did now, being this man's fantasy.

Then she heard his measured footsteps moving away, the scrape of a chair and…silence.

She'd never heard silence so rich, so filled with expectancy and eagerness. She wanted to capture this moment in her mind, wished she had a notebook to describe the sensation as each layer of her world peeled away and her awareness narrowed down to the size of a pinprick, where she heard only hints of Josh's steady breathing, the rustle of a page flipping, the rasp of something…a pencil, perhaps?…scratching across paper.

Surely he wasn't sketching her?

Lennon didn't know, but the idea brought to mind the memory of a scene she'd written recently where her spy hero intruded on the heroine as she sat for a portrait. A sensual, tantalizing scene, with undertones of voyeurism, where the heroine's attraction to the hero builds as he watches her image being recreated by an artist on canvas.

In this moment, Lennon might have been her heroine, might have been living that scene, for the emotions were so similar, so powerful. Like her heroine, she struggled to meet the challenge of appearing calm and unaffected, when the heavy silence and knowledge that he watched her aroused her with an intensity she'd never known before.

She gave over to the sensation, determined to savor this moment where fantasy and reality collided. She let thoughts flow freely from her mind, concentrated instead on how her breasts stretched tight, how her nipples still ached from where he'd touched them, how her desire built slowly, until she could feel the moisture pool between her thighs.

And Josh never spoke, never broke the spell of his steady breathing, of the confident strokes of what sounded like pencil against paper.

Lennon lay in a haze of awareness and heady sensation when she finally heard him move. Before her dazed mind even registered that he was heading her way, she heard the clink of metal as he untied the scarves from the finials and removed them from the handcuffs.

He may have released her, but he didn't remove the handcuffs. He kept her restrained, restricted in movement just like he dominated her senses, her thoughts, her emotions.

Squeezing her eyes tightly shut as he sat on the chaise, she resisted the urge to open them when he guided her bound wrists in front of her. He scooped her onto his lap and maneuvered them around until he rested back against the wall. She felt her nakedness keenly against his fully clothed body.

"Look at me," his gruff voice commanded, and Lennon obliged, gazed up into a face stark with hunger, yet somehow softened by need.

It was a look that touched her on so many levels, made her want to feel him buried inside her, made her want to tenderly caress the tense line of his jaw. Made her yearn to hear loving words that she had no business wanting to hear.

But then he kissed her, chased away thoughts and wishes with a demand so strong Lennon could only kiss him back, tangling her tongue with his, wanting to touch him, yet halted by the handcuffs that still bound her.

But Josh knew, oh, he knew exactly what she wanted, even though she never dragged her mouth away from his to tell him, even though she couldn't use her hands to show him.

With his mouth still devouring hers, he fumbled with his zipper, freeing his erection from the tangle of fabric. Lennon responded to the sight with an urgency she couldn't control, a need to feel him inside her. Maneuvering off his lap, she hooked her bound wrists behind his head, straddled him.

Josh groaned—a raw sound that erupted from his mouth—and broke their kiss—to guide his mouth down, down, toward her breast.

He latched on with enough force to make her shudder, from a jolt of pleasure that rocked her from head to toe. She could feel his hot length between them, searing the moist flesh of her sex, and she glided against him, wanting to reach down and guide him inside her, frustrated that the handcuffs blocked her efforts.

But Josh's hands were free and he grasped her bottom, drove his fingers deep into her cheeks, taking care of the problem for her. One slick thrust and he sank in to the hilt, stealing her breath with the sensation, her thoughts, her will.

He sucked on her nipples in turn, and all Lennon could do was bury her face in his silky hair, inhale the musky scent that was Josh's own, and meet his short, driving thrusts. Need mounted. His hands dug into her bottom, lifting her, dragging her back, their motions intensely, perfectly in sync. She felt him arch hard against her and that was just the push she needed. She gasped aloud as her climax burst upon her, her halting gasps mingling with his throaty growl of completion.

Lennon clung to him. She'd never known such desperation, such urgency, such complete and utter absorption in another human being. She couldn't rally enough brain cells to make sense of the thought, or to register anything but an awareness of how Josh's heartbeat matched the breakneck pace of her own, how he looked as staggered and stunned as she felt.

Wrapping his arms tightly around her, he maneuvered and leaned back on the chaise, pulling her with him. "Come here, *chère*," he said softly. "Give me your hands."

He fished a key from his pocket and freed her wrists. Tossing the handcuffs onto the floor, he cradled her against his chest, his lips brushing lightly across the top of her head.

She buried her face in his neck, the fine silk of his shirt cushioning her cheek as he stroked her hair, soft gentle caresses that made her think of lovers in the afterglow, of couples who cherished each other, of tender scenes she'd written when her heroes and heroines had professed their love.

But avowals of devotion had no place between her and Josh, Lennon reminded herself fiercely, grasping at the reins of her runaway emotions. They'd signed on for a fling, and she couldn't let herself interpret his actions as anything beyond that. She wasn't a teenager in the throes of a first crush, and she certainly wasn't her mother in paroxysms of the first bloom of grand passion. She was a responsible woman who'd made her choices, and right now she'd chosen to become involved in a *fling* with this man. No more.

But why, oh why did that thought make her so sad?

"So what were you doing over there, Josh?" Lennon asked, a diversionary tactic. "It sounded as if you were drawing."

"I was," he said simply.

Lennon tugged out of his arms and launched herself off the chaise, putting desperately needed distance between them. "I didn't know you could draw."

He just shrugged. "How well will be for you to decide."

She could feel his gaze following her, but any vulnerability she might have felt from her nakedness evaporated beneath the weight of her surprise the instant she viewed his sketch.

The dimensions, the balance, the movement of the drawing took her breath away. With a commanding technique she'd had no idea he possessed, he'd created an image on paper so powerful it took her a moment to see past the bold pencil strokes and detailed shadowing to recognize the image was of her.

There was no mistaking the rapt look on her face, the sleepily closed eyes and the parted lips that came to life on the page, and while his unexpected talent stole her breath, it was the context of the image that made tears sting her eyes.

This was how Josh saw her. This exquisite, wanting woman, so vulnerable in her position, yet so strong in her passion, was what Josh saw when he looked at her.

He'd titled the sketch *Sleeping Beauty*.

Lennon simply stood there, absorbing the wonder of his gesture, of this moment, which felt so far beyond sex, so beyond a fling, that her eyes burned with unshed tears.

"Maybe I should have used the camera, *chère,* if my sketch hurts your eyes."

Though his comment was light, his voice sounded oddly

strained, and Lennon knew he was fishing for a reaction as a way to bridge the distance, to give her something tangible to cling to, because he obviously recognized how moved she was.

"I had no idea. Did your grandfather know you could draw like this?"

She managed to drag her gaze from the sketch, hoping he interpreted her tears as appreciation for his artwork and not the thousand soft emotions around her heart. He nodded, but something vaguely sad flickered across his face, making her realize she wasn't the only one struggling to hide her emotions.

"He must have been thrilled."

"He was disappointed I didn't take art seriously," Josh said. "I put myself through school sketching suspects for law enforcement agencies. He wanted me to pursue art as a career."

She held his gaze, not asking the question, not willing to ask him to go someplace clearly painful for him.

"It wasn't in the cards, *chère*," was all he said, and Lennon couldn't help but wonder if she wore her emotions on her face, because in her silence he seemed to hear her questions as clearly as a bell.

"You're very talented."

"I haven't sketched for a long time."

With his shadowed expression, his shuttered gaze, Lennon couldn't tell whether he was reconciled or saddened by that admission. Yet he'd sketched her. Though he'd chosen to live his life separated from creative endeavors and family and love, he'd picked up a pencil and sketched her, made her feel special and cherished while he looked at her…and the memory of how she'd felt as he'd sketched her brought another thought to mind.

"Coming to this studio wasn't just your fantasy, was it?"

His shuttered gaze never changed. "No."

"You read a scene from *Milord Spy?*"

"Your document was open the night I put you to bed."

"Oh." She wondered what else he might have read. She didn't really mind, but the idea that he'd been interested enough to even bother struck another blow to the distance she struggled so hard to hang on to. That he'd wanted to recreate her fantasy stunned her, and even more overwhelming was that in doing so he'd shared such a beautiful, and very personal, part of himself.

A man with the courage to spin fantasies.

Lennon gazed down at the sketch again, the beauty of the image striking her anew, making her long to cling to the man who'd drawn this, not to let him retreat into his isolated world that allowed no time for art or family or love. Or her.

And with tears still stinging her eyes, Lennon stood there, forced to face the fact that she'd gone and done exactly what she shouldn't have—she'd fallen in love with Mr. Wrong.

15

REGINA NEEDED ONLY TO SEE the Do Not Disturb sign hanging from the doorknob of her suite to realize that her son and Davinia had assumed she'd be occupied with the exhibition lectures for the afternoon.

Mistakenly assumed, because she hadn't been able to bear another minute of the recitation on the importance of sex through history and its impact on society's cultural evolution.

She'd skipped the late brunch, as the time had varied from her normal routine, and had intended to place an order with room service, then rest until the banquet that preceded the auction tonight.

Bachelors. Regina shook her head, actually considering knocking on the door and disturbing her son's tête-à-tête. She'd endured too much already this weekend to stand in the hallway in front of a suite she'd been forced to *share*. Then again, if she interrupted Joshua and Davinia, she'd be forced to endure his annoyance and her daughter-in-law's fluttery attempts to cover up what they'd been doing behind locked doors. Regina dismissed the idea, deciding she simply wasn't up to facing two more family members who'd succumbed to this sexfest.

She retraced her steps to the elevator, not at all pleased this weekend wasn't turning out as she'd planned. She'd meant to find out why her grandson had taken it upon himself to surface in a place he had no business surfacing, and, hopefully, appeal to the boy to act in a manner befitting his name and station. She hadn't expected to become a featured guest.

No doubt Quinevere McDarby was laughing like a hyena at the idea of her sitting though a lecture about the imagined symbolism of sucking mouths and thrusting male body parts.

Picking up a house phone, Regina directed the front desk to connect her with her grandson's room, only to receive voice mail—which meant he and Lennon were either out or occupied.

She preferred not to know which. Making her way down to the lobby, she settled herself in for a wait, dismissing the idea of ordering lunch in the hotel's restaurant. Though she knew the food would be exceptionally well prepared, she didn't intend to eat alone, didn't care for the message it conveyed. Let today's women tout their independence all they pleased, but as far as Regina was concerned, a woman alone in a restaurant meant no one wanted to eat with her.

As she mulled over the unsettling fact that apparently no one did want to eat with her, she heard the very last voice she wanted to hear.

"Regina," Quinevere said, approaching with Olaf in tow. "Whatever are you doing sitting alone in the lobby?"

Alone.

"My room's occupied at present. Apparently my son and his wife needed some privacy."

"Oh." Quinevere's big blue eyes widened as she guessed the implications of that statement. "So the sex toys got to them, did they? Well, good. That's exactly what Olaf and I were hoping when we arranged the event. Right, Olaf?"

"Yes indeed, Miss Q." He flashed a wide grin, dazzling against his dark skin, and made Regina wonder what could possibly make this man abandon an upwardly mobile career with Eastman Antiquities to play houseboy to an aging sex maniac.

Some of Regina's bemusement must have revealed itself, because Quinevere asked, "What's the problem, Regina? Don't you want your son to be happy in his marriage?"

"I believe sex belongs in a bedroom," she said shortly, so Quinevere understood she didn't intend to discuss the subject.

"You haven't seen anyone having sex in the halls, have you?" Her voice held such an innocent air of surprise that it took Regina a minute to realize she'd meant the question as a joke—a coarse, tasteless joke, but a joke, nevertheless.

Regina could think of no reply, but Quinevere apparently hadn't expected one, because she said, "If you've got nothing more pressing scheduled, why don't you come with me until your suite's available again? I'm heading up to mine to take tea and rest before the auction tonight. It's just Olaf and me. We've got plenty of room."

Regina wasn't at all sure she'd heard correctly, but when Quinevere said, "We haven't visited in forever—"

Ever.

"—and since you're here, we could take advantage of the time by discussing how best to present the connection between the Eastman Gallery and Eastman Antiquities. I've managed to field most of the questions so far, but more are bound to come up. Especially if Joshua Two starts developing your educational resources."

Business? Quinevere no more wanted Regina's input than she wanted that cut-crystal chandelier above them to fall on her head. She was attempting to make it easy to cross the chasm between them. Pride demanded that Regina say "No, thank you," to the offer, but a tiny voice inside urged her to forgo pride just this once to get out of this lobby where it might appear to the other guests that her family had abandoned her.

She'd managed to avoid dealing directly with Quinevere McDarby for fifty-odd years. Must she really face this now, when all she wanted to do was enjoy her old age and savor the fruits of her labors?

But Quinevere McDarby was a fruit of her labor, that tiny voice inside pointed out. The woman would never have been in Regina's life had it not been for the choices she'd made about her marriage so many years ago.

Regina stared at the nemesis she'd created, remembered asking her late husband what it was about the woman that had made him commit so completely to her. He'd said that Quinevere McDarby possessed the most loving heart of anyone he'd ever met in his life.

Regina remembered thinking he must have been blinded by lust, even recalled feeling a fleeting flash of envy that he'd regarded the woman so highly. But upon closer inspection…she supposed she could look at the way Quinevere had welcomed her and her family this weekend in very much the same way.

If she'd been of a mind to.

She wasn't. But perhaps the time had come to at least talk with the woman.

Rising, Regina said, "I do have some thoughts on how best to…"

AS MUCH AS JOSH WOULD have enjoyed crawling into bed beside Lennon and taking advantage of the lull in their schedule before tonight's banquet, the report he'd just received by fax of the police department's investigation focused his thoughts on work.

He reviewed the report, satisfied with their efforts, yet disturbed that they hadn't discovered anything conclusive.

Josh did, however, notice something about the logistics that raised a discrepancy with his investigation of the flash-and-bang attack.

Digging through his briefcase, he retrieved his handheld tape recorder and replayed the tape he'd made of his initial interview with Miss Q the night she'd called.

"Could you see anything in the alley?" he'd asked.

"It was dark, Josh Three," he heard Miss Q say.

Depressing the button, Josh replayed that segment again.

"It was dark, Josh Three."

According to the police department's follow-up investigation, the city's utility company had just replaced streetlamp bulbs in all the Quarter's dark alleyways in preparation for the Mardi Gras festivities, which meant the alley behind the museum would have been lit up like a stadium.

He depressed the Play button again.

"What direction did the grenade come from?" he'd asked.

"Opposite the streetlamps."

Opposite the streetlamps meant the assailant would have to run right beneath the streetlamp to get out of the alley. Why would someone trying to frighten an old lady make the attempt from a place where he'd be forced to run under a damned spotlight to get away?

As Josh mulled over that question, another hammered at him—what had happened to make the letters stop coming?

Over the past days he'd eliminated most of the suspects, the literary crowd, plus practically all the bachelors, and those left on his list had weak motivation at best. The only thing that had changed yesterday was his relationship with Lennon. That got him thinking in an entirely new direction....

Getting to his feet, he pulled the bedroom door closed so as not to disturb Sleeping Beauty, and headed for the phone to dial Beauregard Armistead, his grandfather's close friend and the lawyer who'd represented the Eastman family's interests for longer than Josh had been alive.

Though Beau was clearly staggered by this out-of-the-blue call, he listened when Josh got straight to the point.

"I've got a question about my grandfather's military artifact collection. Do you know if he kept collecting up until he died, and what happened to the collection after his death? Is it on display somewhere?"

Josh shook his head as the lawyer confirmed his suspicions. After thanking Beau for the information, he hung up the phone.

No damned wonder he wasn't getting anywhere on his search for suspects. There weren't any. Except for the one he suspected of masterminding this entire charade.

And he was going to pay her a visit right now.

Writing a note in case Lennon awoke to find him gone, he left the Carriage House for the main hotel. Five minutes later the elevator dumped him on the top floor and he knocked sharply on the door straight ahead, then strode in when the door opened.

"Olaf," he said, greeting the man who held the door. Meanwhile his gaze scanned the room for the tiny whirlwind who was about to answer his questions.

She sat at the table, smiling cheerily when she saw him. "What a nice surprise, Josh Three. Come sit. Olaf was just entertaining us with the *real* story of how he got his name."

She seemed to think this was significant, but Josh was distracted, and surprised, by the table neatly laid with tea and assorted finger foods, and by the woman he'd never expected to see there.

"Grandmother?"

"Hello, Joshua," she said casually, as though sitting across a table from Miss Q were an everyday occurrence.

Before Josh could even begin to process this unexpected sight, Miss Q asked, "Where's Lennon?"

"Sleeping in our suite."

"You left her sleeping—alone?" Miss Q's eyes grew wide. Her teacup clinked on the saucer when she set it down.

"Wasn't protecting her the whole point of you being here this weekend?" his grandmother asked.

"My great-niece is horizontal in a bed and you're here chatting with two old ladies?" Miss Q asked with something remarkably like disgust in her voice. "Josh Three, I'm surprised at you."

His grandmother's cup hit the table with another loud clink. "Do you ever think about anything but sex?"

"Not if I can help it," Miss Q replied cordially, leveling her a curious glance. "Exactly what is it you have against sex?"

Josh took one look at his grandmother's expression and saw an argument coming. *Time for evasive maneuvers.* "I just received an interesting piece of information," he interjected.

"Really?" Miss Q said raptly. "Something that explains why you've left Lennon alone and unprotected, perhaps?"

"As a matter of fact, yes."

Josh could tell by the flare of amusement in Miss Q's face that she was busted and she knew it.

"You're responsible for the flash-and-bang grenade and the letters, aren't you?"

Josh wasn't sure what he expected, but her casual grin and easy nod wasn't it.

"I am indeed."

"Did you hire someone to set off bottle rockets when we walked into the alley?"

"I wish I'd have thought of it." Her lively face twisted

into a frowning moue. "A stroke of brilliance that had your grandfather's fine touch all over it."

Okay. Josh didn't know what to say. Miss Q seemed to be in command of all her faculties and given the extent of the work she'd done pulling this gallery together, she couldn't be too prone to memory lapses. Which meant she must be crazy. "And you stopped sending the letters because...?"

"I was too busy to keep putting them together. Once you and Lennon became lovers, I didn't see the point."

"I see." He turned to Olaf. "You were in the courtyard?"

He nodded. "I grew up using stones to hunt in the jungle. I could bring down dinner from the branches of a tree at two hundred yards. Lennon was never in danger."

She'd been frightened, and that was enough, as far as Josh was concerned. "You knew about this all along?"

"Not until after we heard those fireworks in the alley. Miss Q explained in the car while we were driving away. She was so thrilled at such a timely coincidence she couldn't keep her secret any longer. She told me everything."

"And you willingly went along."

Olaf flashed a white smile. "What Miss Q wants Miss Q gets. That's my motto."

It looked like Miss Q wasn't the only one shooting with more than a few blanks in her cylinder.

"And where did the grenade come from?"

"I've stored your grandfather's military artifact collection at the gallery until I decide where to place it."

"Did you pitch Lennon to the bachelors to get them to participate in the auction?

She arched a fine brow in an expression very reminiscent of her great-niece. "I wouldn't exactly call it *pitching*."

"What would you call it, then? And what was the point of all this?"

Miss Q scoffed. "Josh Three, you're a private investigator and you haven't figured that out yet? With as close as you and Lennon have become, I would have thought my motive obvious."

"Indulge me." He leaned back against the desk, settling in for what would surely be an explanation he'd have to wrap his weary brain around.

"Please do, Quinevere," his grandmother said. "I'm interested in hearing this, too."

Miss Q settled back in her chair and propped her fingers together before her. "It's very simple, really. Lennon has some very decided ideas about what she wants for her future, which I attribute largely to watching her mother and me make some rather unorthodox choices for our own lives. She wants what she calls a 'normal' marriage."

His grandmother applauded. "Smart girl."

Miss Q scowled. "She planned to find a husband at the bachelor auction, and suffice to say, I didn't like her criteria. I want my great-niece to have the very best in life, and when your grandfather reminded me that he wanted the same for you, Josh, I knew I had to get you two together."

His grandfather reminded her?

There it was again—that casual reference to talking with a man who'd died two years before. Josh made a mental note to ask Lennon about this phenomenon later. He wouldn't raise the question now, not with his grandmother staring as though she'd just realized she was sitting awfully close to a ticking bomb. She'd had enough shocks to contend with for one day.

But to Josh's profound surprise, his grandmother's shock melted away and she chuckled. "You're just as much of a manipulator as I am, Quinevere. I had no idea."

"We must keep an eye on our own, mustn't we?"

"We must," his grandmother agreed with something that looked remarkably like a smile.

And as Josh stared at these two, realizing he was witnessing a meeting of the minds the likes of which had never before been seen—and probably never would be again—both women turned to stare at him.

"The acorn doesn't fall far from the tree, does it?" Miss Q fixed her gaze on him.

Josh suddenly found himself the recipient of two wistful stares. He knew exactly what Miss Q was doing, trying to get his grandmother to openly acknowledge that he was capable of leading his own life without her interference.

"Joshua was a very good man and his grandson is, too." His grandmother shot a look that revealed she knew exactly what Miss Q was pulling, too. To her credit, though, she didn't balk, but carried the thought one step further. "And now you're trying to arrange something between our families. What do you think about that, Joshua?"

A formal connection between the Eastmans and the McDarbys. Just the thought should have made her faint. Yet she'd asked what he wanted instead, reinforcing that times had changed.

Josh knew exactly what he wanted, because falling in love with Lennon had stripped away all his barriers. *Him,* a man who prided himself on maintaining distance with his emotions. He went undercover with drug dealers without a second thought. He handled grenades, dodged crossfire and collaborated with the authorities as part of a normal workday. Yet one gorgeous blond romance writer had managed to span that distance to make him realize what he'd been missing in his life, make him acknowledge just how lonely he'd been.

He knew exactly what he wanted, and hoped his grandmother was ready to hear it.

"I want to marry Lennon," he said. "Maybe you ladies would be kind enough to advise me on how I might help her move past her rather decided ideas about Mr. Right and Mr. Wrong...."

LENNON SAT UPRIGHT in her back-row seat and wished this auction were over. She also wished she knew where Josh had gone to, but she sat with two generations of Eastmans and thought it best to stay put, keep them occupied and wait for Josh's return.

She forced a smile when Davinia commented about the six thousand dollars the last bachelor had commanded—the most generous bid yet. The bidding increased in five hundred dollar increments, amounting to very generous totals that would go a long way toward keeping the gallery solvent until it had earned a reputation of its own.

"He was the most handsome so far," Davinia said, glancing down at her gold-embossed program, which contained the bachelors' biographies. "It was clever of your great-aunt to schedule the auction right in the middle of the events. The bidders seem eager to spend the next two days with their bachelors."

Auntie Q was *something,* all right.

Lennon's head was still reeling from Josh's explanation that her great-aunt had staged all those threats to bring Josh into their lives. Lennon couldn't say she was surprised. Not at all, in fact. The entire scheme was quintessential Auntie Q. And she'd gotten her wish, because Lennon was experiencing grand passion big time.

The trouble was Lennon didn't want just grand passion with Josh. She wanted the whole package—marriage, a future, and yes, lots of babies, no matter how tall they might grow to be.

She'd fallen in love, *love,* for goodness sake, with a romance hero who wanted no more than a weekend of exciting sex. And Davinia's reminder that the weekend was already half over gave Lennon visions of the bleak road ahead, trying to cope with the aftermath. Just the thought of Wednesday's arrival and checkout time made her numb. She'd head home, try to get back to work—she was so behind—and attempt to write a happily ever after for *Milord Spy* when her own heart was breaking.

Linc Palmer walked onto the stage, formally dressed, as were all the bachelors tonight. He smiled as Auntie Q introduced him and prompted the audience to bid high for this handsome doctor.

Lennon remembered Josh's comments about Doc Linc, as he'd called him, being so fixated on physical beauty that he stalked women like he was searching for a winning slot machine. How she could have thought about marrying any of these bachelors was beyond her.

When she thought about marriage, or about passion, or about sex, the only image that sprang to mind was of an intensely handsome man with too-long black hair and deep green eyes. A man who'd completely redefined the meaning of Mr. Right and Mr. Wrong.

Doc Linc commanded a whopping sixty-five hundred dollars, which appeared to please him as he left the stage to join the leggy brunette who just might live up to his exacting physical standards. The auction was finally over and Lennon intended to see where Josh had gone. She only had two days left and planned to make the most of each second. Good thing she'd napped earlier, because she didn't plan to waste any more time sleeping....

"What a wonderful turnout for our bachelors," Auntie

Q said into the microphone, reclaiming the audience's attention. "The founders, family and staff connected with the Joshua Eastman Gallery appreciate your generous support. Your programs indicate that the handsome Dr. Palmer was our final bachelor of the night, but since the programs went to print, we've added another. A man who unexpectedly and very graciously offered himself to help raise funds for the Eastman Gallery.

"But I must caution you that our latecomer has insisted on a stipulation—whoever buys him won't get to just enjoy him until Fat Tuesday. Whoever buys this bachelor gets him for keeps."

For keeps?

The audience buzzed expectantly, and Lennon watched raptly as Auntie Q swept her hand toward the wings and said, "Please welcome our final bachelor."

When Josh stepped onto the stage, the women in the audience went nuts, catcalling, whooping uproariously and good-naturedly accusing Auntie Q of saving the best for last, which didn't go over too well with the other bachelors, judging by all their grumbling as they returned to their seats.

And the tumult continued, which was a very good thing, as Lennon could only stare, trying to draw a decent breath, trying desperately to comprehend what was happening.

This was such an outrageous, audacious move, so completely unexpected, that it took Josh's grandmother leaning forward in the row and saying, "I hope you're not going to leave him standing up there," to snap Lennon out of her daze.

Had she just been given some sort of *blessing?*

Apparently so, because Josh's parents were both watching her with delighted smiles. Lennon's gaze shot back to the stage, where Josh stood, resplendent in his black tux, with his long hair unbound, looking just like a romance hero.

Auntie Q read his bio, but Lennon didn't hear a word as Josh stared directly at her, revealing with a glance that he wanted her...*for keeps.*

In one quick burst of mental math that would have made any teacher proud, Lennon calculated exactly how much her publishing house would be sending in the next royalty check—there would be no bidding war for this bachelor.

She raised her paddle.

"The lovely lady in the back will start bidding at..."

"Seventeen thousand."

Davinia gasped and Mr. Eastman chuckled by her side, while shouts of "You go girl!" erupted in the auditorium. Regina Eastman shook her head and muttered something about fools and their money, but Josh shot Lennon one of those roguish half grins, clearly surprised, but obviously very, very pleased.

"My upcoming royalty check," she explained, and Davinia patted her hand with an approving smile that indicated, unlike her mother-in-law, she thought the money well spent.

"Do I hear seventeen thousand, five hundred?" Auntie Q demanded from the podium.

The tumult died away swiftly, and Lennon had the giddy thought that she'd done exactly what she'd hoped to—shut down the bidding completely.

Raising her gavel, Auntie Q sounded positively rapturous as she said, "Seventeen thousand going once...going twice...sold to the lovely romance writer in the last row."

The gavel hit hard, sealing the deal, and Josh made his way off the stage, hindered from clearing the aisle by swarms of well-wishers who patted his back and shook his hand.

For keeps.

And while he worked his way through the crowd, Lennon sat in her seat, frozen, not daring to believe what had just happened, barely able to breathe until she saw Josh up close and confirmed that he truly meant for keeps.

Davinia held her hand, apparently recognizing her shock, and by the time Josh finally reclaimed his seat, Lennon's pulse raced so hard, she barely managed to sit still.

His grandmother greeted him with a tight smile, but his father reached over to shake his hand.

"Well done," he said.

Josh only nodded, his gaze capturing Lennon's, those deep green eyes mirroring all the love she felt bubbling up inside her.

For keeps.

"You'll make me crazy for the rest of my life."

Josh grinned that romance hero smile, making her heartbeat flutter madly and her insides melt, and said, "Yes, I will."

Epilogue

"MIRACLE OF MIRACLES, Joshua," Quinevere silently whispered with a glance upward at the last slices of gorgeous blue sky fading into twilight. "Not only was Regina in the mood to throw a party, but she has managed to throw a good one."

She smiled. It had been the perfect day and she was glad for a quiet moment to share with the man she loved. "We used to talk about bringing Josh and Lennon together for a grand passion, but after Josh went away it didn't seem likely we'd ever realize that dream." Her gaze misted as she watched her great-niece dance with her new husband over the lush green lawn, looking as though they might have stepped out of the pages of one of Lennon's books. "Look at them, my love. We accomplished so many wonderful things in our life together, but they're our greatest work of art."

She sighed softly. "I don't use the term 'ours' loosely, either, because I know you were up there helping me every step of the way. And those fireworks," she said with a low whistle. "A stroke of brilliance."

Quinevere could almost hear Joshua chuckle in response. He'd always had a dry sense of humor, not unlike his grandson's, and she missed his rich laughter, looked forward to the day when she would hear it again. Until then, though, she had a lot of living to do.

As far as Quinevere was concerned living was synony-mous with celebrating.

From her place on the sheltered veranda, where she sipped a champagne spritzer and sought temporary respite from the summer heat the dusk had yet to cool, Quinevere gazed out over the manicured lawn at the guests who were dancing to the last of the daylight before the reception moved indoors for a formal dinner, more dancing and a host of traditional wedding festivities.

Though she would have enjoyed opening her home, an-other stately Garden District mansion only five blocks away, for the first time since Joshua's death, Quinevere had decided she'd have plenty of time to throw the newlyweds parties.

While this occasion was about two people falling in love and deciding to share their lives together, it was also about Josh coming home to his family, and as such, the Eastman mansion was the perfect place for the wedding.

Besides, with all the prewedding activities, showers, re-hearsals and such, Regina had had a great deal of adjusting to do. While she'd managed admirably, Quinevere didn't think it wise to tempt fate—and asking her to step foot inside the McDarby mansion just might push the woman right over the edge.

They'd tackle that particular obstacle another day. Now was the time to celebrate, and that's exactly what the guests were doing. Photographers from two well-known romance trade magazines moved through the crowd, merrily snap-ping pictures of what they called a real-life romance—no doubt a marketing move by Lennon's publishing house to sell more books—but Quinevere agreed wholly with the premise.

Josh may have technically resembled Lennon's Georgian spy, but Quinevere would always think of him as a swashbuckling pirate, although he'd long since abandoned his ponytail for a neatly trimmed style that made him favor his grandfather more than ever.

And Lennon... Misty tears swelled in Quinevere's eyes as she gazed at her great-niece, at the color in her cheeks, that beaming smile on her face. She was simply exquisite in a white silk and lace creation reminiscent of Scarlett O'Hara.

And she hadn't been the only one thinking along the lines of old Southern charm, either. Lennon's editor, a lovely young woman named Ellen, had suggested Lennon try her hand at spinning a love story set in the Deep South.

A native of the cold, cold North, Ellen had been captivated by New Orleans's sleepy charm, and Quinevere had already convinced her to extend her trip a few days so Olaf could take them to tour the area's historic plantations while Lennon and Josh honeymooned in the South Pacific.

Of course, Quinevere hadn't mentioned that she just happened to know a very handsome young man from an upstanding family who managed one of the plantations for a holding company based in the very same cold city Ellen lived in.

No, she'd save that tidbit for later, although she thought Lennon already suspected what she was up to. But her great-niece hadn't taken her to task. No, she'd simply smiled, gazed adoringly up at her handsome new husband and told Ellen to have fun.

Lennon was obviously well pleased with how her love life had shaped up, and had every confidence that her Auntie Q would take good care of her friend. And she would. With a little divine assistance from Joshua, of course.

Quinevere gazed down at the new Mr. and Mrs. Joshua Eastman III, dancing, whispering intimately and clearly enjoying the celebration of their love with friends, and said, "Don't you think everyone should be as gloriously happy as we were, Joshua?"

Ah, *l'amour.*

HARLEQUIN® Temptation.

Look for bed, breakfast and more...!

COOPER'S CORNER

Some of your favorite Temptation authors are
checking in early at Cooper's Corner Bed and Breakfast

In May 2002:

#877 The Baby and the Bachelor
Kristine Rolofson

In June 2002:

#881 Double Exposure
Vicki Lewis Thompson

In July 2002:

#885 For the Love of Nick
Jill Shalvis

In August 2002 things heat up even more at
Cooper's Corner. There's a whole year of intrigue
and excitement to come—twelve fabulous books
bound to capture your heart and mind!

**Join all your favorite Harlequin authors
in Cooper's Corner!**

HARLEQUIN®
Makes any time special ®

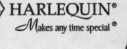

If you enjoyed what you just read,
then we've got an offer you can't resist!

Take 2 bestselling love stories FREE!

Plus get a FREE surprise gift!